ISBN-13: 978-1522778158

For my haters

Fuck you

1
#WTF

"You are supposed to be with me."

What words are these? They startle me, and at first I think I've heard him wrong. He's leaning across the table while our significant others are twenty feet away, waiting in line for our food.

"You and me," he says. "Not us and them."

I blink at him before I realize he's making a joke. I laugh and go back to looking at my magazine. Actually, it's not really a magazine. It's a math journal, because I'm super cool like that.

"Helena…" I don't look up right away. I'm afraid to. If I look up and see that he's not joking, everything will change.

"Helena." He reaches out and touches my hand. I jump, pull back. My chair makes a horrid scraping sound, and Neil looks over. I pretend that I dropped something and reach under the table. Under the table are our shoes and legs. There is a blue crayon lying at my feet; I pick it up and resurface.

Neil is at the front of the line ordering our food, and my best friend's boyfriend is waiting for my response, his eyes heavy with burden.

"Are you drunk?" I hiss. "What the fuck?"

"No," he says. Though he doesn't look so sure. For the first time, I notice the scruff on his face. The skin around his eyes is sallow. He's going through something, maybe? Life is being bullshit.

"If this is a joke, you're making me really uncomfortable," I tell him. "Della is right there. What the hell is wrong with you?"

"I only have ten minutes, Helena." His eyes move to the blue crayon, which is resting between our hands.

"Ten minutes for what? You're sweating," I say. "Did you take something, are you on the crack?" What type of drugs make you sweat like that? Crack? Heroin?

I want Neil and Della to come back. I want everything to go back to normal. I spin around to see where they are.

"Helena…"

"Stop saying my name like that." My voice shakes. I make to stand up, but he grabs the crayon, then my hand.

"I don't have much time. Let me show you."

He's sitting very still, but his eyes remind me of a cornered animal: frightened, panicked, bright. I've never seen that look on his face, but since Della's only been dating him for a few months, it's a moot point. I don't really know this guy. He could be a druggie for all I know. He turns my hand over so it's palm up, and I let him. I don't know why, but I do.

He places the crayon in my palm and closes my fist around it.

"You have to say it out loud," he says. "Show me, Kit."

"Say it, Helena. Please. I'm afraid of what will happen if you don't."

Because he looks so afraid, I say it.

"Show me, Kit." And then, "Should I know what this is?"

"No one should," he says. And then everything goes black.

Kit is there when I wake up. My head is aching, and my tongue is stuck to the roof of my mouth. I must have passed out. That's never happened to me before. I sit up, but instead of being on the floor of the Bread Company, I am spread out on someone's sofa. It's a nice sofa, the kind you see in a Pottery Barn catalog. Five bajillion dollars of treated suede. I scratch at it, and then sniff my finger. *Suede.*

"Neil?" I sit up, looking around. Did they carry me to the manager's office? How embarrassing. Pretty fancy couch for a manager. "Kit, what happened? Where's Neil?"

"He's not here."

I stand up, but it's too fast, and I get dizzy. I slump back onto the couch and put my head between my knees.

"Get Neil, please." My voice sounds nasally. I look up to see Kit's jeans still in front of me. He makes no move to get Neil. With a deep sigh, he sits down next to me.

"Neil is in Barbados on his honeymoon."

"Did he get married on the way back to our table?" I say through my teeth. I'm done with this game. Della is off her rocker if she keeps seeing this guy. He's on drugs, or nuts, or both.

Kit clears his throat. "This is actually his second marriage. He was married to you for a while."

My head shoots up. When he sees the look on my face, he flinches.

A child comes running into the room and flings himself on my lap. I recoil. I don't like kids; they're messy and noisy, and—

It asks me for a sandwich.

"Hey, buddy. I'll get you one. Let's give Mom a minute."

What. The. Fuck.

I'm off the sofa and backed into a corner in five seconds. Kit and the small human are already gone from the room. I can hear their voices, high and happy. The Pottery Barn room. There is a lot of navy blue everywhere I look. Navy blue picture frames, navy blue braided rugs, navy blue planters, spilling with healthy ferns. I walk to the window, convinced I'm going to see the parking lot in front of the Bread Company. Maybe they carried me over to the Pier One. Instead, I'm looking at a pretty garden. A knotty oak stands in its center, a circle of white stones around its base.

I'm backing away from the window when I walk into something. Kit. He grips the top of my arms to steady me. I tingle where he touches me. I'm allergic to nuts.

"Where the hell am I?" I ask, shoving him away. "What's happening?"

"You're in your house," he says. "214 Sycamore Circle." There is a long pause, and then he says, "Port Townsend, Washington."

I laugh. Whoever did this got me good. I step around Kit and run through the house. A dining room opens into a large, airy kitchen. I can see water beyond the windows, its surface prickled by rain. I am staring at the rain when a small, lispy voice says, "What are you wooking at?"

The kid. He's sitting at the kitchen table, stuffing his face with bread.

"Who are you?" I ask.

"Thomas." When he says his name, wet bread flies out of his mouth and sprays the table.

"Thomas who? What's your last name?"

"Same as Dad's, but not the same as yours," he says, matter-of-factly.

My skin prickles.

"Thomas Finn Browster. And you are Helena Marie Conway."

He fist pumps the air. *Browster!* Neil's last name.

I hear Kit behind me, and when I turn to look at him he's leaning against the fridge, frowning.

He lifts a finger to his lips when he sees me watching him, and then glances at the boy.

"You have another one," he says.

"Another what?"

"Child." He pushes away from the fridge and walks toward me. All of a sudden I'm noticing the gray at his temples and the fine lines around his eyes. He doesn't look like the Kit from the Bread Company.

He steers me toward a bedroom and opens the door. A nursery. A tiny head with fluffy black hair. I peer into the crib, my heart racing.

"You said Neil was on his honeymoon, but she's just a bab—"

"She's ours."

I swallow. "Yours and mine?"

"Yes."

My heart is freaking out. I can feel it pumping all the blood to my brain.

"Are you a time traveler?"

Kit smiles for the first time. Deep smile lines cut into his cheeks like he does a lot of it. Funny, I can't remember seeing Kit smile. He always seems so serious, which is what Della likes about him. *Della.*

"Where's Della?" Oh God. I had a baby with her boyfriend. I look down at my hand, but there's no wedding ring.

He walks out of the room. I glance back at the baby before I follow him out.

When we're in the hallway, he closes the nursery door.

"We're not exactly on speaking terms with Della," he says.

I feel such grief. Della and I had been a thing for over ten years. Kit sees the look on my face and quickly averts his eyes.

"This is a dream," I say. Kit shakes his head no. I catch a glimpse of myself in the heavy, gilded mirror behind his head. My hair is short. Highlighted. "No, a nightmare," I say, reaching up to touch it. "I look like a mom."

"You are a mom."

In this alternate universe, or time travel, or dream, I am a mom. But I am just Helena in my mind. Child-free and flat-bellied. And before me is Kit. The guy my best friend thinks is "the one." It is not possible that I would ever look at him that way. I look at him now, trying to see him in a different light. He is so different from Neil. Stocky, a little scruffy. Neil shaved his arms; Kit's arms are covered in black hair. Neil has dark eyes; Kit has light eyes. Neil wears contacts; Kit wears glasses. Della and I have never shared the same taste in men, which suited us just fine. Made chicks before dicks easier to live by.

"Where is she?" I ask.

"She's still in Florida. We moved here two years ago."

Kit takes my hand. "Let me show you something," he says.

It feels all wrong. Our fingers don't fit well together. His hands are large, his fingers broad. My hand feels stretched and awkward in his. Della always said that hands should fit together like puzzle pieces. Hers and Kit's fit. She told me that!

The little boy suddenly appears from the kitchen. Kit lets go of my hand to swing him into his arms.

They seem very comfortable together, considering he's not the boy's father. Neil is his father. So where is Neil? And what happened between us?

"What happened to Neil? Why aren't we together?"

He glances at the little boy … what was his name? Tim? Tom? And sets him on his feet.

"Go put in a movie, little man, and I'll be in there in a minute to watch it with you."

He's a good kid, I guess, because he nods without arguing and runs off, his bare feet slapping the hardwood.

"Neil cheated on you," he says. "But it's not as simple as it sounds. You aren't mad at him. You understood."

Heat rises to my face. Neil cheated on me? Neil wasn't the type, not to mention he worshipped the ground I walked on. "He would never," I say. Kit shrugs. "People are people. Things change."

"No," I say. "This is a Pottery Barn life. I don't want it."

"Like I said, it's not that simple. He had his … reasons."

Before I can ask what those reasons are, the baby starts to cry. Kit glances at her door and then back at me.

"She only wants you. She's teething. If I go in there and get her, she'll freak out."

"I don't even like babies."

He grabs my arms and spins me around 'til I'm facing the nursery door.

"You like this one," he says, giving me a little shove.

"What's her name?" I hiss, before opening the door.

He grins. For whatever reason, my stomach does a little flip.

"Brandy."

I give him a disgusted look. "Like the liquor?" I hiss.

He tries not to smile, but all of a sudden I see where those deep lines on either side of his mouth come from.

"It's what you were drinking the night you got pregnant."

"Oh God," I say, pushing open the door. "I grew up to be a goddamn cliché."

Brandy is sitting in her crib, screaming. Her arms go up the minute she sees me. I've never had a baby reach for me before; they like me less than I like them.

I pick her up, and she immediately stops wailing. She's little. Petite. And she has so much hair she looks like a little lion. I guess if I liked babies, this one would be considered cute. I carry her out to her … father. "Here," I say, offering her to him. He shakes his head. "You hold her."

I do so stiffly as we walk toward what looks like another living room. This one less Pottery Barn adult, and more Pottery Barn kids. God. If this was all real, what happened to me? I didn't like shit like this. My apartment looked like a garage sale gone wrong.

"Why does everything look like this?" I ask him.

"Look like what?"

"Like I have no personality."

Kit looks surprised. "I don't know. This is what you like. I've never thought about it before."

"How long have we been together?"

The corners of his mouth twitch, and before he says anything, I know he's going to lie.

"Few years."

"And we love each other?"

He stops rifling through a drawer to look at me.

"Do you know that feeling you have right now? The bewilderment, the fear, the fascination?"

I nod.

"That's what I feel every day. Because I've never loved someone like I love you."

My stomach does this involuntary flutter thingy. I feel guilty that my best friend's boyfriend made my stomach flutter. Luckily, Brandy yanks on my hair so it looks more like pain than a reaction to his words.

He goes back to his drawer and pulls out a coloring book. At first I think he's getting it for the little boy, but then he hands it to me.

"Do you want me to give it to Tim?" I ask, confused.

"Tom," he says. "And no. That's what I wanted to show you."

I flip to the first page and find what I'm not expecting. Beautiful pictures of castles made of candy, fairy houses perched in fruit trees, and princesses fighting dragons. The type of coloring book I would have wanted as a child.

"What's this?" I ask, not looking up. I want to see more.

"It's yours," he says, taking the baby from me.

I laugh. "I can't draw. I'm not artistic at all." I slam it shut and hand it back to him. This is such a strange dream. I pinch myself, but I don't wake up, and it hurts.

"That's how you bought this house, moved to Washington. You have a line of them, and they're very popular. There are even posters and notebooks. You can buy them in Target."

"Target?" I repeat. "I'm in school to be an accountant," I say. "This is silly. I want to wake up."

Why am I getting upset? If this is a dream, I should just go with it, right?

Tom comes running in just then and announces that he spilled grape juice on the floor. Kit leaves in a hurry, and I am left alone to tend to the little girl. I sit her on my lap and touch her mane of silky hair. She sighs contentedly, and I figure she likes it. "I like it too," I tell her. "One time I fell asleep at a funeral because my dad was playing with my hair." I keep doing it so she doesn't cry and alert Kit to the fact that I know nothing about babies. When he comes back, we are sitting on the couch, her half-drugged against my chest. I'm still trying to wake myself from this strange dream. He leans against the doorframe, smiling that half-smile he does.

"She's just like you."

"You don't know what I'm like," I say.

"Really, Helena? Don't I?"

I hesitate. I don't know anything.

I keep expecting the dream to end, but it doesn't. I spend what seems like hours with Kit, Tom, and Brandy as they move through their day. I try to be a good sport, pretending to fit in with his life, even taking a walk with them through the greenest woods I have ever seen. Do dreams really go on this long? Why when you wake up, do dreams seem so hazy and distorted? We stop at a lake, and Kit and Tom skip rocks while I hold Brandy, who really, to my horror, doesn't want anyone but me. I scoop some of the rich, wet dirt onto a fingertip and taste it. Dirt shouldn't have a taste in a dream. Or it should taste like Oreos. It definitely shouldn't taste like dirt. After the walk, Kit cooks us all dinner. Fish he caught himself. He grills it outside on the patio he says that I designed. Again, I remind him that I'm not creative enough to have designed something as majestic as the patio. It reminds me a little of the coloring books, with their carved wood tree houses, and lanterns hanging from trees. The fish is delicious. By the time Kit carries Brandy and Tom inside to give them their baths, I am in full panic mode. I reference the movies I've seen to help me: *Inception*, *BIG*, *The Wizard of Oz*. When Kit comes back carrying a bottle of wine and two glasses, I'm crying and ripping the paper napkins into confetti.

He doesn't say anything about my tears. He opens the bottle and fills a glass, setting it in front of me.

I throw it back like a college girl. Because I am a college girl—not a mom.

"This isn't real," I say. "Where are all of my memories if it's real?"

He sits down next to me and throws an ankle over his knee.

"The day I fell in love with you was the first day you found yourself. You weren't even mine yet."

He looks all blurry and distorted through my tears; I let them slip down my face as I listen to him.

"You always insisted you were left-brained, but I didn't believe you. An artist can always recognize another artist. We sniff each other out. One night we were all drunk and hanging out at Della's place. She said she wanted to color, so she carries out all these coloring books, crayons, and markers. And we all lay on our stomachs on the floor and colored like five year olds. It was one of those nights you don't forget, because it was so bizarre," he pauses, "but also because I fell in love."

I want him to keep going. The story he's telling has never happened, but it sounds so real.

"I was lying next to you on the carpet, and Neil was on your other side. Your picture was the best. It wasn't just good; it was surprisingly good. Everyone freaked out, but I felt smug like I already knew it. We started joking about you being an artist, and it was then that you said you wanted to be great at drawing so you could have your own coloring book line. So I told you to do it."

I find that my lips part, and my eyes become glassy when he speaks to me like he knows me. It's intimate. I've always wanted to know myself and have never known where to begin.

"I can't—"

"Draw," he finishes. "Yes, so you've said. You took classes. Didn't tell anyone but me."

I want to pick up a pen and see if it's true, if I have some hidden talent I never knew I had. And I want to know, of all people, why I told Kit. If this isn't a dream...

It's a dream.

"Wh-what sorts of things do we do together?" I ask him.

Kit licks his lips. "You and I are the same," he says. "Don't look at me like that."

I snort when I laugh, covering my mouth with the back of my hand.

"We are very different." He smiles. "I'm an optimist, you're a pessimist. I avoid confrontation, you charge into it."

"So how are we the same?"

"We were both on the search for something true at the same time. Sometimes a person's truth is another person's love."

I don't know what he means, and I'm ashamed to admit it.

"Do we like to do the same things?"

"Yes." His face is in shadow, but I can hear his fingertips as they rub at the scruff on his chin. "We like art. Food. Small moments that last forever. We like to have sex. We like our babies—" I get goosebumps at that last bit. "We traveled a bit before we had Brandy. We hope to do more of that. We have a list of all the places we want to make love—"

"What's on the list?" I cut him off. My mouth feels dry.

His voice is low when he speaks. "The Blue Train."

"What's that?" I lean forward.

He smiles at me. "It's a train in South Africa that runs from Pretoria to Cape Town."

I sit back. "A train? Oh."

Kit raises his eyebrow at me. "It's chartered. It takes you through some of the most breathtaking views in the world. Private cabin, private chef."

I raise my eyebrows.

"What else?"

"A graveyard during a full moon. A treehouse."

He leans forward and pours himself another glass of wine.

"What do I … what do I like about being with you?"

"You want to be you," he says. "And that doesn't offend me."

Again, I have no idea what he's talking about. I was supremely inoffensive. Boring. Being me took minimal effort.

We drink the bottle of wine in silence, listening to the toads, and the water, and the trees. A cacophony of God's things. When I stand up my head spins. I sway and have to catch myself on the back of my chair. Kit stands up, too, and I don't know if it's because of the wine, or the fact that I've convinced myself this is a dream, but I walk boldly to him. *It's been done before.* That's the feeling I get when his hands and arms find me. Everything about him is familiar—the solidness, his smell, the callouses on his fingertips. This is not the awkward embrace of two people touching for the first time. He's unclasped my bra and pulled off my shirt before I've reached his mouth. I kiss him for the first time, naked from the waist up as his thumbs trace the line under her breasts. The air feels erotic when it blows across my skin. Hands so different from Neil's long, slender ones touch me. Heavy, warm hands with broad fingers. He tastes of wine. When I kiss his cheek, the stubble scratches at my lips. It's not entirely unpleasant. I tug at his shirt, and he takes it off. I like how solid he is, and then I really like how solid he is when he picks me up and sets me on the table, and my legs strain to reach around him.

This isn't real. You aren't cheating. I close my eyes. He pulls off my pants, kisses me through my panties, and slides on top of me. Our wine bottle goes crashing to the floor, and I turn my head to look at the shards even as he's kissing his way down my neck and his fingers are in my underwear. My skin is tingling, my hips angled up in demand. Demand of … Kit. His head is bent. I can see him, as he gets ready to push himself inside of me. Then I can feel him, right there. I grab at his arms, frantic. And in that moment I don't care who he is, and whom he's supposed to belong to. This feels natural, Kit and I acting on something that was already there. My eyes roll back in my head as he slides inside of me.

And then I wake up.

2
#DRANKTHEKOOLAID

I wake up in my car. Light stabs sharply through the windshield, and I squint my eyes. There are greasy fingerprints on the driver's side window. Hands that pressed and slid. They've been there for a while … something about being drunk and eating fried chicken, then not being able to find my keys. I keep meaning to clean them off, but I'm so … busy. I look for Kit. Where is he? No, I'm not supposed to be looking for Kit. It's Neil I'm with. Neil I love. My mind is still caught in my … dream? I raise my seat and rub at my heart. It's hurting. Like for real. This could be a heart attack; I feel like I have high cholesterol. No, no—it's something else. I feel so sad. How could a dream have so much detail? I've never experienced anything like that. The screen on my phone lights up. It's Neil. They're in the restaurant looking for me. Neil, Della, and Kit. *Kit.* I remember now. I arrived an hour early and wanted to close my eyes for a few minutes before everyone got to the restaurant. All the late nights studying are catching up to me.

I get out of the car slowly and look around. I haven't been sleeping well with finals in a week. And then I graduate. And then I'm grown up. Not quite like the grownup I was in the dream, with children and a house, and a Kit. I can still feel his lips on my neck. I reach up to touch my sweet spot, right below my ear. I laugh as I walk to the door of the restaurant. So stupid. I've never even thought of the guy in that way. The dream will dissipate soon, but as I walk through the doors, and toward my boyfriend, it's still there, sticky and thick. I do not feel like Helena of now, but rather the Helena of my dream. I look for Kit. He's sitting next to Della, listening intently to something she's whispering in his ear. I wait for him to look up and see me. I don't know what I expect to see in his eyes, familiarity maybe. It's so stupid. No such thing happens. When Kit sees me walk up to the table, he smiles politely, his eyes flitting, non-committal. How they should be since we hardly know each other. Della's greeting is much more enthusiastic. I smile blandly as she jumps up to embrace me, commenting on my shirt. Kit is looking at the menu. I want to snatch it from him.

Don't you see me? We had a baby together!

I blush at my own thoughts as Neil pulls out my chair, kissing me on the cheek. I close my eyes and try to be pulled in by him. But he smells off, and his fingers are too long and pokey as he kneads my neck.

Oh my God. It's like I'm on drugs.

"What's wrong?" Neil asks.

I take a sip of my water, spilling it on myself. "Nothing," I say. "I'm just really hungry." He flags down the server, and as he does, I wonder if he would really cheat on me. Neil, who likes things to be simple and easy. Cheating takes work. A complicated smorgasbord of emotions that he isn't wired for.

When the waiter comes, I order wine. Neil raises his eyebrows. I don't blame him, I suppose. I've been a beer drinker until this very moment. "I thought you didn't like wine."

"I didn't," I say, shooting Kit a look. "I guess I do now. It's, like, super hot in here."

Kit orders wine too. Della and Neil make fun of us. Old people, they say. I would have said that too … last week, this morning, an hour ago. Can a dream really influence your palate? I don't think so.

They talk about all kinds of things, but I barely hear them. They are not things I care about anymore. I pull out a pen from my purse and start to draw on the paper placemat. I am trying to draw the things I saw in the coloring book, but I'm terrible.

"What are you doing?" Della asks me. "You're totally zoned out." She's leaning into him, her hand rubbing his thigh. She picks up the placemat and examines it. "Is this … a treehouse?"

"Yes!" I say excitedly. She giggles, and I feel sad.

"Don't quit your day job, Helena," she says. "You're the math girl." I take back the placemat and put it face down on the table. Kit looks at me for the first time—like really zones in.

"Do you like to draw?" he asks. I like to compare people's eyes to sweets. Kit's eyes are chocolaty—melty and warm. I'm not a big chocolate person, but Neil has cough drop eyes, and right now I just really need something sweet.

"No," Neil answers for me. "I've known her for years, and I've never seen her so much as doodle in a notebook."

I look back at Kit, hoping for something. I think about saying that thing about wanting to illustrate a coloring book, but it's not true, and I'd feel silly saying it. Maybe I'm scared.

"I don't know," I say to Kit. "I'm not very good at it."

I wait for him to encourage me, but the server comes with our food, and all is forgotten. They spend the rest of dinner talking about a trip we are all planning to take over the summer. I spend it thinking about the dream. A life I never knew I wanted. I want to go back. I want to fall asleep again to see if I can visit Helena and Kit's Pottery Barn house in Port Townsend, Washington. When Kit says something, I listen. He's kind of the same person I knew in the dream, maybe not as self-aware. But, for the first time, I notice how attentive he is to my best friend. How touchy-feely, and not in a smothering way. He just likes to touch her, and I feel jealous. When he speaks, it's never without purpose. He says things that make Neil nod thoughtfully, and make Della look up at him with a dreamy look on her face. This is crazy. I stand up.

"I have to go," I say.

"Why?" Neil protests. "We are supposed to go to a movie."

"I don't feel well," I say. I lean down and kiss him on the cheek. There is no stubble to graze my lips. "I'll see you tomorrow. Bye guys." I wave at Della and Kit and walk quickly to my car. I look over my shoulder, expecting one of them to be following me, and I feel a pang of sadness that they're all talking at the table like I was never there.

I drive home and let myself into my apartment, still unable to shake the weird feeling I've had since waking up from the dream. Instead of taking out my textbooks to study, I find an empty notebook and begin writing down the details of the dream. *So stupid. Such a waste of time.* I tell myself this, but I don't stop doing it, until there are ten pages of scrawling, blue ink. When I'm done, I'm exhausted. From the emotion of it, yes. But more so, because I feel changed. Shifted. Redirected. I drink three glasses of water, take a shower. When nothing can distract me from the strangeness I feel, I open my laptop and find Kit's Facebook profile. We became friends recently, after the first time Della introduced us. It always seems like the thing to do when you meet someone new—add them to your life on social media. *We are now friends!* Now you can see what I eat for lunch, posted in my very favorite filter, and see pictures of my running shoes as I take an above shot to let you know I work out. And read my sentimental posts about how I date the best guy in the universe (posted on his birthday or our anniversary). Every pretentious, made up moment of my life will be yours. Welcome, follower!

After we tapped our way into each other's media lives, I never took the time to go back and look at Kit's profiles. Though I apparently follow him on Twitter, Facebook, and Instagram, Kit doesn't post very much. I find a picture of Della sitting on his lap and study them both intently—her white, perfect teeth, his tight-lipped grin. Where did they even meet? I try to remember. He was a musician, I think. She went on and on about that. I look for clues on his Instagram, but he only posts sunsets and beach shots void of humans. Really good ones actually. He played his camera phone pretty well. I slam my laptop shut, ignore a call from Della, and crawl into bed. Maybe I'll get lucky and go back to Port Townsend in my sleep. Maybe the dream will turn into a nightmare, and then I'll *want* to forget it. Tomorrow, my head will be clear. Tomorrow, Kit will just be Della's boyfriend, and I will be in love with Neil, and I'll have my whole life ahead of me.

3
#SOCKS

I wake up and stalk all of his profiles again. Nothing has changed since last night, but it's the first thing I think to do. I have seven missed calls from Della and Neil. I call Neil first while lying on my stomach, studying a picture Kit took of a seagull perched on a piece of driftwood.

"The movie was great," he tells me. "I don't know if either of them saw any of it; they were all over each other."

I report Kit's picture as inappropriate out of spite.

"What do you mean?" I ask. "He's not really that touchy-feely."

"I think they really like each other. They were making jokes about eloping last night."

"What? No!" I stuff a pillow over my mouth and roll onto my back. Luckily, Neil thinks I was upset about Della.

"Relax. You know how boy crazy Della is. She's not actually going to marry him."

I make the sign of the cross as I stare up at the ceiling.

"They asked us to go with them to Barclays tonight, but I told them I didn't know if you could since you have to study."

"I'll go," I say quickly. I roll out of bed, trying to land on my feet, but instead I get caught in the sheets and roll onto the floor. Neil doesn't hear the thump, or my cry of pain.

"Pick you up at seven," he says before hanging up. He doesn't wait for my goodbye. I stay tangled in my sheets and pretend I'm Frodo when Shelob the spider spins him into his web. I almost fall asleep again, but my phone rings. Della this time.

"Neil says you're coming tonight," she says. "I'm so freaking excited. Listen, I know this is going to freak you out, but I really think Kit is going to ask me to marry him."

My *What?* is muffled by the blankets.

"I know, I know," she says. "But when you know, you know. That's what everyone says."

I fight my way out of the blankets and jump to my feet. I catch sight of myself in the mirror and flinch. Topknot gone wrong, crooked and spilling out, lion mane hairs around my face sticking up in every direction. I'm wearing my Lion King pajamas from my middle school days. I can't bear to toss them, because Simba and Nala had a beautiful love. There's a knock on my door. I'm already opening it when Della says, "Oh yeah, Kit should be there in a few minutes. I sent him over to get my laptop bag." It's too late to slam the door shut. With his girlfriend yakking in my ear, I open the door to my dream husband. Not the husband of my dreams, just my dream husband. Except I'm not even sure we were married, just having babies out of wedlock and living in Port Townsend like a bunch of hippies. Kit raises his eyebrows when he sees me.

"I have to go," I say to Della. I hang up without waiting for her response.

"Hakuna Matata."

"So predictable. Running errands for the queen?"

I think about reaching up to smooth down my mane, but if I opened the door like this, I might as well own it.

"She left her bag here?"

"Yes." I step aside so he can come in. When he breezes past me, I get a whiff of his cologne. Not the same as the dream, but good. Neil doesn't wear cologne. I watch him look around the room for Della's bag. I know where it is, but I want to watch him. I also want to be mean to him because he's ruining my life. "It's there by the barstool," I finally say. Kit bends down to pick it up. We never have much to say to each other, and it's always a little awkward. But, now I feel like I know him. I head past him into the kitchen and take out the bacon.

He hesitates, not sure if he's supposed to leave or make small talk.

I don't really want to share my bacon with him—it's the expensive, peppercorn kind—but I'm curious about who is he. Or who he is. Or whatever.

"Hungry?" I ask.

"Is that the kind with the pepper on it? From the deli?"

I nod.

He sits on one of my two barstools and folds his hands on the counter. "I don't know how to cook. It's a severe handicap."

I shrug. "There are videos on the internet, cooking shows, and lessons you can buy for fifty bucks an hour. You just need some drive and you can be rehabilitated."

He laughs. His smile isn't centered on his face; it's all up on his left cheek like it's drunk. You wouldn't really know that since he rarely smiles. He looks younger, mischievous.

"Maybe I should do that," he says. "Become a self-made sous chef."

"I predict you'll love to cook in ten years," I say, turning the bacon. "Then you'll have to make me something great, since I started your love of cooking."

"All right," he says, looking at me. "What would you like?"

"Fish," I say quickly. "That you caught yourself."

"And after that, I'll chop down a tree for you."

I feel myself tingle, so I look down at my bacon. That happened so easily. The banter. The first time we've ever had a discussion alone, and we're simpatico. I get the eggs and cheese out, too, because I need to stress eat.

"So you just—"

He makes the whipping motion I'm using to scramble the eggs.

"Yes," I say. "Want to try?"

He does it to humor me; I know he does. Who wants to whip slimy eggs around in a bowl? He splashes them all over my counter, but it's cute that he's trying. I make him pour them into the pan, then, when I see he's a willing helper, hand him the spatula. He watches as I finish the bacon and sprinkle cheese on the eggs. I wish I felt self-conscious about my hair, but truth be told, I look hella cute with psycho hair.

Too much? I ask myself. *Who cares?* I portion our food onto plates and walk ahead of him to my tiny dinette. While he sits, I go back for coffee.

"I don't drink coffee," he tells me.

I take a long sip from my mug and stare at him over the rim. "That's why you never smile. You'd be a better man if you drank coffee." He laughs for the second time, and I feel a little high as I hand him his mug.

"What's a Muggle?" he asks, taking it from me.

"I save that mug for special people, Kit. Don't ask questions."

Kit drinks his coffee. I wait for him to flinch, or make the usual complaints that non-coffee drinkers make. But he downs it like a pro, and I decide he's not as bad as I thought. Maybe a little stoic. Melancholy. But, man, when you get him to laugh, it feels like a real goddam treat.

"Thanks for teaching me to stir eggs, and also for feeding me," he says when it's time to go.

"No problem, Kit. See you tonight." I sound all business. I want to pat myself on the back for not swooning.

"Tonight?" he asks.

"Yeah, Neil and I are coming with to Barclays."

"Cool," he says. "I didn't know."

"Della makes plans for everyone," I say. I want to see how he reacts to that. If he's annoyed by Della's tendencies to control everyone's free time. But he just shrugs.

"See you later then."

When I look in the mirror after he leaves, I find egg in my hair. Also, I don't look nearly as cute as I imagined.

Della shows up later while I am sorting through my box of mismatched socks. She walks right in, tossing her designer shit on my sofa.

"Oh no," she says. "Why do you have that out?"

"What? No reason." I try to hide the box, even though she's already seen it.

She grabs me by the shoulders and looks in my eyes. "You don't get that box out unless you have high anxiety," she says. "What's wrong?"

Della is correct. My box of socks has been around since I was a kid. My mom would complain that one of my socks was missing, and she'd throw the loner in the trash. Five year old me would get it out of the trash when she wasn't looking and stuff it in my pillowcase. The other sock would turn up. I knew it even then. I was just keeping its partner safe until it did. When my mother changed my bed sheets, she freaked out about all the socks in my pillowcase. I heard her telling my dad I was a hoarder. I remember feeling shame. There was something wrong with me; my mother had said it with such conviction. *Hoarder! Sock hoarder!* Later, when my dad came to my room to speak to me, he told me that when he was little, he used to keep all the caps to the toothpaste tubes. He couldn't bear to throw them away. He gave me a shoebox and told me to keep my socks in there instead. I hid it under my bed, my shoebox of shame, and when I felt anxious or lost I would pull it out and touch all of my socks. All loners. All waiting to be reunited with their twin. I eventually outgrew the shoebox … and by that I mean there were too many socks.

4
#SMUTLOVER

Kit doesn't come to Barclays. At the last minute he calls Della and tells her something's come up. I don't know who's more disappointed: Della—who starts to cry—or me, as I sulk in a corner pretending to listen to Neil as he talks about rocket science, or some shit like that. We order drinks, and I pull out a pen to doodle on my placemat. Once again, Neil and Della have a conversation without me. I wonder when I became the weird one. The little social pariah who sits in the shadows, trying to discover her hidden artistic talent. I even ordered a different drink than my usual cranberry vodka. It seems so childish to order, now that I've furnished a house with Pottery Barn. I order another glass of wine. White this time. The night ends early, and Neil drives us both home. Della asks me if she can sleep over. I say yes, but I don't like it when she spends the night. For all of her beautiful, smooth skin, and bright blue eyes, Della farts in her sleep. It gets really uncomfortable. Most nights I go sleep on the couch and then sneak back to the bed before she wakes up. Neil walks us to the door and kisses me goodnight.

"I was hoping we'd have some time together tonight. To … you know…" He waggles his eyebrows at me.

"To what?" I ask dryly. Neil doesn't get my humor. It's nothing against him, really. But sometimes I like to make him nervous.

"To do things." He glances over my shoulder to where Della is taking off her shoes and picking up the remote.

"Like?"

"Have sex," he whispers.

"What? Why are you mumbling?"

"To have sex," he says louder.

"Ew!" Della says from the living room. "I'm right here."

I watch him turn bright red, and I giggle. Neil is cute.

"Plenty of time for that next week, lover," I say. "After finals are over."

He gives me a really good kiss goodnight. I almost get glassy-eyed as I remember all the reasons I love him.

1. Good kisser
2. Kind
3. Goofy
4.

Della makes me cook her a snack. Cook. Like I actually have to melt butter and chop garlic for what she wants. She sits on the couch, with *Teen Mom* on mute, and talks about Kit the whole time. She thought a proposal was coming, but now he's possibly cheating.

"I have been distant," she tells me. I wonder when that was.

"Emotionally distant?" I ask. "Or physically? Because every time I look over, you're on his lap."

"Emotionally," she says, without skipping a beat. "Last week I sent two of his calls to voicemail. I was on the toilet. And yesterday, when he asked me what I thought about his bass playing, I gave him a really generic response."

"Ouch," I say. "Wedding's off."

"This isn't a joke, Helena! He's the love of my life. My soul mate!"

I scrunch up my nose. Hadn't I read somewhere that there was a difference? I think about telling her about my dream. Maybe that's what I need. A good laugh about me with Kit. But she'd probably say that Kit and I have nothing in common. And then I'd get mad. She didn't see us at breakfast. She didn't know that I changed his mind about coffee. Or that I was working hard to be a coloring book artist, because in my dream he told me I was. All these things.

I carry her snack to her and sit as far away from her on the couch as I can.

"Come snuggle with me," she says.

"No."

She turns back to the TV, glassy-eyed, checking her phone every thirty seconds.

"Has he not answered any of your texts?" I ask her.

"No. I think he's asleep."

I wait a few minutes before picking up my phone and typing in his name.

Hey Kit!

It takes a few, but eventually the talk box pops up. I wait, my limbs tingling.

K: Hey kid!

I glance at Della out of the corner of my eye. She's enraptured by Tyler and Catelynn.

Drink anymore coffee?

K: I want to be a better man.

Lol. Why haven't you texted Della? She's freaking out.

His text box shows up for a few seconds, then disappears all together. After that, I don't hear from him.

Shunned by association. Maybe Della was right. He is cheating on her. Asshole. There is no way I am marrying someone like that, let alone having his baby. I have to stop this nonsense. It was just a freaking dream.

"Tell me about him," I say to Della. "What's he like and why do you think he's so great anyway?"

She turns to look at me, her eyes large and filled with tears. "He's so good. Ten times better than anyone I know. He cares so much about other people. And not what they think—he doesn't give a shit about what anyone thinks—he just cares about *them*."

"What else? Is he smart? What is he into?"

"He's ... really smart. But, he doesn't throw it around, you know? He's quiet. Listens, even when you think he isn't. And he notices details, crazy details. Like he always knows when I've had my eyebrows waxed, or change my nail polish color. And he likes ... I don't know. We do the same things."

Since Della's life consists of sleeping late, shopping for bikinis, and going to the occasional late night concert, I'm not sure it says much about Kit.

"He's just busy," I tell her. "It's not about you."

She nods, and just like that, her glassy eyes turn back to the TV, and she's zoned out. That's the thing about Della: if someone's not in love with her, she stops being able to function.

Kit disappears for a week. And, during that week, Della will not leave my apartment. She follows me from room to room, asks for snacks, and cries into my throw pillows. I suggest she go to his job and ask him what's up. But she says only trashy girls chase men, and instead stalks his Facebook.

I try to leave my apartment as much as possible, but she asks if she can come with me when I leave. I'm smothered in places a person shouldn't be subjected to smothering: the grocery store, the dry cleaners, the gas station where she gets out of the car to stand next to me while I pump gas. I sneak out once, when she's using the bathroom, and ten minutes later she blows up my phone until I answer.

"Where are you?" she sobs.

When I tell her I ran to the bookstore, she says she'll meet me there, and shows up in huge sunglasses and a tight black dress.

"Why are you dressed like that?" I ask. I am crouched in the trashy novel section, looking for cheap thrills and deep skills.

"Kit is here," she says. "I saw on his Instagram."

Shoot. I didn't. He hardly ever posts pictures.

"Were you going for the clubbing-in-the-middle-of-the-day look?" I ask her.

"Shhhh," she says, flapping her hand at me. "Here he comes."

I have *The Barron's Lust* in my hand when Kit comes walking up. I stand up, so I'm not at crotch level, and glance at Della. Her face is indifferent, but I can see her hands trembling. I'm caught in the middle of a couple's quarrel, and I don't know what to do with myself.

"Easy Dells," I whisper. "He's just a boy who has a lot of explaining to do."

Her shoulders straighten up, and I see her pointy little chin jut forward.

Kit notices my book first. "Whoa!" he says. "Bet it's at least ten inches."

I put it back on the shelf.

"Where have you been?" Della growls. I flinch, but try to look supportive.

Kit makes a face. "Nowhere new. Why are you wearing sunglasses inside?"

Della rips them off her face to reveal two swollen eyes.

"You haven't returned any of my calls. I've been a mess."

I take a few steps back, trying to ease out of the smut aisle before they start fighting.

Kit rubs a hand across the back of his neck. "Oh. Sorry about that. When I'm writing, I get distracted."

"Writing?" Her face is screwed up in confusion.

"Yeah," he says. "I've been working on something new."

"What do you write?" I blurt.

He notices me at the end of the aisle and gives me a funny smile.

"Nothing serious," he says. "I just tinker." He looks at Della. "But, this time I'm into it. I haven't slept in forty-eight hours." And then, with a side-glance to me, he says "I've been drinking a lot of coffee."

Join the club, I want to tell him. On the sleep *and* the coffee.

"I … I didn't know," Della says. "It felt like you didn't want to speak to me."

Kit sighs. Deep.

"Sometimes I'm not good about keeping in touch. I disappear. I don't mean to upset anyone, I swear. I just get involved with what I'm doing."

"Oh," she says. "Now I feel stupid."

"Don't."

And then they kiss in the smut aisle. And my initial thought is that I'm watching him cheat on me. Or maybe not me—dream Helena. But it feels weird and gross.

I drive home, book-less. At least I'll get my apartment back.

5
#ART

After finals, I sign up for an art class. I don't even tell Neil. It's stupid, I know. You have one lousy dream, and you think you're destined for coloring book greatness. But my instructor is a kooky old guy named Neptune who walks around the classroom barefoot and smells like Vicks Vapor Rub. I'm totally into him. He tells us that when he was a young man, Joan Mitchell commissioned him to paint her nude. If I can't be Neptune's favorite at the end of this eight-week session, life isn't even worth living. I want him to want to paint me naked. Is that creepy? Oh my God, I'm so creepy. I'm not particularly good at any of the assignments, but one time Neptune tells me that he likes my interpretation of a sea horse.

"It's like a seahorse who was born in the sky," he says. I smell vodka on his breath, but still. Weren't all of the greatest artists junkies and alcoholics? I frame my airborne seahorse and hang it in my bedroom. It's just the beginning. I'm going to be so super good at this one day.

Della invites us to dinner at her apartment a few weeks later. I haven't seen either her or Kit since the smutty bookstore kiss. And I don't want to. I've managed not to think of him at all. Even in art class when I draw a tree house that looks more like a minivan. Even when I scramble eggs. It's easy to forget a guy who has melty smurf eyes and a melancholy face. I'm not about that life.

TARRYN FISHER

"I don't want to go," I tell Neil. "I have to look for a job. I'm a grown up."

"Being a grown up can wait for a night," he says. "Della's been complaining that she never sees you anymore."

Della hasn't been complaining to me. I wonder why she'd talk to Neil about something like that.

"Okay," I say. "But she can't cook, so maybe we should eat dinner before we go."

Neil agrees, and we make plans to eat at Le Tub before we head over to her house. Le Tub is a Miami oceanside restaurant that uses old bathtubs and toilets as decoration. If you're really lucky, you get a table by the water where you can see the manatees as they swim by. Someone once told me that it was one of Oprah's favorite restaurants, but seriously, Oprah has a lot of favorite things—it all sounds like lies at this point.

I make sure my hair is blow-dried this time, and put on my nice silk shorts and a peasant top. Neil whistles when he sees me, and I make a mental note to try to look nice more often.

"Legs for days," he says.

"All the better to wrap around you," I say, then immediately blush. I never say things like that. So embarrassing. Neil likes it. He makes me drink three glasses of wine, and when we hug in the parking lot after dinner, he slips his fingers under my shorts and kisses my ear.

I'm like a real life seductress. Who knew wine could unwind me?

Della announces that we smell like steak when we arrive. She leans in to sniff my hair, and I swat her away. We lie and say it's the air freshener in Neil's car, and I hand her a bottle of wine. It feels different in here. Like, not as Della. I eye the living room suspiciously. Everything is neat and orderly. No sign of a male live-in. But still…

She ushers us into her pink living room where a tray of appetizers is set up on the coffee table.

* 30 *

I blink. Fancy shit. I forget I just ate dinner and try it all. Salmon canapés, miniature meat pies, baked brie. I spill mango salsa on my shirt, and I don't even care. The button of my shorts is digging into my stomach. Della pours me a glass of wine, and while I'm trying to wipe off the salsa, wine splashes onto my shirt.

"Where did you buy this?" I ask through a mouthful of cheese.

"I didn't buy it," she says. "Kit made it."

The cheese gets stuck in my throat, and I cough. It's awful, like my whole life flashes in front of my eyes, and it's so boring. Lying little shit. Neil hits me on the back. I'm bent over and watery-eyed when Kit walks into the room, a tray of something perched on his steepled fingers.

"Don't like it?" he asks.

I eye his ripped blue jeans, and shake my head. *Filth. Chef scum.*

"It's delicious," I say. "It's the work of a talented chef. Someone who's had a *lot* of practice in the kitchen."

He smirks and sets down the tray. "Eh, it's not that hard. Like scrambling eggs."

I choke on my wine.

"What's wrong with you tonight?" Neil says, handing me a napkin.

"Just doing everything too fast," I say. "Choking and whatnot."

"You have cheese in your hair," Kit says. "Right there." He motions to the spot. I don't pull it out. Let the cheese have my hair.

Della claps her hands and takes a bacon-wrapped scallop off Kit's tray. "Now I'll never have to learn how to cook!" she says gleefully. "Kit can take care of it!"

I wonder when she ever had plans to learn how to cook. Especially since I'd been her official snack-maker since tenth grade.

"What's for dinner?" I ask, sinking into the couch.

"Fish," Kit says. "That I caught myself."

I balk.

"Lovely," I say. Then, "Neil, can you pour me more wine? That's right. Fill it all the way to the top…"

It turns out that I can eat a lot more than I think, especially if it's delicious as fuck. By the time we are finished with dinner, I can't even stand up straight. Neil has fallen asleep with his head on the table, and Della is singing karaoke by herself in the bedroom. Kit leads me to the living room, suspiciously sober, and helps me onto the love seat.

"I'll make some coffee," he says, moving toward the kitchen.

"Did you lie about the coffee too?" I hiss. I cling to the cushions so I don't roll off the couch.

He's holding four wine glasses between his fingers. He stops to consider what I've said, and all I can think about is how he's able to hold all four wine glasses without them slipping out of his hands.

"No. That was true. It's probably why I started writing that book. I got addicted to coffee and stayed up all night. Thanks for that."

I roll my eyes.

"Hey, I got you something."

I make a face. "You got *me* something?"

"Yeah," he says. "Hold on."

He disappears into Della's bedroom and comes out carrying a brown paper bag.

I take it from him, gingerly.

"What the what?" I say.

I reach into the bag and pull out a book.

"Drawing for beginners," I read. My brain is a wine slushy, but the situation is still eerie enough to give me goose bumps.

"It's a start," he tells me. "If you're going to doodle, you might as well learn how to do it really well."

I swallow the lump in my throat. "Why did you choose this particular book?" I ask, looking up at him.

"There were lots of kinds," he says. "But I thought you'd like the castles and unicorns."

My heart does this racing thing. For the first time in days, I don't think I'm crazy. I think everything is crazy. I'm trapped in a dream. The dream has invaded my world. *What the hell?*

6
#SOOVERÏT

I read the book Kit got me, then I text him to thank him. He plays it off like it was nothing. Typical. He has no idea how *not* nothing it was.

When are you going to let me read the book you're writing?

His text comes back almost immediately.

K: Wow! You'd want to?

I roll onto my back, excited. Maybe reading his book would give me some kind of insight into who he is.

Of course! I love to read.

K: Okay, I'll send it over. But I have to warn you, there aren't any throbbing penises or heaving breasts in my book.

I drop the phone on my face before I can respond. I may have a black eye tomorrow, but also Kit's unfinished manuscript.

What in the world would give you the impression I read that sort of thing?

K: I don't know. It was a stupid thing to say. You're way too uptight to appreciate a good fucking.

I frown. I don't know if we are still kidding around, or if he really thinks that about me. It doesn't really matter anyway. I'm a tiger in bed. Right out of one of my smutty novels with the embracing couples on the cover. That's a lie, but only to myself.

After texting him my e-mail address, I pull out my sketchbook. It dawns on me that since my dream I've become obsessive about making it come true. At least portions of it. Why else would I sign up for art classes when I've never drawn a serious thing in my life? And what happens if I never get better at it? Does it mean my dream failed? Or I failed?

I don't do anything that day but wait for Kit to send his manuscript. I should be looking for a job—a nice, cushy accounting job to rest my fat numbers brain on. I was top of my class at UM. There are already e-mails gathering in my account, so-and-so's uncle who is looking for an accountant. My mom's gynecologist who knows someone who is looking for an accountant. Even my uncle Chester is looking for an accountant for his snow cone business. All the free shaved ice I can eat.

I draw instead. Neptune looked at a tree I did last week and made a weird sound in the back of his throat. I'm no grunting expert, but it sounded like impressed approval to me. I've imitated that sound twice since then—once at a restaurant with Neil who asked me if I had something lodged in my throat, and once on the phone with my mother who wanted to bring me soup for the cold I was coming down with. Some people aren't good with expressive communication. It's not their fault. Finally, Kit sends me his novel. It appears in my inbox with the title: Doers Don't Do. I have no idea what that means. But when I transfer it to my iPad, it's only six chapters long. I'm disappointed. I was expecting *War and Peace* after all of the time he took off from Della. I settle down in my bed with a bag of cashews and my dream husband's book. Not the husband of my dreams, just the one from my dream, I remind myself.

Kit's story is about two boys who love the same girl. One of the boys is rash and impulsive; he enlists in the army and almost gets his arm blown off. The other is a librarian—deep thinking, kind of stalkerish. He stays in town to moon over the girl,

Stephanie Brown. Who the hell names their character Stephanie Brown? Kit is who. Stephanie is lackluster. She has all the pretty things pretty girls have, but I can't figure for the life of me why George or Denver would want her so badly. It will come, I think. Slowly, Kit will unfold the story, and the obsession, and in the end I would be madly in love with Stephanie Brown, too. I close out the document after chapter six and pull up my e-mail.

I want more.

I hit SEND. It doesn't take him long to respond. I am in the middle of tossing cashews into the air and catching them in my mouth when I hear my e-mail ping. His response is enthusiastic and just one word.

Really!?

I like his use of an exclamation point and a question mark. It hits the spot.

Yes, I send back. *Have you written past chapter six?*

Almost immediately, there is a new file in my e-mail. *Six more chapters!* But they'll have to wait. I have art class. I dress in all black to channel my inner artist and put my hair up in a bun. When I walk into class, Neptune nods at me. Everyone is taking me more seriously lately. I wonder if he nodded like that at Joan Mitchell when he was a young man. We are given reign of our own art today.

"Draw anything you like!" Neptune announces, punching the air. I feel inspired today. I draw George, Denver, and Stephanie Brown. All holding hands, standing by the fishing boat they restored together. Except they don't look like regular people. Instead of arms, I give George guns, and Denver has a giant computer as a head. Stephanie Brown, I draw drab, with soppy, weak shoulders. Neptune gets really excited when he stops by my work area. He claps his hands.

"All this time you draw trees and submarines, and here is your real talent," he says. "Pop art impressionism."

I beam. I take my work home that night with the intent of showing Kit. But, when I get home, Neil is waiting on my doorstep. He looks so angry I almost turn around and go back to my car.

"What's wrong?" I ask, as I pull out my key. Neil has a key, right on his key chain. I'm not sure why he's waiting out here.

"You forgot the dinner," he snaps. And when I just look at him, he repeats it, only with more emphasis. "The dinner."

The dinner, the dinner, the dinner…?

The whoosh of failure hits me hard. I feel pitiful, and sorry, and sick to my stomach. Neil's dinner. That his boss threw for him. To welcome him to the firm. It was important and exciting. We bought a bottle of champagne to celebrate, and I planned out my outfit—not too sexy, not too serious. How could I forget Neil's dinner? I don't know how to verbally express my sorrow with words. This results in my mouth opening and closing in a speak failure. Neil is waiting for me to say something, his hair sticking up and his tie pulled loose.

"Neil," I say. "Why didn't you text me? I—"

"I did. All night."

I reach for my phone. It's dead. How long has it been dead? I forgot to charge my phone.

"I'm so, so sorry," I manage.

"Where were you?"

I guess now would be the right time. I open the door, looking over my shoulder at him. He's hesitant to follow me inside, and I wonder if he came here with the intention of breaking up with me.

"I'll explain." I say. "Just come in. You can break up with me after."

He sloths inside and sits on the couch. His head is all droopy, and his shoulders are sad. I feel the knot inside my stomach coil tighter. I am such a selfish cunt.

"I have been secretly taking art classes," I blurt. "For six weeks. And I lie about looking for a job. I don't want a job—I mean, I do—not a boring accounting job. And that's where I was tonight. I forgot about your dinner because I'm selfish and stupid, and I was screwing around with charcoal and paper."

He's quiet for a long time. Just looking at me like he's never seen me before.

"Art?"

I nod.

"That's why you've been drawing on everything lately?"

I nod again.

"This is weird."

I face palm. "I know. For me, too. I guess I'm trying to find myself and doing a shitty job if it."

Neil looks perplexed. "I've known you for years, Helena. One of the things I've always loved about you is the fact that you have always been the girl who knows herself. While all the other girls fumbled around with life, you were the one who did your own thing."

"People change, Neil. You can't expect me to be one thing my whole life. Shit, I've only been alive for twenty-three years, and you're already making a big deal about me changing something."

Neil holds up his hands to ward off my anger. "I'm not saying that. I'm just surprised is all. People rely on you. You can't just go down a different path and not warn anyone. Even Della—"

"Even Della, what?" I yell. "And how long have you and Della been talking behind my back?"

"It's not like that, and you know it. We are worried about you. Your parents, too. No one has heard from you in weeks."

He is right. My parents had gone into debt, taken out a second mortgage on their home to pay my way through college. All so that I could have a good life. I was a numbers girl, accounting seemed like a given. All through my kid years I had never shown any kind of artistic talent. Even when I had taken piano lessons, my fingers had seemed fat and clumsy. I took them for two years and could barely play "Chopsticks." I sink down onto my couch and cover my face with my hands. God, what would my mother say? This is a nightmare. *No!* This *was* a dream!

"You're right," I tell him. "I'm sorry. I feel so stupid."

He's next to me in an instant, rubbing my back, reassuring me. I lean into him and feel so tired. What have I been doing?

"I'll get it together," I say. "I don't know what happened."

We don't talk about the dinner I missed anymore, or art class, which I stop going to. I find a job; I go back to being me. I don't remember my dreams anymore.

7
#HERO

I have an unhealthy addiction to Kit Kats and Kentucky Fried Chicken. It's not something I talk about. I don't burden people with the ugly things about me. Sometimes my hair will smell like grease and perfectly crispy chicken breast, and sometimes you'll find a log of chocolate on my bedroom floor. Let's not talk about those things. I keep them in the shade.

I have different, less realistic dreams about Kit, but horrifying nonetheless. As a consequence, my tongue is stained red from the wine, and my thighs fill with lard. I start my new job with new pants from Express that I had to buy, because … KFC. Luckily everyone sort of started their new jobs at the same time, and social gatherings take a backseat to job acclamation. Kit did not go to college with Neil, Della, and me. He went to community college and graduated a year earlier than us. According to Della, he's studying for his master's, while working nights. So when I get a flat one morning on the way to work, and I have to call Triple A, I am surprised when Kit pulls over in his white pickup. He has on silver Ray Bans, and he's chewing on a toothpick.

"Yo," he says, walking toward me. "I came to rescue you."

"Nice flannels. And Triple A is already on their way. Thanks for the chivalry though."

He grins as he crouches next to my car, inspecting the tire. "Nail," he says. Traffic whizzes by his back, blowing his shirt up and revealing his tanned skin. I want to tell him to be careful, but it's such an obvious statement. So I stand off to the side, my arms crossed over my chest, and gripe. When Kit finally stands up and walks around to where I am waiting, I wipe my palms on my plump thighs and try not to make eye contact.

"It's hot," I say. "I hate Florida."

"Florida hates you. You should move somewhere cooler."

"Like where?" I ask. I chew on the inside of my mouth while I wait for his response, but I already know what he's going to say. *Wa-Wa-*

"Washington. It's perfect there."

"Oh yeah? Have you been?"

"I'm from Washington," he says, wiping his hands on a blue bandana he produces from his back pocket. "Port Townsend."

I throw my head back and look at the sky. I want to stress eat all the fried chicken. All the Kit Kats.

"I think you've mentioned that," I say. Though he hasn't. Not that I can remember anyway. But, if it was lying in my subconscious somewhere that would explain…

"I haven't. I don't like to tell people where I'm from unless they ask."

I look at him. "Why not?"

"Because then they think they know you, and I don't want to be known."

"That's stupid. Everyone wants to be known." I crane my head to look for the Triple A rescue truck. *Please hurry, please hurry.*

"Except those who don't."

"Why did you tell me then?"

He looks up at the sky, and I can see the clouds reflected in his sunglasses.

"I don't know," he says.

My eyebrows dance around for bit. I'm glad he's not looking.

"How did you know I was here, anyway?" I ask.

"I have eyes."

I pull my lips tight when I look at him, so he can really see my displeasure.

"I was driving by, Helena. You're hard to miss."

Hard to miss? Hard to miss? Was it because of my thighs? It doesn't matter because the rescue truck bounces up like an overeager golden retriever.

Everything in my life is bad timing.

Kit waits with me while a guy who looks like Ben Stiller changes my tire.

"How's my Blue Steel?" he whispers to me, making a face.

"Of all the movies to remember him in," I sigh. "What is this? A school for ants?"

Ben Stiller's lookalike dusts his hands and is off to save someone else.

"Thanks for pulling over," I say. "And keeping me company."

"No problem; you're kind of a lonely heart."

A lonely heart. Am I? I look away.

"I'm not lonely," I say.

Kit grins. "Really?"

I look back at him, dumbfounded. He looks so smug. All that smirking.

"See ya, Helena."

It's the way he says my name and smiles at the same time. No one else smiles like that when they say my name. Do they? It's never been good enough for me to notice. Certainly not Neil, who hardly smiles at all. Della mostly whines my name, and my parents call me Lena in purring, adoring voices (only child).

By the time I've got his name out of my mouth and say goodbye, he's already in his truck, pulling away. It isn't true—any of this. My fascination with Kit, my sudden inclination to art. I am having a quarter-life crisis. I read about them online after Googling: *What the fuck is wrong with me?* The website was a dot-org so I know it is legit. Anyway, it said that sometimes when a person experiences a huge life change, they lose all grip of reality and try to create something new that they're more comfortable with. That's what is happening. I think about commenting on the article, validating the author with my story. I picture him checking the article every day waiting for someone like me to share my personal breakdown with the dot-org community. In the end I am too ashamed to admit to any of this.

The South Florida heat has sucked me dry, or rather made me the opposite of dry. I lift my arms and air out my pits. *Fuck it.* I am calling in to work. Car troubles. I drive in the same direction Kit went. He lives in Wilton Manners. I've seen his apartment complex in the recess of his Facebook pictures. That's what Florida is—not an apartment building—but a whole sprawling apartment village, painted various shades of orangey-pink, with a gym and a pool. I can find that. What if he is at work? Where does he work? He is getting his masters—Della told me that once. And he bartends nights at some place downtown. Facebook tells me where he works. Perfect.

I blast the AC and set off to find Kit Isley. A staged run-in, maybe a little private conversation to turn me off. After all, Della and I have completely opposite taste in men. I can get this shit out of my system once and for all. I'll be back to normal by Monday, coasting down the highway of my smooth, well planned out life. Neil in the driver's seat. Neil. Neil.

Neil

Neil

Neil

8
#FUCKLOVE

Kit works at Tavern on Hyde. I walk in at six o' clock and park myself at the bar. It's trendy, and not what I was expecting as his place of employment. Maybe something more dive-ish. I know, I know, I'm a judgmental asshole. I order a glass of wine from a female bartender with facial piercings who tells me her shift is over, and Kit will be taking care of me.

"He's not here yet," she says. "Should be any minute."

"Do you have any Butterbeer?" I ask as she's walking away. She doesn't hear me, and that's a good thing.

I send Neil's call to voicemail, and sit up straighter when I see him walk into the bar. He's wearing a white button down, black pants, and suspenders. He's not my type, but the getup is pretty sexy. Like, put your brother in suspenders and he might become hot too. Okay, that was too far, and I need to stop watching *Game of Thrones*. Kit goes straight to the computer and clocks in. Before he can turn around and see me, I spill wine on my shirt. Leaks right out of the corner of my mouth, per usual. I really need to see a doctor about my gappy lips. I'm scrubbing at my top when he says my name.

"Helena?"

"Yes," I say. "It's me."

He leans on the bar in front of me, watching. I'm wiping incessantly at my boob. I stop.

"You're so awkward."

"Maybe because you say really awkward things," I point out.

"This is why we can't have nice things," he says, handing me a cup of seltzer and a rag.

I'm getting really weirded out by all of his "we" comments.

"It was on sale," I say. "Twelve dollars at Gap."

"See," he says, walking over to another customer. "That was awkward."

I shrug. I have bigger problems, like my gappy lips.

The bar gets busy after that, and Kit comes around a couple times to give me new drinks. He doesn't ask what I want; he just brings me things. First, a martini that has a slimy white thing floating in it.

"It's a lychee nut," he says. "You'll like it."

I do. He switches back to wine at some point, white this time. Food that I didn't order arrives: scallops on mango quinoa. I've never eaten scallops, but he tells me they're his favorite. They have the texture of a tongue, and I briefly consider that he's sending me a message. By the time I'm onto dessert, the bar stools are mostly empty, and Nina Gordon is playing over the speakers. I'm way buzzed. I'm thinking how fun it would be to dance to this song in the empty restaurant. Since I am not a good dancer, I know this is an unreliable boozy thought.

Kit comes to sit on the barstool next to me. What I really like about him is that he has never once asked why I'm here. Like his girlfriend's best friend showing up at his job, and getting wasted alone, is completely normal.

"We close in an hour. May I drive you home?"

"I can Uber," I say. "It's no big deal."

He shakes his head. "I'm just afraid for you," he says. "If the Uber driver sees how dirty your clothes are, he may think you're not good for the fare."

"That's true," I say. There are several glasses of flat seltzer on the bar in front of me. He stacks up the plates left over from my dinner. I pull out my wallet, but he waves me away.

"I fed you tonight."

I'm too lightheaded to argue.

"We can leave in about an hour-thirty. That okay?"

I nod. When he leaves, I summon the Uber, and scribble a quick note on my napkin. I slide it under my empty glass, along with a twenty.

I should never have come. I should never have stayed. I should never have written the note. I almost go back, but I'm uncertain on my feet, and the driver is looking at me like he's thinking about leaving.

I wake up on my couch. My couch smells like patchouli. I fucking hate patchouli. I cover my nose and roll onto my back. I didn't even make it to the bedroom. Which is cool, because I also threw up on one of my throw pillows, and no one likes vomit in their bed. I stumble over to the trashcan and stuff the throw pillow inside. Then I take a shower. I'm halfway through soaping my hair when I remember the note I left for Kit at the bar. I groan. I jump out of the shower, not bothering to grab a towel, and run for my phone. God. A gazillion missed calls from Neil, and my parents, and Della, and my job. *Blah blah.* Soap is running down the back of my legs. I scroll through the texts until I see Kit's name.

> K: WTF

That's all it says. I cover my mouth with my hand. What did the note say? I close my eyes. I remember how clumsy the pen felt between my fingers. How the nub ripped the napkin in some places, and I had to pull it taut to write.

> I HAD A DREAM. DON'T MARRY DELLA

I groan. Suddenly, I need to throw up again. Instead, I take a selfie. My hair is globbed up on one side of my head, and there is mascara streaking down my face. I put the photo in an album called Mortifying Emotional Moments, and I title it Soggy Napkin Note. The last selfie I posted in there was of me on the day I graduated college. My perfectly made up face is happy … relieved. I called that one: Sallie Mae Can Suck It.

I finish my shower and feel more hopeful. I'll never see Kit again. That will solve all the problems at hand. Somehow I'll find someone better for Della, someone taller, with a less satirical face. She'll be happier with a doctor or an investment broker anyway. Someone to fund her lifestyle, who wouldn't infringe on her independence. Or I could find a new best friend. Elaine, from college, always liked me. I liked her hair.

Neil wants to go to the beach. He says "just us," but you know how that goes. Always seeing someone you know when you're in a bikini and your stomach is bloated from all the drinking and eating you did from the night before. I go anyway, and wear a monokini. I still feel whoozy when I step out of my shorts and lay on my towel, my head underneath an open book. Neil's been talking about his job for the last forty minutes. He hasn't asked me a damn thing about my job. When he takes a break to laugh at his own joke, I tell him about my flat, and he balks.

"Why didn't you call me? I would have come to get you. They let me take thirty minutes extra for my lunch break because they think I'm really good."

I roll my eyes behind my sunglasses. "I called Triple A. Plus, Kit saw me and pulled over." I added that last bit without thought.

"Kit? Della's Kit?"

"Well, she doesn't own him," I say, annoyed. "And how many other Kits do we know?"

"You don't think that's weird?" he asks.

I sit up. "That the guy dating my best friend sees me stranded on the side of the road and pulled over to help?"

Neil huffs. "Well, I guess when you put it that way…"

"There's no other way to put it."

He looks all crestfallen and lamby. I am about to lean over and kiss him when his phone lights up to tell him he has a text. I don't mean to look; I'm not like that—a snoop. But I see a girl's name. He grabs for the phone, but I'm faster. It's automatic. My hand punches in his passcode and …

all
I
see
are
tits

"Helena…"

Why is he saying my name? Why is he even saying my name? We are both standing up now, me still holding his phone looking at the tits. The pictures are still coming. I didn't know tits could be selfied from so many angles. I'm shaking. The phone drops from my hand, into the sand.

"I have to tell you something," he says. He's advancing on me, slowly. Like I'm some a-bomb about to explode. *BOOM!*

"You're a cheating douchebag?"

"Helena, let me talk."

"Hold that thought," I say. Then I punch him. Right in the eye, and like my dad taught me. Pull back, throw forward. His head rolls, then snaps forward like a bobble head. *Boing, boing, boing on his skinny turkey neck.* He lifts his hand to his eye, and I slap him so that he has a hit on each side of his face.

"Helena!" he yells, holding out his hand for me to stop.

I like the shock on his face. I like that we're both shocked.

"Let me explain," he tries.

I raise my hand to hit him again, and he flinches back.

"How long has this been happening?"

His face blanches.

"Not long."

"How long?" I yell.

"A year," he says, dropping his head.

"A year," I whisper. Suddenly, there's no more hitting in me. Just wasteland. My shoulders slump forward.

"Why?" I ask. And then as a noise rises from my throat—a sob—and I say the most pathetic thing. "What did I do wrong?"

Neil drops his head. "Nothing, Helena." And then, "She's pregnant."

I can't stand. I drop hard onto the sand and look at the surf. There are no waves in this part of Florida, so instead of surfers, you get little kids in Dora the Explorer swimsuits.

"You've been busy," he starts. "It just happened, and it was a mistake." Saying it was a mistake doesn't make it hurt less; in fact, it feels starker underneath all of this sun, and heat, and sand. It's like they're punishing me too.

"I'm sorry," he says. But there's not a sorry big enough for a betrayal like this. *A year.* Neil was the one I was making plans with. Talking about the future with. After the initial shock, the hurt surges forward. I stand up. I can't be here. I can't look at him. He has a zit on the side of his neck: bright, and red, and bulbous. I'm so revolted that I ever dated him.

"Please, Helena," he says. "It was a mistake. I love you." But I'm not having it, and his use of the word 'love' makes me laugh. *Love is faithful, love is kind, love is patient.* Love is not—*I wasn't thinking.* I grab my things, stumble away. *The dream,* I think. *This was in the dream.* And her name is Sadie.

"Avada Kedavra," I whisper at Sadie.

I walk home. Not because I can't call someone. Hell, Della would be there in a second with a machete. I just need to think. I take a selfie while I wait at a red light and send it to the MEM folder. I call it, *Fuck Love.*

9

#BEFOREHECHEATS

Neil doesn't want to be with Sadie, though Sadie wants to be with Neil. Isn't that a funny thing? He wanted her enough to risk my heart. I hear this all through phone messages, e-mails, texts, and Della. Apparently, during my quarter-life crisis, Della and Neil became close. I'd feel betrayed, but Neil already took care of that one. Sadie is keeping the baby, of course, because her dad is a minister, and she is pro-life. Not pro-abstinence. Neil says he will be in the baby's life as much as Sadie will let him. He wants to work things out with me. I don't like working out of any kind. Not the body or the heart. Just thinking about working things out makes me tired. I am sleepy for working things out. I tell Neil to go to hell, and then I cry for two days. Was it me? Was I too cold? Too inexperienced? Not pretty enough? Not good enough in bed? And when disloyal, seed-sowing scum buckets slept with other girls, why did women look inward to find fault in themselves? It wasn't my fault. Actually, maybe it was. Fuck it. What did it matter anyway?

I go get drinks at Tavern on Hyde. I haven't heard a peep from Kit in weeks. His girlfriend, on the other hand, has been camped out in my bed, this time in support of me. She still asks me to make her snacks, even though I'm the one with the broken heart. She even tells me that it'll keep my mind off things. *"You need to stay busy."*

I am avoiding her tonight, though apparently not her boyfriend. All I can think about is Kit and the dream. How he was almost warning me. Perhaps in my subconscious, I knew. Neil hadn't been Neil for a long time. In hindsight, we hadn't connected in … a year.

I stumble into Tavern on Hyde with a severely tangled braid, and dark circles under my eyes. Kit is talking to some of his customers on the other side of the bar when he sees me. He does a double take, and I wonder how rough I look. *You look rough in a vulnerable, pretty way*, I tell myself. Though I should probably start combing my hair again.

"Hello," he slides a drink in front of me before I've even had the chance to sit down. "How's your heart?"

"I feel sober, and I want to feel drunk," I say.

"I'm sorry that happened to you." He wipes the bar down with a rag, then leans on his elbows and studies me. His eyes are really lovely and sad. "The sadness comes in waves, yes? It's like you feel something different every ten minutes."

"Yeah," I say, wondering who broke his heart. What a cunt. I drink my purple drink and stare at my phone. But every time I stare at a phone, I see tits in my mind. You can't get those things out of your head, you know?

Della is texting me. *We should get dressed up and go out tonight!*

To dance with men who will later break my heart?

D: *You have to be positive*, she texts back.

Fuck that.

D: *I'll meet you for drinks then,* she sends.

I'm already drinking. I just want to be alone.

She doesn't text back, and I know her feelings are hurt.

I put my phone away. Aside from the unbearable heart pain, feelings of inadequacy, sporadic tears, and hopelessness, I kind of like being single. You're not responsible to tell anyone where you are or who you're with. It's freedom and loneliness, exhilaration and inner calm. You don't have to shave. It's the best high and the worst low. The motherfucking pits. I choose to ignore Della and my parents, and there's not a thing they can do about it.

Kit doesn't mention the note I left him, thank God. Maybe he's forgotten, or maybe he thinks I was too drunk to know what I was doing. We make small talk between his other customers, and I check out his suspenders when he's not looking. He has really broad shoulders; he could be too stocky, but everything narrows out at his waist. He's not my type, but it's okay to notice things. I don't want to be the type of self-centered person who only notices things about themselves. So, really I'm practicing being a good person by checking out Kit's suspenders. And that's what it's about—the suspenders. He sings me a song about cheating and tells me that it's on Carrie Underwood's album. When he hits the high notes, he closes his eyes and points a finger in the air. It all reminds me of Mariah Carey, and that's a bit uncomfortable.

When he's in the kitchen getting someone's food, I leave cash on the bar and sneak out. I don't like goodbyes, especially when they're directed at me. I think I'm clever until I get to my car and see Kit sitting in my front seat.

"You think I don't know you by now?" he asks. He gets out to make way for me.

"You were busy," I say. "I have things to do."

"Like what?"

I lick my lips because they still taste like lemon.

"I have to wash my hair."

"Clearly," he says. He closes the door once I'm in and bends down to lean his elbows through the open window.

I am shaking I'm so nervous. He's going to ask me about the damn napkin, I just know it. I'll say I don't remember, and who is he to argue?

"Helena…" He smiles. "Goodnight."

God. Fuck. He steps away, grinning. A terse smile, and I throw the car into reverse, trying not to look at him in the rearview as I cruise out of the parking lot. It's not until I'm home and getting out of the car that I notice the napkin on my passenger side seat.

I pick it up. It's the same kind they keep at the bar.

Give me a reason not to

I groan. *No, no, no, no, no.* I stuff the napkin in my purse and head inside. Della will be here. Della is here.

"Where have you been?" she asks when I walk through the door. She's in pajama pants and a bra—both mine. I resent her large tits. They remind me of bad texting times.

"I was at a Harry Potter convention. Why? Do you need a snack?" I ask.

"I was worried."

"Dells, you could go home, you know. I appreciate all the love, but I don't need a babysitter."

"People commit suicide all the time after breakups."

"I'm not going to commit suicide. I stopped for a drink at Tavern on Hyde," I tell her.

Her face lights up. "Did you see Kit? Is he still hot?"

"I did see him; he was wearing suspenders and a long-sleeve shirt in this weather. Super hot."

"He doesn't like me to go in when he's working," she says. "He says it's not professional to have your girlfriend drinking at your place of employment."

I nod. Della was a sloppy drunk; she always ended up fondling a stranger and singing En Vogue at the top of her lungs. Kit was probably just trying to save himself the embarrassment.

"He's really nice, Della," I say. "A good guy."

I hate using the good guy cliché with Kit, but what else is there to say. It's true. Della beams. She's so happy with this she makes *me* a snack. She's already named their children, and has a board on Pinterest for their wedding. As we eat our snack, she pulls it up and shows me the new centerpieces she's found.

"A winter wedding," she says. "Because they're much more romantic." In Florida, winter is sixty-five degrees, but I don't say this. I nod and approve of her lantern centerpieces. *Fucklovefucklovefucklove.*

Give me a reason not to

I kiss the top of her head. There isn't a good reason. They are cute together. It doesn't matter that I already know the name of his daughter. That was just a dream.

10
#FOODPORN

One night, as Della and I are listening to Carrie Underwood's "Before He Cheats," there is a knock on my door. I go to answer it, only to find Kit on my welcome mat, a bag of groceries in his hand.

"Since you've stolen my girlfriend, I've come to make you both dinner," he announces. I feel unreasonably disappointed that he didn't come just for me. *I'm sort of your wife! We had a child together for God's sake.*

"Great song." He steps around me and kisses Della.

"Yeaaah."

I put Carrie on mute, but Kit keeps singing it from the kitchen. Even when he thinks no one is looking, he does the closed eye, finger pointy thing. It has deep potential to be adorable, but he's not my type. And *God*, stop stealing shit from Mariah.

He doesn't ask me where anything is, or for help—not that I would have given it to him anyway. He bangs around in the kitchen while Della and I watch reruns of *Teen Mom*, until he announces it's time for dinner.

"What did you make?" I ask, sitting at my table and feeling strangely like a guest.

"Ropa Vieja."

I scrunch my nose. "Old clothes?" My Spanish is limited to four years of high school, so I could be wrong.

"Yes. Delicious."

Della doesn't question Kit's dirty laundry, so I don't either. Turns out it's extra fucking good. I want to take a picture for my

MEM folder and call it: I'll Eat His Old Pants, but that would risk questions and judgment. They both might get the wrong idea. Kit does cleanup and dishes, and shoos me out of the kitchen when I try to help.

"He's perfect," Della announces. "Let's stay up all night and play games." Forty minutes and four beers later, she passes out on my sofa. Kit and I are playing Mancala, but he really sucks.

"It's your strategy," I tell him. "You have none."

"Wanna go for a walk?" Kit asks. We both look at Della who won't be waking up any time soon.

"Dells," I say, shaking her shoulder. "Let's go for a walk."

She moans into the sofa cushion and slaps me away.

I shrug. "She hates the heat anyway," I tell him. "It frizzes her blowout."

"Yeah, I know," Kit says, smiling. "She's my girlfriend."

I feel my face flush and hurry to the door ahead of him. *Of course. Of course.*

I don't have a blowout; I just have a messy bun. Kit pats the top of it when we step out into the thick air.

"It's like a hair hive," he says. "Small creatures could live in there."

"I had a snail as a pet once," I say. "Its name was SnailTail."

"Your weirdness never ceases to amaze me," Kit says.

"I was taking art classes," I blurt.

Kit looks at me funny, his head cocked to the side. "Was?"

"I stopped going because it was affecting my relationship. Neil made me feel like I was cheating on him when he found out."

"Ah, well, good ol' Neil was probably feeling a little guilty about his own extracurricular activities and looking for something to blame."

"I wasn't very good," I tell him.

He shrugs. "But you are very good at passion. And if you have enough passion, you can almost learn to do anything well."

I stare at him.

"How come Justin Bieber never gets any better at being a thug?"

We both laugh.

"Maybe I'll try something new. Hey! How's your book coming along? Do you have more to send me?"

I haven't thought about Kit's book since the night I had the fight with Neil about missing his work dinner. I can't believe I forgot about it.

"I feel good when I'm writing. It seems to be all coming together."

He glows a little when he talks about it. I wish I had something to make me glow like that. We walk past the lake, which isn't really a lake. There is a jaunty fountain in the middle, spraying water into the still air. The air is so warm I want it to blow my way.

"Can I ask you something?" I say.

"You just did."

I pull a face.

"Are you in love?"

Kit stops walking, and I panic. I've gone too far, asked something too personal. I pull on my earlobe and stare at him until he starts to laugh.

"Calm down, leave your ear alone."

I drop my hand to my side. So awkward.

"I was engaged before Della," he says.

My head jerks up. I'm surprised. I feel like that's something she would have told me.

"She doesn't know," he says.

"Oh."

"We just decided early on not to talk about our past relationships. Anyway, since we aren't dating, I can tell you."

I'd rather he not. We've been married.

"You can't tell. This is in confidence."

"She's my best friend. Do you really think I'm not going to tell her?"

"Actually, yes. If you tell me you won't, I'll believe you."

He's right. I thrive on owning people's secrets. Makes me feel superior to know I have them, even if no one else knows.

"Whatever," I say. "I make no promises."

We come to a junction in the path, and Kit chooses left. I always go right. It feels weird that he didn't ask me which way to go, or that he just chose so decisively. Neil would have fumbled over that one.

"She was my high school sweetheart. We were beautifully cliché. Even down to the part where she cheated on me with one of my friends."

Aha! The cunt!

"I mean, I know it was a mistake, and we'd only been with each other, so I get it. Still hurts though. I was looking for a reason to run away after that. So, I packed up and moved here."

I hesitate. "So, you love Della, but you're still not over your ex?"

"Something like that," he says. "Just taking it slower this time. I was in a relationship for five years."

"Gotcha."

"Don't do that," he says, looking at me.

"Do what?"

"Be all formal and weird. Just say what you're thinking."

"Okay…"

I've never been called out on my use of conversational words. But, I suppose they're a bit of a copout if you really think about it.

"Do you speak Parseltongue?" I ask.

"What?" His face screws up.

I shake my head. "Never mind. I think she's super into you. And you're only half in. And that sounds like someone, namely Della, is going to get hurt."

"I like her a lot. She's funny, and she doesn't take herself too seriously. She has a good heart."

I agree with all of those things. But I don't want to marry Della, or live with her. In fact, I really want her to go home and stop eating my popcorn.

"If you weren't so hung up on…?"

"Greer," he says.

"Ew, seriously?"

He nods.

"If you weren't so hung up on Greer, would you feel differently about Della?"

"Don't know. I think that the right girl can wipe away the memories of the wrong girl."

Wow. Okay.

"Sure." But I don't think that. If that were true, there wouldn't be so many humans pining for their long, lost love. We didn't always want what was right. We wanted what we couldn't have.

"You're hopeful and positive," I tell him. "But don't break one girl's heart because you're trying to heal yourself of another one."

"Yes, ma'am," he says. "But something tells me that won't be my problem. I see a whole different shit storm in my future."

I narrow my eyes at him. "You have a commemorative Greer tattoo, don't you?"

His eyes grow wide, and he scratches a spot on his cheek while making a face.

"Ha!" I laugh. "Let me see it. After that guess, I deserve it."

He shakes his head. "No way. No one said I had one. You're making stuff up."

He's smiling, and I know I've caught him.

"I'll just ask Della," I say. "She's obviously seen it."

Kit shakes his head. "No, no she hasn't."

I cock my head. "That's impossible. You've … you guys have…"

"It's in white ink. You can only see it in black light."

"Oh." I wait a few minutes as we trudge along the path, the warm air pushing up my nose, making me want to scream.

"What's it of?"

"It says…" He stops. I wonder if he's reconsidering telling me. "It says, 'Don't fear the animals.'"

And then Della finds us. She's half asleep and slurring. "I got scared," she says, running her fingers through her hair. Her eyes are sleepy, still drunk.

"I kind of want my own bed," she says, looking at me. "Do you mind if I go home tonight, Helena?"

She wants Kit in her bed, and in her, but I nod. They don't even come back inside. I walk them straight to Kit's car where he helps Della in, and then jogs around to the driver's side.

"Night, Helena."

"Hey, night. And thanks for dinner."

"Sorry I'm such a lousy cook." He grins.

"You're an excellent liar, though. It makes up for it."

"You're pretty … excellent."

I feel so lonely when they're gone.

11
#KITELLA

There are definite, solid lines in life that should never be crossed. Developing a crush on your best friend's boyfriend is one of them. Showing up to his job frequently and drinking his fruity cocktails is another. I don't like him as much as Kentucky Fried Chicken, but hell if that boy didn't look at me and tell me I was pretty … excellent. Excellent, which is above normal. Like I'm better than regular girls. Not your basic bitch. Finger-licking excellent. I realize I'm vulnerable and most days I feel like a worthless human—someone a guy can cheat on, and call it a mistake. I don't want to be someone's 'girl who got away.' I want to be someone's 'girl who'd I'd never let get away.' I sign up for another class, and this time I try something a little different: clay. I like the feel of the cool, wet clay between my fingers. Clay is about numbers and proportion that you can control with your palms. I'm better at clay than I am at drawing. My hands feel less clumsy. I make coffee cups, vases, plates, then serving platters. All of them lacking symmetry, but I am so proud of them I throw out the cheap set I bought from Wal-Mart and place my handmade dinnerware in my kitchen cabinets. I paint everything white and splatter them with black paint. I am fighting the Pottery Barn taste that, according to my dream, is set to emerge in ten years. The carefully placed Chinese pots and decorative, stained knots give me hives. *All a dream. All a dream,* I tell myself. I focus on creating my style out of mess and mixed color. A Pottery Barn girl is for Neil, not Kit. Kit's girl is color and texture.

When I realize that I'm avoiding Pottery Barn because of Kit, I go to their online store and buy a pair of ceramic French bulldogs. Nothing will control me, not Kit or Pottery Barn. To even things out, I replace my old throw pillows with ones I find at the flea market, but I won't touch them. Or put them on my couch. I buy replacements at Pottery Barn. I stop drinking wine, too, since that was a manifestation of the dream, but some nights when I'm really sad I sniff an old cork I keep in my junk drawer. It's not a cork from the wine Kit brought over; I don't think so anyway. It was something I found near my trashcan. So when I start putting it on the spare pillow and sleeping with it, it has nothing to do with Kit. It's just a random wine cork I've grown attached to. During the day, I put it in my purse where it travels with me to work, then art class. Clay is over; I register for an oil-on-canvas class, hoping for better results than my first class with Neptune.

On weekends, Della insists I tag along with whatever she and Kit are doing. She swears it's not pity, and I'm no longer on suicide watch, and that Kit genuinely enjoys my company, while she needs me around for moral support.

"Moral support for what?" I ask her.

"Best friend moral support. Like, I just like having you around, you make me feel good."

I love Della, God I love her. I've known her since we didn't have real personalities, and we relied on *Tiger Beat* to tell us which boys to have crushes on—JTT for me, Devon Sawa for her. But people grow up, change, they are sorted into different houses— Slytherin for Della, Ravenclaw for me. They become what life dictates, and Della and I took two different routes. Della's dad won the lottery. I shit you not. Five hundred thousand on a scratch-off ticket during our sophomore year. He doubled his money on investments, and all of a sudden, Della was a rich girl. Vacations to the Greek Isles, Christmas cruises to the Bahamas, a brand new Range Rover senior year. Our *Tiger Beat* years were replaced with glossy *Vogue* years, during which Della's family took me on every vacation, and every outing on their boat. If they bought Della a pair of Kate Spade sunglasses, I would get a pair too. It was fun at first, but then I started to feel like a poor, charity tagalong. I still feel like that.

The only time I didn't feel their cloying pity was when Kit sent me chapters of his book. Only me. That wasn't pity; he genuinely wanted to share those with me. I was getting really attached to George, Denver, and Stephanie Brown. If I could put them on my pillow next to the wine cork, I would. Instead I read what he's sent me over and over. I understand the *Twilight* craze, the *Fifty Shades of Grey* craze. For the first time, I am not just reading a book; I am invested in the book. If George, Denver, and Stephanie Brown don't get their shit together, I am never going to read another book again. Kit enjoys my commitment to their story, but we don't talk about it in front of Della. Della was part of the *Twilight* mania, and after reading one chapter of Kit's untitled manuscript she asked if there were werewolves or vampires in the story. Kit shut her down real fast after that. She pouted but agreed to wait until he was finished to read the rest.

I am at an estate sale with Kit, Della, and our friend, June, who we've hung out with on and off since high school. June and I are on the front lawn, looking though boxes of old books, while Kit and Della are in the house looking at the furniture.

"Do you think Kitella will be moving in together soon?" June asks.

I look up surprised. "Kitella?"

"Kit and Della," she says. "Kitella." June is an odd bird. I know I'm an odd bird on the inside, but June is an odd bird on the inside and the outside. I eye her floral hat, and the paperclip necklace she's wearing.

"Kitella," I snort. "I don't know. Della's apartment is so … Della. I can't see a guy moving in there."

"They'd change things for sure. Make room. They've been together a while now."

"Only like eight months," I say defensively. "Not that long."

"Come on, Helena. Della doesn't usually make it through the three-month mark. Her wedding board is growing on Pinterest. Those two are serious."

It is true. She has a menu and flower girl gifts now. Della always found something wrong with the boys she dated. Charles was too needy, Tim was too jealous, Anthony had an annoying twin sister. Kit is perfect; she says it all the time. And they are furniture shopping as we speak.

"Do you like them together?" I ask June.

"Yeah, they're cute. I think he balances her. He's not as shallow as some of the other guys she's dated."

June wanders off to look at a lamp, and I feel like sinking into the sea of grass. Why did all of that feel like bad news? It isn't because I don't want my best friend to be happy, because I do. I just want her to be happy with someone else. I go find them in the house. They're looking at bookcases.

"I saw ones just like this in Restoration Hardware," Della says. "For four times the price. This is a steal."

Kit doesn't look convinced. "We don't have enough books combined to fit on these things."

"We can buy more!" Della says. Then she turns to me and her pink lips are spread so wide I can see every single one of her teeth.

"We're moving in together!" she squeals and claps, and I stand there dumbfounded, wondering if June has psychic ability.

"Into your apartment?" I ask, because it's the only thing I can think to say.

"No, silly. That's too small. We are going to buy a house."

I look at Kit, but he's avoiding my eyes.

"That's so great," I say. "Congratulations, guys." And then I say I have to go to the bathroom, but I go outside instead. I need air, space to hide my falling face. It's the dumbest thing I've ever experienced, but that doesn't mean I don't feel it anyway. That's the most pathetic part of being a human, the emotions you don't ask for or want, they just rush you anyway. I roll my wine cork between my palms. In a house nearby, someone is frying bacon. I can hear a man's rackety, wet cough, and I can feel sorrow spreading from brain to heart. I know that life is not simple because I am not simple. In fact, I am learning that I am more than simple and less than normal. To fall in love with a boy is one thing, but to fall in love with your best friend's boy because of a dream is … well, I'm fucked.

12
#OLFUCKERY

You don't start searching for truth until something goes terribly wrong and you realize that you need it. There's no going back after that. The emotional concrete is poured. A foundation laid. *This is what it feels like to go mad,* I think. It feels like I've skipped ten years and just did the growing up without having to do the actual time. Willful blindness belongs to the young. In my case, I learned of my depravity early enough to rid myself of it. I cannot hate Sadie; Sadie would have happened with a different name. Maybe when I was already married. Sadie is just the name of Neil's inability to be faithful. Perhaps she saved me from a lot more. I cannot hate the dream; the dream woke me up. But, that's all it was—a dream. I keep art, because I never knew I loved it until I became a coloring book artist. I carry a knapsack with me now, filled with charcoals, pencils, a sketchpad, a wine cork. I give up listening to the beach music that was with me through college, and I make playlists that sound yearning and pathetic. I am what I am. I marvel at how yearning can make you disintegrate. And to keep from disappearing all together, you must rebuild yourself. I get a tattoo on my wrist, but I don't tell anyone, and I hide it underneath my watch. *May* is all it says. Because that's when my perspective shifted.

I help Kitella move into their new home. A tan house with white window boxes. It's the first time I'm seeing them in over a month. Kit hasn't been able to work on his story because of the move, so

I've no communication with him either. When I pull up, it's not Della but Kit who comes outside and throws his arms around me. I'm stiff at first, but then I lift my arms and hug him back. The worst part of a hug is the smell. If you hug a person enough, their smell becomes familiar, and you associate it with comfort, intimacy, and closeness. Kit always smells like gasoline and pine needles. *Gasoline and pine needles*, I think as I release him. *How ridiculously appropriate.* An olfactory experience turned olfuckery. Now I won't be able to smell gasoline without seeing his pretty face. I follow him into the house; he seems excited. Della is unpacking dishes into the kitchen cabinets, a pink bandana tied around her hair. I hate to say it, but she's glowing. "Helena!" She launches herself at me, and I stumble backward into Kit. We all fall, and we all laugh on Kitella's new kitchen hardwood.

"This feels so right," Della says. "All back together." I roll away from them and toward the fridge. I pull a can of Coke from the bottom shelf, while still lying on my back.

"I'm already tired from this move. Can we just do this all day?"

Kit hauls me to my feet, and I'm given the job of unpacking and organizing Kitella's closet. This is nothing new. Della has been making me organize her closet since freshman year of high school. As payment for the service, I get to choose one thing I want from her extensive wardrobe. I find a pair of designer jeans I like and set them aside. *Mine.*

'Don't touch those Rag and Bone jeans," she yells from the kitchen. I put them back and take her favorite blazer to spite her.

Kit's clothes put me in a bad mood. There's too much plaid. No one should wear this much plaid. I sniff a shirt, and then I sniff it again. The third time I sniff it is just to even things out; I like groups of three.

"Did you just smell my shirt?"

I spin around. He's leaning on the closet door, arms folded, and of course blocking my escape.

"It smells moldy. Don't you think?" I hold it toward him, but he doesn't reach for it. He has a pretty intense stare. What disturbs you more than the stare though is the smirking.

He doesn't know shit, I tell myself.

"It smelled moldy…" I say again. He looks at my mouth, and I squirm.

"Della wants to get dinner."

I look down at my raggedy, moving day clothes. "Can't we just order in?"

"She's sick of being here. She wants to get out for a bit."

Not even unpacked and already sick of being in her house.

"You've got your topknot going," Kit says. "That's all the dressing up you need."

Della must have taught him that word. I liked hair hive better.

We decide on sushi. But Della doesn't do hole-in-the-wall sushi, where she says the fish is fishy. We have to go to the big, fancy place downtown. I wear my new blazer, though, which makes me cheerful. June meets us at the restaurant. I think Della invites her places so I don't feel like the third wheel. But truly, I feel like the third wheel even when I'm alone. June waves to us when we walk up to the restaurant. It's robust waving. Like she's just been shipwrecked and needs us to see her. She's wearing a turban on her head, and her T-shirt says *Cou Cou*.

"I like this girl," Kit says. I grin. Me too.

We're not even in the restaurant when we see Neil and pregnant Sadie. She is heavy with child, as I am heavy with topknot. Neil flushes when he sees me. He looks from me to Sadie with cornered rat expression.

It feels shitty to see them here. They were supposed to go away, evaporate into a cloud of infidelity and lies. My first instinct is to run. Why would I be the one running? They're the liars and cheats. I'm standing close to Kit, and all of a sudden I feel the pressure of his hand on my lower back.

Neil opens his mouth, but I hold up my hand.

"Don't hurt your brain. This is awkward for all of us except June, who likes being awkward. Hello, from us to you. Now move aside; we are hungry for raw fish." Kit snickers, and Della elbows him in the ribs.

Neil and Sadie move along quickly. I don't look at Sadie, so I don't know how she takes all of it, but Neil looks stricken. When we walk through the doors of the restaurant, all three of them start laughing. Kit kisses me on top of the head, right by the topknot. "Brilliant," he says. "You're all the muse I'll ever need." This sends me into tingle/butterfly/confusion overload. I sit as far away from him as I can and flirt with the waiter. It's brotherly. I know that. He's a kind, kind human, and I am a whore for that dream. By the end of dinner I've ruined my new blazer with soy sauce and Sriracha.

"There's a whole market for you in disposable clothes," Kit says.

Della glares at me, but she really has no right. It's *myyy* blazer. June and Kit walk up ahead, and Della links arms with me.

"Hey," she whispers. "I may be pregnant."

When my eyes grow wide, she hushes me. "I haven't told him. Don't say anything."

"What does 'may be' mean? Like you've taken a test? You've missed a period? What…?"

Della glances at Kit to make sure he's still distracted. "Well, I haven't taken the test yet. I am a week late. A *week*," she emphasizes.

This is not the first time Della is a week late on her period. It is, however, the first time she looks happy about it.

"Well, let's get one then," I say around the emotion clogged in my throat. "We should know so we have peace of mind."

Della nods, glowing eyes and a small happy smile on her lips. I'll be happy for them. I swear to God I will. I'll just need some time to adjust.

13
#NEGATIVE

Della's test is not positive. I watch her wrap the test in toilet paper and push it to the bottom of the trashcan. She's wearing a look of severe disappointment. It's a strange thing to grasp, that just a little while ago the worst thing that could happen was a positive pregnancy test. Now, my best friend, who once spent an afternoon in hysterics because of a broken condom, was grieving the fact the she wasn't pregnant. She wanted this badly. Why? I do not know. She already has Kit. His eyes are fixated on her. She doesn't need a baby to gain his attention, nor to keep him. She comes from a good family, the kind that gets together on Tuesday nights for no reason other than to spend time with each other and to eat their Nonna's Sugo.

"One day," I say to comfort her. It's not what she wants to hear. She turns away from me and opens the bathroom door. She sent Kit to the store for milk so that we could carry out our mission in secret. She thought that when he got back there would be something to celebrate.

"Why are you upset, Della? I thought you would be relieved."

"I am relieved," she lies. I am the one who is relieved. I think of what Kit told me that night we took a walk. How unsure he was about his feelings for her. Things may have changed since then, but something tells me a few months aren't enough to cure a man of his past.

"Della," I say. "You like to do things in order. First, a beautiful wedding, then a beautiful baby, okay?"

I hug her, and she starts to cry.

"I wanted to give him something," she says.

Her gray eyes are misty, her lashes damp. She is so achingly beautiful, feminine, and vulnerable. I understand why men take their feelings for her so seriously. She's Della.

"Maybe start with a smaller gift," I say. "Like a watch, or a kitten, or something."

She laughs through her lovely tears and throws her arms around my neck. "You always know what to say. Thank you, Helena."

I stroke her hair like I used to do in high school when I was the pretty one, and the boys she liked couldn't see past the braces and sharp knees. *They'll all be sorry one day,* I used to tell her. And they all were.

Kit's pickup pulls into the driveway, and she pulls away from me to go to him. It's all right. I do not covet Della's emotional dependence. I'm rather relieved that the responsibility is no longer mine. I watch as she runs out the front door and flings herself at him, wrapping her legs around his torso. He drops his bags to hold onto her. Of all the things that have happened tonight, that's what affects me most. The way he so effortlessly drops his bags to catch her. I don't have much reference since Neil was my one serious boyfriend, though I know he never would have dropped his bags to catch me lest something broke. That causes an ache deep in my chest. To know that there are guys willing to drop their shopping bags to catch their girl. And I want someone to love me that effortlessly. Or maybe, I think morosely, I want *Kit* to love me that effortlessly. To raise my son, and to nurture the art that lies dormant in me. It's such a bad time to do this, but I think of baby Brandy. Della wanted to have Kit's baby, and in some other life I already had. I start to giggle, and by the time Kit and Della walk back through the doors, I am full out belly laughing.

"What?" Della asks. She looks around like there's a joke she missed. Kit's mouth twitches, and then he starts to laugh too.

"What's wrong with you guys?" Della perches her hands on her hips, but she's smiling.

I can't even stand up straight. I slide down the living room wall as my stomach rolls with laughter. Have I ever laughed like this? No, and I don't even know what's funny.

"She just caught the giggles," Kit says, shaking his head. There's a short smile attached to his mouth. "She doesn't even laugh; that's a cackle."

Della nods. "I always thought her laugh sounded evil."

This makes me laugh harder; the fact that Kit noticed right away, but it took Della ten plus years, and her boyfriend, to know that I have an evil laugh. She wanders off to the kitchen, shaking her head. It's a bad time to catch Kit's eye. He's still standing in front of the closed door, bag in hand. He's not laughing or smiling anymore. His lips are folded in, and his eyes are narrowed. When our eyes catch, my laughter is gone. Just like that. It's the Kit I saw in my dream, the one who grabbed my hand and said, *"You are supposed to be with me."*

I lean my head back against the wall, hands dangling between my knees. Drunk and not drunk. Sober and not sober. Locking eyes with Kit Isley in his newly purchased love nest doesn't make me feel good. It makes me feel like shit. I look back at his face because I want to know what he's feeling. I can see Kit's chest heaving. Deep breaths because … what? Maybe he had a dream too. Maybe he feels a connection too. It's probably all in my head, and that's what makes me feel truly crazy, that I might be making all of this up. I don't know what propels me to say it. Obviously, I've been doing a lot of crazy shit lately.

"Hey, Kit." My voice is barely audible. I touch my lips to make sure they're really moving. "I had a dream."

I move the hair from my eyes so that I can see him clearly, and hold it back out of my face.

His eyes get wide; his lips unfold.

"So you've said." His voice is soft. "What was your dream about?"

Now that he's asking I don't know how to say it. Thick tongue, thicker thoughts. How does one declare lunacy? My chest begins to ache. This was a huge mistake. I am still feeling the alcohol from dinner.

Then Della drops something in the kitchen. A glass shatters along with my moment. Timing is everything when you're about to tell someone you dreamed him into your heart. Fuck if that's not the corniest thing I ever heard. Kit's head turns toward the kitchen where Della is cursing loudly, calling for help. He glances back at me regretfully. His eyes drag over my face one last moment, and then he is gone. I don't even say goodbye. I sneak out while they are in the kitchen. I won't be missed. I've always been the weird one anyway, expected to do things like this. Della likes being around her friends, but ever since she started dating Kit she's needed us less and less. Which is good. Except not, because I can't do what I'm thinking. I can't.

14
#OMG

The next morning I open my e-mail to find something from Kit. Last week someone hacked his e-mail and sent me a virus in the form of skinny pills, so I don't open it right away. I wash my face, make coffee, and put Pat Benatar on the record player. When I finally settle down with my computer, I see that the e-mail is untitled. I brace myself for another virus, but when I open the file, it's a chapter. I feel giddy that he's writing again. I sip my coffee and scroll through to see how long it is. It's been a while since the last time Kit sent me a chapter, and a while since I read a good book. Last I read George, Denver, and Stephanie Brown were stuck between a rock and a hard place. Denver broke his leg and lost his job, and Stephanie, being the ever-kind soul that she was, let him move in with her. George was now at a disadvantage and hoping to injure himself as well. I picture them all living in Stephanie Brown's small apartment and giggle. People didn't really take such desperate measures for love. Poor Stephanie Brown was running herself dry with all of their neediness. But when I scroll down, it's not their story I see. It's something new. Something that makes the hair stand up on the back of my neck from sheer creepiness. I close my computer. Drum my fingers on the case. Open it again. It's still there, and I'm not dreaming.

CHAPTER ONE

THE DREAM

When I am finished reading, I shut down my computer and go back to bed. I feel safer in my cocoon of creamy sheets and fat pillows. How? How on Earth did he write that? What did it mean? How could he? I stare at the cold coffee on my nightstand and feel ill.

I'm so embarrassed. What was I thinking telling him that? I gave Kit a few words, some ill guarded emotion, and behold! Chapter One: The Dream. Did Chapter One come out of him or me? I don't know much about artists, but I'm beginning to feel as if they possess sorcery.

My lease is up in a month. I can move. God, haven't I always wanted to get out of this hot cesspool of sweaty, tanned people and sharp palm trees? I have a disease called *can't keep your fucking mouth shut*. And seriously, if you know you're going to implode, isn't it better to get to the going?

"Calm down, Helena. You can't leave town because your best friend's boyfriend has psychic powers."

I crawl toward my phone and check my text messages. There's a message from Kit.

K: I wrote five more chapters last night.

What happens in those five chapters? I want to know. His characters have no names; he simply calls them He and She. *He does this. She does that.* It's elusive, and his male character's use of portmanteau words makes me smile. That's Kit. Fralad for a fried chicken salad, which the character doesn't think is a salad at all. Smust when he's not sure if he's smitten or in lust. Priend for an acquaintance that thinks they're a friend. And then I find myself searching for myself in the woman, who Kit describes as being aloof, preoccupied, and disconnected from the world around her. Was I those things? Or was I self-absorbed to think she was me? It crosses my mind that my words to him last night could have struck an idea, and the similarities could be coincidental.

I text back. *What is this book going to be about?*

His text bubble appears as he starts to type, then abruptly it's gone. It starts, then it's gone again. He's typing things then erasing them. I strangle my phone, then slam it on the bed a few times. It's lying facedown on the comforter, and I lift the corner to peek at the screen. There isn't a text. I go to the kitchen for a snack, then circle my bed a few times while I spoon peanut butter into my mouth from the jar. I'm scared that he's texted. I'm also scared that he hasn't.

"You chicken!" I yell. I lunge for the phone, dropping the peanut butter jar on the floor.

The first text message is from Della: *CALL ME NOW!*

All caps. We reserve all caps for emergencies.
Kit's text is underneath Della's.

K: You tell me.

I don't know what that means. Is he telling me that since I inspired the story, I have say over where it goes? I call Della.

"The test was wrong!" she screams into the phone.

It takes a minute to register what she's talking about. The test was…

"What?!"

"I took another one. I took five. They're all positive."

My head is spinning. I sit on the edge of the bed and put my head between my knees. I'm waiting for my feelings to catch up to my shock. Somehow I know they're not going to be good feelings, happy ones. Though they should be because my best friend is having a baby.

"Have you told—"

"No," she says quickly. "I haven't told him yet. I'm scared."

"Scared of what?" I ask dryly. "You wanted this."

"Yeah. But it's not like we planned it or talked about it or anything. I don't really know what he's going to say."

If she doesn't know what Kit would say, she doesn't know Kit very well. I could picture him being surprised, taking a few hours to let it process, then he would let resignation turn to happiness. Kit is the kind of guy who shows up.

"Wow," I say. "Everyone is having babies." It's a stupid thing to say, and I immediately apologize. "Sorry, I'm just in shock. And obviously not everyone is having babies ... just you and Sadie."

I bite my lip waiting to see how she'll take that one. I keep making stupid comments, and I don't mean to. Honestly. I'm happy for her. I think.

"It's not the same," she snaps.

"Of course not," I say quickly.

"Sadie got pregnant on purpose."

"Yeah..." My voice trails off. God, I just want this conversation to be over.

"When are you going to tell..."

"I have to go," she says. She hangs up before I say anything else. I stare at Kit's text for a long time, trying to decide what to do. He's going to have a baby with my best friend, which means I can't cut him off completely. But I have to cut off some parts. Like the part where I'm sort of into him. So maybe this texting bullshit has to stop. And sending me stories. I feel genuinely depressed about that one. And the hovering thing he does at parties and such. And—okay—I have to stop showing up at his job. I delete his texts without reading the last one. Then I delete him from my phone. I send Della a text that I know will repair what we lost in the last phone conversation. She's easy like that.

Let's pick out names!

Her text bubble appears almost immediately.

Daphne, she sends.

Hell no! I type back.

She gives me an *lol,* and just like that we're back on track. Helena and Della. The quirky one, and the pretty one.

Kit doesn't text me again. I check in with Della three days later to find out if she told him.

Yeah, she texts back.

Well?! What did he say?

D: *He was ecstatic. Couldn't be happier.*

Right away? I'm pushing it, but I want to see how right I was about him.

D: *Yes, right away.*

She's lying.

15
#YOGI

Della loses the baby. Kit calls to tell me. His voice is even and somber. I've never been on the phone with him before, and I wonder if he always sounds like this or if this is his grieving voice. I leave work right away and drive the two miles to their house. I know Della asked Kit to call; it's her thing. Makes the situation bleaker when you need someone to make your calls for you. I'm not being harsh; it's how she is. When she got her period for the first time, she made her mom call to tell me something had happened. People never really change, do they? When I arrive at 216 Trinidad Lane, her whole family is congregated in the living room. The sight of them all sitting there depresses me. It's like a wake. Each of her family members hugs me in turn, then I am sent off to Della and Kit's bedroom where she is lying on her bed in the dark.

"Hello," I say. I climb into the bed with her, and she snuggles into me. "I'm so sorry, Dells."

She sniffles.

"I'm not going to say cheesy, comforting, and slightly offensive things," I tell her.

"I know," she says. "That's why I like it that you're here."

"Who said the worst thing?" I ask. "Out of all of them."

"Aunt Yoli. She said my womb may not be fertilized enough to take seed."

We both snort with laughter, and that's what best friends are all about. Turning the bleak.

"Aunt Yoli once told me that my breasts would never make a hungry baby full," I tell her. "I was only thirteen."

We laugh some more, and I take Della's hand.

She turns on the TV, and we watch *Desperate Housewives* until Kit relieves me, and comes to lie with her on the bed. We barely exchange a glance, but as we cross paths I grab his hand and squeeze. *Sorry about the baby.* He squeezes back.

I go to their house every night after work. Della is taking it hard. Harder even than I thought. I make their meals and stay with her while Kit is at work. And, once again, my life is consumed by Della's grief. I don't mind except that I'm tired. And I still have a little of my own grief to deal with. June accuses me of being an enabler. I think about the way I encourage June to wear ugly hats, and I know she's right.

I am cleaning up the kitchen one night after she's fallen asleep when Kit gets home from work. I see the lights from his truck, and I can't help but feel excited. A non-depressed person to talk to! He hoists himself on the counter next to where I'm washing dishes.

"You have to take care of you too," is the first thing he says to me. And then I start to cry. It's so stupid, nothing bad has happened to me. I have no right.

"I'm sorry," I say. "I don't mean to make this about me."

Kit laughs a little. "You never make anything about you. Maybe you should."

I wave him away. "I'm fine. Everything is good. What about you? You okay?"

Kit shakes his head. "You can't change the subject and try to distract me."

I watch the water drain out of the sink. "I'm really uncomfortable talking about myself. I'd rather you tell me about you."

"All right. What would you like to know?"

"Had you told your family about the baby?"

His face doesn't betray a thing. He's basically unreadable. "No. It was early."

Fair enough.

"How do *you* feel about it?"

He chews on his bottom lip. "I don't know. I barely had time to process the pregnancy before it was over."

"Are you sad?" I press him. I want to know something. He gives so little.

"I don't know."

"For someone who seems to know so much about everyone else's feelings, you seem to know so little about your own."

Kit grimaces. "Maybe I don't like talking about myself either."

"Hmmm," I say, grinning. "What ever will we do?"

He jumps down from his perch. "Go for a walk," he says.

I look back toward their room. "Okay. Should we leave a note?"

"Did she take her sleeping pill?"

I nod.

"She'll be out 'til morning then."

I follow him out the door and down the drive. I try to predict which way he'll turn down the street, and I get it wrong. The air smells slightly of the ocean, and gasoline from the highway. It's the smell of escape and freedom. I wonder if Kit notices, and if it makes him want to jump in his truck and drive, drive, drive away from perfection.

"Kit," I say. "Are you in love?"

He grimaces. "Why do you ask me that every time we go on a walk?"

"Why do you never answer the question?"

"It's uncomfortable," he says. "And none of your business."

I laugh. "Fair enough, Kit Kat."

Kit sighs. "Please don't make me relive high school."

People called him Kit Kat in high school. That's cute. I wonder what he was like.

When I think he's not going to answer my question, he does. "I want to be, Helena. I've tried."

I know he's shared something incredibly personal with me so I try not to react. I want to grab him by the lapels and scream, "WHAT THE HELL?!" and "That's my best friend's heart you're messing with!"

Instead, I clear my throat. "Oh yeah? You almost became a dad, Kit. That's a scary life cocktail you're mixing." He's quiet for a long time.

"You've been friends with Della for years, Helena. You know how she is. There have been a couple of times when we've come close to ending things. She … threatens herself."

I am surprised. I am. I've never known Della to use suicide to make a guy stay. I've also never known Della to try to get pregnant. People change I guess.

"I don't know what to say, Kit. I'm not sure that's a good reason to stay, though. Sounds pretty unhealthy."

"I care about her. So much."

"I think you really, really need to love someone to have a baby with them. And even then, sometimes couples don't make it."

"Why are you talking in that weird voice?" He's looking at me sideways, and I get swirly whirlies in my belly.

"It happens when I'm nervous."

"You sound like Yogi Bear."

I throw my hands up in the air. "Oh my God, I'm never going on a walk with you again."

"Yeah, yeah Yogi."

"Every house in this place looks the same," I say, trying to change the subject. "It's sort of nauseating."

Kit laughs. "My house is different," he says. "Della made sure no one has shutters the same color as we do."

"You're right. You have the best shutters." And then at the same time we both say, "Aubergine," and start to laugh. She couldn't call them purple, or violet, or anything simple. Della liked for her things to sound as fancy as possible, and aubergine was the very fanciest way to say purple.

"One more question," I say. Kit groans.

"How do you know, and I mean really know, when you're in love with someone?"

We are standing by the little retention pond that all of the houses in the development are built around. I can see the backs of all of them, facing the pond with glowing windows. While I peek in people's windows, Kit bends to pick up a rock, and skips it across the water. *One … two … three … four.* I count his skips, impressed.

"It all feels like a dream," he says.

"A dream," I repeat. Ain't he right.

16
#AWKWARD

"It's weird. You and Kit."

"Huh?"

Della is holding a dress up to herself in front of the mirror in Nordstrom, yet her eyes are not on her own reflection, but on mine.

I play it cool and push hangers aside, study ugly shirts, and avoid meeting her eyes. Why are we here again? Oh, because she wanted to come.

"You guys seem close. Probably closer than you and I have been in a while." She looks at the dress, tilts her head to the side, and purses her lips.

"We get along pretty well." I shrug. "Where is this coming from?"

She suddenly looks guilty. "Nowhere. It's stupid. I've become this jealous monster. I've never felt like this about anyone before. It's more intense, you know?"

I don't know. I'm not the jealous type.

I shake my head at her. "You always want me to be friends with your boyfriends. You've shoved them on me in the past. Now you have a problem with it?"

She chews on her lip. Big, fat lips that match her big, fat eyes.

"I told you. It's different with Kit. And … he likes you. He's always talking about you."

I try to be cool, but I knock over a display of bracelets. "Shit. Oops."

Della bends down to help me pick them up, glancing up at me nervously every few seconds.

"Don't be mad, okay? I'm just being stupid."

I am mad. But at myself. How bad is it that Della is noticing something off? I have to lay off, leave Kit alone.

"You're not stupid," I say. "You're in love. Besides, what is there to say about me? I'm boring."

"That's not true. I like you, don't I?"

I don't answer. Della likes people who cater to her. I'm a professional caterer. It doesn't make me feel used, just needed.

"He just always wants you around. He shares his stories with you and not with me. And you guys always seem to have an inside joke, you know?"

"Don't you have inside jokes together?"

Her brows draw together. "Not really. I don't think he thinks I'm very funny."

"He thinks you're kind," I say. And then I tell her the nice things Kit said about her.

"And honestly, Della, I think he's laughing *at* me not with me. I'm only funny because I'm awkward."

"That's true." She nods. "You are very awkward."

I pull a shirt off the rack and hold it up to myself. She rolls her eyes. "It's beige. You're such a beige bitch." I put it back. Who wants to be a beige bitch? I watch my best friend admire herself in the mirror. It's the strangest thing to watch. The conceit battling the insecurity. I never knew a woman could be both until Della. A beautiful woman, racked by jealousy. *Of what?* I think. How many girls would love to be her? I wouldn't. It must be exhausting to be that consumed with yourself. Boring even. I feel guilty about the thoughts I've been having about Della. If I were really honest with myself, I'd say they started around the time Kit showed up. Can one person make you view someone in a different light? It shouldn't be that way. I'm disloyal.

A week later I am at Kit and Della's for a BBQ. There are twenty or so people in their small backyard, some sitting on lawn chairs, sipping beer, while others are hiding out in the air conditioning, gathered around the guacamole. I am part of the outside group. We quickly nickname ourselves The Outsiders—for more than one reason. Kit is not among us, but he comes over in between grilling. June sits next to me. She is pensive and fidgety tugging on the tassels on her skirt.

"What's wrong with you?" I ask her. "You're acting like a girl."

She glances back into the kitchen. That's when I sort of know. Della must have spoken to her about something. June hates being put in the middle. I put a hand on her arm, narrowing my eyes. Before I can say something, the back door slides open, and Della walks out with a plate of meat. June spins around, not looking at her. She's wearing hot pink shorts and a white tank. No bra. *We all know you have nipples, Della. Thanks for that.* I crack my neck as she hands Kit the plate and wraps her arms around his torso, pressing her face to his back. When all he does is smile at her, she goes in for something more drastic. She's wanting attention. There are too many girls here, and Della needs to know she's the best one. God, it sucks to know someone this well. It used to bother me less.

Someone's passing around a joint. I take it and suck down a little too eagerly. My coughing fit disrupts the group. Out of the corner of my eye I see Kit pull away from Della to come check on me. *No! No! No!* I wave him and everyone else away. I don't want any more trouble. I don't like the way she's been looking at me lately, like I'm a thing of danger that needs to be watched. Kit plucks the joint from my fingers.

"It'll subside," he says.

I can't say anything back because I'm too busy coughing, but I manage to shoot him a dirty look. Della watches from near the grill, one arm folded across her waist, the other tugging on a strand of her silky hair. June is watching Della. *Dammit June!* And Kit is still watching me watch everyone else.

"I'm fine," I say between my teeth. "I've smoked before, you know."

"Didn't look like it."

It makes me angry that he's singling me out. I'm just another guest at his house, and I want to be left alone, not chastised.

I'm not going to be drawn into a fight with someone who should be minding their own business anyway. I take the joint back from him and do another hit, then I pass it to the person next to me.

One of my fellow Outsiders cheers me on. "Thatta girl, Helena."

Kit glares at me for a few more seconds before returning to his post at the grill. I glance at Della out of the corner of my eye; she looks sour. All life gone. June is whimpering beside me like a puppy.

"Shut up, June," I say. "Awkward social situations are the building blocks of life."

"We should talk," she says. "But not here. She's watching me."

She is. She's watching both of us. I look straight on at Della, because I'm not afraid of her. I'm afraid of what we're becoming. Our relationship is tearing, twisting. The friendship part is slowly blurring, and something else is coming into focus. We used to look at each other and find solidarity in our knowledge of each other. Now our looks are assessing. Sizing. That's the worst thing about being young. You really have no clue about all the changes that are coming. And when they come, no matter how people have warned you, you are genuinely surprised.

17
#BYETHEN

I meet June for a late lunch on Saturday. I want to go to brunch, because I like brunch most, but June is a vegan.

"Please, Helena. It's all eggs, and bacon, and sausage. Brunch is the anti-vegan."

"I just want normal friends," I complain to her. "Ones who eat animals."

"Then be friends with a vegetarian. I am a vegan."

She shakes out her flowery dress as we wait for a table, and gives me a dirty look.

The tiny hostess leads us to a table on the patio where she spreads two menus in front of us. We are both itching to talk, but wait until our server has greeted us and asked for our order.

"She thinks you're after Kit," June finally tells me. And even as we sit a dozen miles away from Della, in a busy cafe, June looks cautiously around like she might appear at any moment. I tap my fingers on the table, annoyed.

"Why would I be after Kit?" I ask. "Why isn't Kit after me?"

I don't know why this bothers me more than my best friend talking behind my back. That she would blame this on me and not on him. I've sought him out ... a couple times. But he's the one always wanting to take walks. And everyone knows what happens when you take walks with a girl.

June rolls her eyes. "Because she's a girl in love, and it's never the man's fault. Only the competition."

"Oh, so now I'm the competition?"

I fold my arms across my chest and pout. June pushes her glasses up her nose. "Kit pays too much attention to you. That's the problem."

My head jerks in her direction. "No, he doesn't."

She laughs. "The reason Della sees you as competition is because you are. Kit has a thing for you. You're blind if you can't see that."

My heart is being awful. I wish it would stop dancing. It's wrong. But I also know it isn't true. Kit is thoughtful and kind. People often misinterpret those qualities for something else.

"Della and I are nothing alike," I say. "Kit has a thing for Della."

"Maybe that's his problem." June leans back so the waiter can put her food down. "They aren't much suited, are they?"

"Opposites attract."

"You're beautiful, Helena. You just don't see it. Which truly makes you more beautiful."

I put down my fork I'm so uncomfortable. "Ugh. Stop. Why are you saying these things?"

"Look, you've obviously known Della a lot longer than I have. But I became friends with her because of you. And vice versa. It's not like someone like Della would ever choose to be friends with me normally."

"What does that mean, June? That's crazy."

June waves her hands in the air and laughs. "I'm not offended. Trust me. I just know how things work. Let me speak your language so you can understand. Della is Cho, and I am Luna Lovegood."

I hit the tabletop. "You are Luna! Oh my God!" Why hadn't that clicked for me?

"Exactly," she says.

"I love it when you speak *Harry Potter* to me. Who am I?"

"You're a muggle who wants to be magical."

I frown. "That's so mean."

June shrugs. "So go be magical. It's a choice."

Maybe she's right. I started to, didn't I? When I took those classes. I feel so pouty. I am just a muggle. A beige bitch muggle. It's a sad day in Helena Land.

Before we part ways, I hug her big. "I'm going to talk to Della," I tell her. "Try to make things right."

She won't look at me. And that's when you know June has more to say.

"Sometimes you can't. Just be okay with that, all right?"

"Sure, June. Sure."

But Della and I had worked through puberty together. When she started cheerleading junior year and made new friends, we worked through that. And when I started dating Louis from the debate team, and didn't see her as often, we worked through that. And when we had our first serious fight about the way she had changed, we worked through that. And when we had nothing in common anymore, we worked through that. We work through things. That's us.

All the way home I'm thinking about what June said. How much of this is my fault. What could I have done differently? I am not good at flirting. I don't try to flirt. Had I flirted with Kit in front of Della and not known I was doing it? If I've done something wrong, I want to own it. I've tried to be friendly to him, aloof. But, that dream … it made me different. And if I were to be really, really honest with myself, I'd say that the dream affected my ability to forgive Neil. All of a sudden I had ideas about things being better. About my loneliness being gone.

I call Della as soon as I get home. I have it all planned out— everything I'm going to say. She picks up on the third ring. There's a lot of noise and shuffling in the background.

"Hello? Dells?"

I hold the phone away from my ear, and I'm about to hang up when I hear it. A long moan, heavy breathing.

"Della?" I say.

Della answers, but its Kit's name she says, followed by a series of yelps. I hang up quickly and feel heat climb my face. She must have accidentally answered while they were having sex. Oh God. I cover my face with my hands. I'm scarred for life.

I feel something else too. What is it? I push it away and go open a bottle of wine. I don't even bother to get a glass; I drink straight from the bottle. The wine hits the back of my throat, and I treat it like water. So classy. I wish I had something stronger—like that bourbon Neil used to bring over on special occasions. Five sips and you felt like you were made of fire and courage. I needed courage. I was a wimp.

She calls me later that night as I'm climbing into bed.

"Hey, sorry I missed your call." Her voice is flat. Dry. I'm still loopy from the bottle of wine I drank.

"Oh. No problem."

There is a long pause, which makes me wonder if she's waiting for me to say something about what happened. Does she know? And then I feel like the dumbest fuck. Of course she knows. Because she didn't miss the call. She did it on purpose.

My voice is colder than it would have been without the realization.

"Just calling to check in. Haven't spoken to you since the BBQ. You were acting weird."

"Everything is fine," she says. "Same as always."

I nod. *Well then.*

"Okay," I say.

"Okay," she says. "Bye then."

She hangs up first.

That is it, isn't it? She has nothing to say to me, and I have nothing to say to her. It hurts.

"Hos before bros!" I yell at the phone. But it's too late. A bro came, and both the hos are in turmoil.

"Fuck you, Kit Isley," I say under my breath. But I don't mean it, and Della already has that covered. The saddest part is I don't have anyone to talk to about this. Normally, I'd talk to Della. Kit. Kit is the one I really want to talk to. Ha! She's right, isn't she?

I take out my phone, hold it above my head, and snap a picture. I call it, The Muggle Loses a Friend.

18
#GRAVİTY

I don't talk to Kit or Della for a month. That's thirty days of isolation from a person I've never gone without, and also, a person I don't want to go without. I'm mostly depressed about it, but I keep myself busy with work and the new art classes I'm taking. Be magical, June said. So, I'm trying. I just want to earn my wand. Martin and Marshall from work talk me into going to the Broward County Fair. To even out the girl/boy score I ask June to come. Martin is stout and red-haired. He fancies himself a wine connoisseur and likes to make the rest of us feel inferior. I swear to God, even his voice changes when he's lecturing us on the delicate skins of pinot grapes. I sink lower into my seat because I don't know which grapes those are. The red ones? Martin's favorite movie is *Sideways* with Paul Giamatti. I see the similarities. Marshall, on the other hand, is Puerto Rican and bitterly confused as to why his parents would name him Marshall when his brothers are named Roberto, Diego and Juan Carlos. He suffers from a self-professed identity crisis. I like them both very much, though June thinks they're weird. Which says a lot. We spend the night wandering from ride to ride as Martin educates us on the difference between Pinot Gris and Pinot Grigio. (Answer: They're made from the same grape, but Pinot Gris is produced in France, while Pinot Grigio derives from Italy.) I'm half-interested and keep asking him questions. The boys take a bathroom/food break, and June grabs my arm, digging her nails into my skin.

"He keeps asking me if I'm interested in moving to China," she hisses. She glances at Marshall, who is waiting in line for a funnel cake. "I think he's trying to wife me."

"You're not seeing anyone," I offer helpfully. "And you love Chinese food."

"Ugh!"

She marches off to the bathroom while I get in line for the Gravitron.

"Cool, Helena," I say to myself. "Piss off your one remaining friend."

"I'll be your friend."

I turn around to find Kit standing behind me, a shit-eating grin on his face. I get over my shock as quickly as I can, and push back my shoulders.

"Doubtful," I snap. "Your girlfriend wouldn't like it."

Whoa! Suppressed anger much?

I look at him apologetically and duck my head.

"Sorry," I say.

"It's okay," he says. "The truth is often angry."

"How've you been?" I'm trying not to obviously search the crowd for Della, but I can't help it. My eyes are dancing around like a crack head.

"She's in the bathroom," he says. "She'll probably run into June and take a few minutes extra to chat. That's who you're here with, right?"

I wonder if he saw us, or if he stalked our Instagram pictures.

Marshall chooses that exact moment to shove a funnel cake in my face. I smile tightly.

"Marshall, this is my friend, Kit."

"Hey man," Marshall juggles his drink and plate to shake Kit's hand, then he shoves the funnel cake at me again.

"Nope. No. Nothing's changed since twenty seconds ago."

Kit shoves both hands in his pockets and looks from me to Marshall. He has a funny look on his face.

"So—" he says.

"Ah, here come the girls and Martin," I interrupt him.

Our pack thickens as Della, June, and Martin walk up. Della is dressed in ridiculous leather shorts and a matching leather top. I'm not sure if she's an erotic trapeze artist, or a girl desperate for everyone to look at her. I wish I hadn't worn beige. She's arm in arm with June when they approach us. I look at Kit to see if he likes that sort of outfit, but find him looking at me.

"Hi," Della says. "Fancy seeing ya'll here." She is introduced to Martin, gives me a short hug, and latches on to Kit.

I look away.

"So are you going to ride this thing?" Della asks, looking around the group. "Because I am definitely not."

"I don't really want to either," June says. "Let's go on the Ferris wheel."

Della smiles brightly at her and nods, then sticks out her bottom lip and looks up at Kit. "Come with us," she says.

"I'd rather ride this," he says. "You go ahead."

"I want you to come with," she insists.

I can feel it, the tension.

All of a sudden I want a piece of Marshall's funnel cake. I take the plate from him and start putting chucks in my mouth.

"I thought you didn't want any," he complains. I hand back the plate and take his Coke. Kit and Della are having an argument. She's insisting he come, and he's refusing to leave.

"I'm just really craving a kebab right now," I say. "Anyone want to come with me to get a kebab?" I look at Martin, who looks at Marshall, who looks at June.

"You're next in line," June says. "You can't leave now." I see her eyes dart nervously toward Kit and Della.

"Let's go, June," Della says, breaking away from Kit and marching off in the direction of the Ferris wheel. June mouths *HELP* to me, and then scurries after her.

"I'm going with them," Marshall says.

"Dude!" Martin looks put out. He watches his friends chase after the girls, and then turns to us.

"You have to ride in twos." He looks at Kit when he says this.

That's not true. The Gravitron can be ridden alone, but Kit plays along.

"Yeah," says Kit. "So, are you riding by yourself?"

I stifle a laugh, but, Martin isn't having it. He squares his already square shoulders and glares at my friend, Kit.

"Helena came to hang out with me tonight."

I jerk in surprise and make a face. Kit sees it and laughs.

I'm about to tell Martin that I pretty much came because they begged me, and that just because I came didn't mean I had to be glued to his side, when we're suddenly at the front of the line. Kit grabs my hand and pulls me up the three stairs to the entrance of the ride. We're herded into the Gravitron, which smells like popcorn and sweat, and the mix of metal and grease. It's disgusting and exciting at the same time.

I glance back and see Martin scowling at us. I didn't know he was into me until that moment. It's funny what people don't see. I'm still holding onto that thought when all of a sudden I literally cannot see.

We stumble forward, searching for the nearest wall. Kit finds us a spot in the back, and we stand with our backs to the padded sides of the Gravitron, never letting go of each other's hands. This has always been my favorite ride—completely enclosed, with padded panels lining the inside wall. Riders lean against these panels, which are angled back. As the ride rotates, the rider is glued to the pad behind them by centrifugal force (Neil told me that). It's a combination of spinning, the inability to move my arms and legs, and the dark that thrills me. I close my eyes as the music begins to play. Kit lets go of my hand, and I force my head left to see why. He's using both hands to cover his face. I laugh, but it's swept away. I reach for his wrist to pull his hand away; it's a struggle, and I'm moving in slow motion. My whole body flips to its side, and now I'm facing Kit. I can't stop laughing. Kit peeks out from beneath his fingers. Even in the dark, as strobe lights flash across his face, I can see that he's a little green.

"You could be riding the Ferris wheel," I shout. Kit laughs, and then flips on his side to face me. All of a sudden we're separated by a pathetic three inches. I can't really go anywhere since the Gravitron is in the middle of its most fierce spin. It's hard to move, and suddenly, it's hard to breathe too. I'm glad it's dark, and that Kit doesn't have access to my expression. He has a different kind of access, and I finding myself daydreaming about a kiss. It's sick, and I've never done that before. But I've also never been this physically close to Kit Isley. I close my eyes to fend him off. And then. And then I feel his hand on my face. Longing can come to a person at the most inopportune times. Like when you're on a fair ride and gravity is holding you down, and your dream husband puts his warm hand on your cheek, even though it's really hard work to do that. I won't open my eyes. I don't want to see what's happening in his. I'll fucking die if he looks at me like I look at him. I keep them shut and feel a tear squeeze its way from the corner of my eye. It struggles down my cheek and rolls onto Kit's hand. And then the ride is over. The spinning slows, and we are given back control of our arms, and legs, and head, and hands. Which is why I'm surprised when Kit's hand doesn't immediately leave my face. We're thrown to our feet as the music ends, bodies still closer than they should be. The doors haven't opened yet, so we stand like that for a minute—my forehead on his chest, his hands around my upper arms. It's a suspended moment, both inappropriate and innocent at the same time. I cling to him, smell him, wish he was mine. And then the doors slide open, and I'm running.

19
#FINDMAGIC

I take a selfie. Call it, The Muggle Searches for Magic, and then I pack a small overnight bag and drive the five hours to my parents' house. My mother hasn't been speaking to me. She wanted me to forgive Neil, which was fine. There was room in my heart for forgiveness; there wasn't room in my life for someone who constantly needed it. She wanted to plan a wedding, and I'd foiled her plans of tulle, and pearls, and cake tasting. My father is working in the yard when I pull up. He tips back his Yankees cap and comes to say hello to me.

"Didn't know you were coming, Hellion. Your mother is going to be so happy to see you."

"I didn't know either. And don't lie to me, Daddy. She's still pissed." He smiles like he's caught.

"She's at the market, so hide your car around back and get her really good."

I nod. Nothing better than scaring your overbearing, controlling mother. My dad liked torturing her too; he'd been putting ideas in my head since I was a little girl. *Move all of the paintings in the house to different rooms. Rub butter on her reading glasses. Wrap cello wrap around the toilet seat.*

My poor mother (who really deserved it). At least she only had the pranks of one child to worry about. My dad comes inside to make me a prime rib sandwich left over from their dinner the night before.

"You coming here to tell us something, Hellion?"

"Yup." I sip spiked lemonade from the Mason jar he hands me. God bless him.

"Good or bad?" he asks. My dad can't keep still. He's never been good at it. I watch him move from the sink, to the fridge, to the back door.

"Why can't you just ask me a question directly?" I ask him. "What are you here to tell us?" I imitate his deep voice. He shakes his head.

"I don't sound like that. But, fine," he says. "What are you here to tell us?"

"I'm moving."

"To where?"

"It's really none of your business, Dad."

He comes to sit down across from me. "Is this about Neil?"

I'm shaking my head before he's finished his sentence. "No, it's about me. I've always been that girl who you can count on—steadfast, predictable, mousy brown hair. That's why Neil liked me—well, he wanted me to dye my hair blonde—but the other parts. And you know what? I don't even think that was me. I think it's what everyone expected from me, so I just went along with it."

"So, you're telling me that on the inside you're a wild, unpredictable blonde?"

"Maybe. I'd like the chance to find out."

"Why can't you find out here?"

I put my pale hand over his brown, calloused one. "Because I'm not brave enough to change with everyone watching me. I want to do it alone. I want it to be real."

He sits back in his chair and narrows his eyes. I think he learned that look from watching too many Robert De Niro movies. My dad is a handsome guy, his hair is all white, but he spikes it up. He has a tattoo of a flamingo on his forearm. A dare from his college days. I always wanted to be like him, but my personality veered more toward my mother's.

"Your mother is overbearing and controlling," he says. "Now, don't get me wrong, that's the reason I fell in love with her. All five feet of her, not afraid of anything, and always telling me what to do. It's pretty hot."

"Eww, Dad."

"Sorry. Anyway, it's nature. Overbearing mothers usually give way to one of two things in their children: rebellion or passivity. In your case, the latter." He dips his finger into the honey jar that sits in the middle of the table and rubs it across my forehead.

"Go child," he says. "Be at peace. Let no one overbear you."

"It's supposed to be oil," I say. "You're supposed to anoint my head with oil."

I can feel the honey dripping down my forehead toward the bridge of my nose, and then it hangs like snot from the tip of my nose. I lick it off.

"Your mother just pulled into the driveway," he says. "Go hide in the pantry and scare her." I hear her tires on the gravel and stand up.

Two days later, I leave my parents' house, confident as fuck. I even have a little bounce in my step that's normally not there because of my really bad posture. My mother was hesitant at first, but after an afternoon of sulking and moodily sipping Zinfandel, she decided that the men in Florida weren't suited for my reserved and articulate personality. The men in Florida. That's why I was given her blessing to leave. Family is a wonderful thing, mostly when they're not projecting their shit on you. She called a friend, who called a friend, who had a job secured for me in less than five hours.

"Tell me," I heard her say over the phone. "Are there handsome, single men working there?"

I had a date with Dean lined up for a week after my move. "Dean," my mother said, clapping. "A handsome name for a handsome man."

My dad shook his head behind her shoulder, his eyes large.

Before I left, my dad and I poured her bottle of Zin down the drain and refilled the bottle with a hot sauce concoction we'd been working on all day.

"Don't forget to video her reaction," I whispered in my dad's ear when I kissed him goodbye. "She's going to divorce both of us if we don't stop."

My dad guffaws. "She'd have to learn to pump her own gas," he calls out.

"Never gonna happen!" I wave goodbye.

Two down—the most important two. Now I just had to tell Della and June. Thank God. I give eight weeks' notice to my job. I haven't been there long enough for anyone to really care that I'm leaving. They throw a party for me anyway, and spell my name wrong on the cake. I wait to tell Della last.

"What the hell do you mean you're moving to Washington?" she says. "How could you just make a decision like this and never talk to me about it?" I sit there for a while, thinking about how to answer her, running the tip of my finger over the grooves that mark the edge of the table. We are at that age that balances between independence and conferring with your friends about every miniscule decision you make. I've never liked that part of adolescence, but tried my hardest to play along. *Should I get bangs, Della? Do I want a silver car or a gold car? The dark wash jeans, or the light?*

"Well, because I'm a grownup, and I don't need to confer with my friends about my decisions."

We are sitting at a sidewalk cafe in downtown Ft. Lauderdale. The waiter drops off our sangria, and, sensing the tension, disappears almost immediately. She pulls out her phone to text Kit—fast thumbs, a childlike pout.

"Hey," I say, touching her hand. "We can visit each other. Think of how fun that will be."

There are tears in her eyes when she sets her phone down on the table. "I don't want to be here without you." A second later I see a text from Kit pop up. "What?!"

"Nah, you'll be okay, Dells. You have Kit, and your new house. You guys want to get married…" My voice trails off on the last one. I take a sip of sangria. The glass is sweating.

Della sniffs. "Kit's on his way," she says.

"Oh, no. Dells, why? This was supposed to be just girls!"

I get panicky. Take more sips. Signal the waiter for another.

"Well, everything changed when you announced you were moving away."

We mostly small talk. I make fun of myself because it always makes her smile. But, today Della is focused, and nothing can distract her.

"Who will save me from my family?" she asks. "Who will show up to make me snacks?"

"Kit," I say. "That's his job now."

Kit arrives, and the mood of our lunch changes. He doesn't feed into Della's depression; instead, he lights up the whole restaurant with his wit, and his suspenders, which he's wearing because he has to go straight to work after this. We are signing receipts, and closing our wallets when he turns to me.

"Why?"

"Not you too; just leave me alone about it," I say. Della sniffles and leaves to go to the bathroom to cry.

"Why?" he asks again when she's gone.

I look at him long and hard. He doesn't look away.

"Why not? I'm young, I'm boring, I'm hurt. Seems right."

"You're running," he says.

I wonder why he's looking at me so intently, and why he's clenching his fists, and why he looks so great in suspenders.

"You should know," I shoot back.

His mouth tightens, but I've got him there.

"Where are you going?"

This is the hard part. I haven't told anyone but my parents where I'm going. I want it to stay that way until I move.

I shake my head.

"You're going to Washington," he says.

My mouth twitches. Bad, bad poker face. How the hell does he know that?

"No."

"Yes, yes you are," he hisses.

I look over his shoulder to check for Della. She's still drying her tears.

"No, I'm moving to Dallas."

"You're lying. It's hot there, and you hate cutoffs and boots."

How does he know that?

"Are you leaving because of me?"

Ooof, ouch, the heat from his eyes is burning.

I try to look offended. I even roll my eyes. I'm not good at eye rolling, Neil used to say it made me look gassy.

"I told you why I'm leaving," I tell him, standing up. He grabs my hand, and it's like the dream. So much that I yank away from him and take a few steps back. Where's the crayon? I see it, lying on the floor under the table. *God.* Is it blue? *You're being stupid,* I tell myself. *This is a restaurant, there are always blue crayons lying on the floor.*

"You're not crazy," he says. "I—"

"Kit," I interrupt him. "Della's coming."

Della calls me later that night. "Look, I know we've had our differences lately, but you're still my best friend, and I love you." I let that sink in along with guilt. "We'll make this work."

"Sure, Dells. Of course we will."

"I have to have someone to call to update about my life," she says.

"Of course you do." I smile against my phone. "That person has always been me, hasn't it?"

20
#FUCKFEAR

When people resolve themselves to something, it becomes very difficult to feel anything but that resolve. And so, as I board my plane to Seattle, wearing a Sounders sweatshirt that June gave me as a goodbye gift, I do not cry, I do not worry, and I do not have feelings of self-doubt. This was what I had decided to do, and that was that. I pull my wine cork from my purse and hold it tightly in my fist as I take my seat and stare out the window. The Florida rain is hard and slanted. I wonder if it will be raining when I reach Seattle, which I hear has more of a gentle mist. I do not think of Kit, who is at a doctor's appointment with Della. I do not think of Della, who is at a doctor's appointment with Kit. I think only of my new adventure. In fact, it's the only adventure I've ever taken, which makes it more exciting. A first. I want to be a magical folk, and not a muggle. I pull out my worn, dog-eared copy of *The Goblet of Fire*. It's the same book I've kept on my nightstand since I first read it six years ago. My favorite of the seven. I brought it with to read on the plane, for courage. To remind myself of why I am doing this. It's my Felix Felicis.

"*Harry Potter*," a voice says from my left. "Have you tried reading the Bible?"

A woman, mid-forties, judgment scribbled all over her pinched, powdered face. Why do Bible lovers always have that constipated look on their face? *Don't stereotype, Helena!* I do my best to smile politely.

"Is that the book where that lady turns into a statue after looking back at a burning city after God told her not to?" I say.

"And where three defiant men are thrown into a furnace and don't burn. Oh, and isn't there a gal who feeds and puts to sleep the general of an enemy's army, and then uses a mallet to drive a tent peg into his brain?" She looks at me blankly.

"But those are true. And that," she says, pointing to Harry, "is fiction. Not to mention devil worship."

"Uh huh, uh huh. Devil worship? Is that like when the Israelites made a cow god of gold and worshipped it?"

She's enraged.

"You would love this book," I say, shoving *The Goblet of Fire* at her. "It's PG-rated compared to the Bible."

"You, young lady, are part of a depraved and lost generation."

She gets up, and I see her march to the front of the plane where the flight attendant meets her. I point my straw at her back and whisper, "Avada Kedavra."

She doesn't come back, and I get lucky because the middle seat stays open.

"Thank you, Jesus; thank you, Harry," I say.

There are mountains. Great big ones that poke through the clouds, tipped in snow that looks like whipped cream. My heart. It is not raining when my plane lands at Sea-Tac. The sky is so cloudless I press my nose to the window and stare around in disbelief. *Liars! Where is the rain?* There is no one to meet me at baggage claim; that's what makes the whole thing feel sore. There is no mother to hug me, and no father to load my luggage into the trunk while making jokes about how heavy it is. I am alone in all things, singular and frightened and excited. I collect my bags and a cab drives me the short fifteen miles to Seattle proper. I can see the city rise in a pageant of lights from the highway. There are cities that take your breath away by their sheer size; some by the beat of their rhythmic culture, but Seattle gives you your breath back. Fills your lungs. I take it in and feel like I can breathe for the first time in my life. My God, it's like I've been looking for this place all along. My hotel is nice; I made sure of that. You never know what type of serial killer you'll meet in a seedy hotel. Things may get rough in the coming months, but for the next four days, until my apartment is ready, I am a tourist. Kit sends me texts of places to go see.

It's sweet, except it keeps him present on my mind all day, the notifications on my phone with his name flashing up at me. I explore the city first, the fish market, The Needle, and the Nordstrom that started it all. I get a cramp walking up one of the steep hills, and a homeless man wearing a grubby pink beanie offers me a cigarette. I take it, even though I've never smoked a cigarette before. I don't want to be rude to my fellow Washingtonians.

"I like your fucking socks," he says, pointing at my feet with a dirty finger. I'm not wearing socks, so that's super cool that he sees them anyway.

"Thanks," I say. "I knitted them myself."

He nods, looking thoughtfully at my feet. "Hey, do you have a couple bucks to loan me? It's my birthday."

I reach into my purse and pull out five ones. "Hey, happy birthday," I say.

He looks confused. "It's not my birthday."

"Of course it's not."

He shuffles back down the hill. I stick my cigarette behind my ear, grinning at the lunacy. *Magic, I tell you.*

Kit texts me: *What are you doing?*

Having a birthday smoke with a friend, I send back.

K: *Guy or girl?*

I make a face, and then type: *Guy*

He doesn't send anything for a while, so I tuck my phone back in my purse while I browse a paper shop until I realize how nerdy it is and leave. Ten minutes later I hear the ping that signifies I have a message.

I feel jealous… that you're there and I'm not, he sends.

I type a response, and then delete it. Too flirtatious.

K: *What were you typing?*

I laugh out loud. *Nothing. Go away.*

He sends a sad face.
And then…

> K: *Are you going to go see Port Townsend?*

> *Should I?*

I sit down at a cafe for lunch. Actually, I sit down at a cafe so I can text Kit. I'm not really that hungry.

> K: *YES! You'll have to take a ferry.*

> *That scares me*, I send back.

> K: *Precisely the reason you should do it.*

He's right, isn't he? That's why I came here—to kill the things that control me.

> *I'll think about it.*

Kit sends a thumbs up.

> K: *Also, for being in my state- #Fuckyou.*

> I chew on my lip for a few seconds before
> I respond: *In a Range Rover on the ferry.*

It takes him a minute to get it. He responds with a shocked-faced emoji.

> K: *Range Rovers aren't very spacious. Someone's going to get hurt.*

I can't anymore. I'm blushing so hard I turn my phone off and bury it in my purse. I can't believe I instigated that. And why a Range Rover? God, I'm so pathetic.

I decide to go to Port Townsend, though. I look up a place to rent a car, and catch a cab over. They have a Range Rover. It's way expensive, but I get it anyway. And why? All because of a conversation I had with Kit that I'm still embarrassed about? Maybe it's because he challenged me not to be afraid. I check out of my hotel and load my suitcases in the trunk. I'm the last car to be loaded onto the ferry, and it scares me that I'm so close to the water. *It scares me.* I get out of the Rover and walk around until I'm standing with my back against the trunk. The wind has cold fingers; it pulls me toward the water. I'm shaking.

I hear the high-pitched voice of a woman yell, "Here goes the feeeerry!" just as we pull away from the dock. I'm terrified. A car on a boat. Me, in a car, on a boat. The Rover could just roll backward and sink into the Sound, taking me with it. I envision all the ways this ferry could kill me, but I stay where I am. All because I'm scared, and I don't want to be. When it gets too much, I close my eyes and let the wind touch me. She's not as aggressive as I thought. Maybe she's not trying to push me into the water; maybe she's trying to make me see the water. I step forward and look down. The ferry is spitting out a thick stream of wake. It froths and churns. It's beautiful. I look back at the city of Edmonds, the hill with the houses—someone called it a bowl. It does look like a bowl of houses. I like that. I imagine a giant spoon scraping all of the houses off the hill and into the Sound. Is that sick? Who cares? I'm okay; this is okay. To me, this ferry is a novelty, but to the people who live here, it's part of the landscape—a way of life. I want to join them. There are people getting out of their cars and walking up a flight of stairs. I decide to follow them. But, before I go, I take a picture of the side of the Rover, outlined by the water, and Instagram it: #Helenatakesonherfears.

There are four decks on the ferry; two are for cars, the third is an enclosed area. There is a little cafeteria with booths, and past that are different areas to sit and watch the water. The top deck is open, and the braver people are up there walking around and taking pictures. Children hang over the railing and it makes me feel ill to watch them. I grab a paper container of French fries from the cafeteria and find a seat near a window. The fries are epically delicious. I'm soaking them in ketchup when I get a text from Kit.

K: #Fuckfear

We're talking in hashtags now. I like it. I don't answer him. Fuck fear, and fuck Kit, and fuck love. I don't need any of that muggle shit.

21
#VICTORIANSEAPORT #HISTORICAL #ECLECTIC #OLD

In my dream, Port Townsend was emerald-glossy—a place where nature is given reign to be free and loud. It is so in real life, too, but I didn't imagine all of the water. Water with the Cascades etched in a jagged shadow behind it. Cold, blue water, where if you watched long enough, you'd see a seal break the surface and then dip back down, its body a glossy black. All so crisp, like a postcard. I arrive on a day when someone is blowing giant bubbles down Main Street. "This isn't real. Is this real?" I say to myself. It's okay to talk to yourself here; I saw someone else doing it.

The store windows are decorated for fall. They're perfectly curated—plump pumpkins piled next to rosy-cheeked scarecrows. The air already smells like nutmeg and crushed leaves. A shop owner is hanging scarves on a rack on the sidewalk. She smiles at me, her long gray hair catching in the breeze. "You look new," she says.

"I'm visiting," I tell her. "I love it here."

"Here loves you," she tells me. "Mutual love is a magical thing."

I buy a scarf from her because she's an excellent salesperson, and for five minutes I wasn't thinking *fuck love*. I find out that her name is Phyllis, and she's a lesbian. I know this because as she bags my scarf, she says, "My partner loves this scarf. She says it looks like wet pavement."

"Your business partner?" I look around for the partner.

"My life partner." She points to a picture behind the register of a woman with spirally red hair.

"What's her name?" I ask. Phyllis laughs.

"Ginger," she says. She hands me my bag, and I feel like I've made a friend. Two friends: Phyllis and Ginger. But, that's the way of Port Townsend. I step out of the store and find a bench where I can watch.

The people are painted in expression and art. Tattoos, hippies with long hair, punks with no hair, the elderly, and the young, children who say hello to you as you walk by. No one is guarded, or jaded, or tired. It's all witchcraft. I've found it, the place of non-Muggles. Kit's openness is not so strange when you meet people like Phyllis. I feel light as I walk down the street, marveling, hoping my car doesn't get towed away from where I parked near an old clam cannery that sits on the water. How could he leave this place for muggy, flat Florida? Greer must have long reach. That scares me. I feel like I understand Kit less after coming here. Perhaps I underestimate Greer. Now, all I want to do is find her. My mental image of her is of a girl with straight brown hair, tied back in a low ponytail. She wears camp T-shirts from her counselor days, and has bright blue eyes. That's what Kit loved the most about her—her eyes. They were full of open honesty. I imagine that's why he gravitated to Della, because she is Greer's polar opposite. This is a hippie town, so she probably wears Birkenstocks and carries a woven backpack. When she's older she will look like Phyllis and braid flowers into her pubic hair. I wonder if she's moved on since Kit. Bought a house with someone … had a baby. *I need to know, I need to know, I need to know.*

I eat lunch at a little place that only serves soup. I listen to the clanking of spoons on porcelain and think it sounds more musical than it would anywhere else. I pay my bill, and I'm looked in the eye when I'm told to have the best day. I *am* having the best day, thank you very much. I take a long walk along the water, take some photos of a beautiful old boat called The Belle, and upload them to Instagram. Kit likes them right away.

He texts me and says: *I know the lady who owns that boat!*

There are two hotels in town, and both are said to be haunted. I check into the Palace Hotel and suddenly feel incredibly lonely. It's all fun and games until you realize you don't have a home anymore, and Phyllis probably isn't your real friend. This has to be the dumbest thing I've ever done. I fall face down on the bed and pretend cry into the comforter. I don't have real tears; I'm in survival mode. The comforter smells strangely of peanut butter, and that creeps me out. What am I really doing here? Am I here for Kit? Sort of. I may really be here for Greer. I've seen one of the girls Kit chose to be with; I know her so well I can read her mind. There is nothing so terribly deep or fascinating about her gray matter. So, now I need to see the other woman. The one who started it all. I need to make a comparison and know why he chose Della. And all for what? To understand why the man in my dream was so different from the man in real life? Why Dream Kit would choose me over Della and this Greer person?

Wait. Do I have an obsessive personality? I obsess over this for a little while, before changing into something warmer and heading out for dinner. I take pictures because I want to remember this place and all the things it made me feel. *What does it feel like?* I ask myself. *Like cold air in your lungs after too much warm air.* Maybe this is how you feel when you find your place in the world.

22
#WHYYOUSOOBSESSEDWITHME

I go to the library first, and, as I climb the stairs, I assure myself that I am here because of my deep, abiding love of books. I need to smell them, touch them, and be near them. Books, beautiful books! I am really here to look for Greer. Do I have an obsession to see the girl Kit loved? Absolutely not. I am merely curious. Mildly so. It's always been my nature, and my third grade teacher, Mrs. Habershield, told me that curiosity was a beautiful thing. I ask the librarian where I can find the county yearbooks, and then make my way to a dusty, forgotten corner of the library. Kit is three years older than Della. I find the right yearbook and flip to the index. Kit Isley is listed as being on pages 20, 117, 340, 345, 410. Popular. I was only on one page of my senior yearbook. If they were high school sweethearts, Greer will be in some of the pictures with him. My prediction is right. Greer Warren stands next to Kit Isley at Prom, wearing an amethyst dress. She is full of braces, smiling widely yet still quite pretty. She has a purple streak in her brown hair, and Kit has given her a purple carnation corsage, which juts ornately from her wrist. I presume purple is her favorite color, and when I find additional pictures of her on page 45, 173, and 211, I find that she was on the yearbook staff, played volleyball, and started a program her junior year to donate one weekend a month to big brother Seattle's inner city kids. She was voted Kindest, Most Likely to Start a Charity, and won Best Looking Couple alongside Kit. I stick out my tongue. Overall, high school Greer Warren was a kind, athletic, humanitarian with a super hot boyfriend. I linger longer on Kit. He smiled more back then, dressed in what would be considered skater boy attire, and for the most part, he kept his hair cut short. I prefer his flannels and ripped jeans, the longer hair and scruffy face. I close the book and slide it back onto the shelf. I want to keep it, but I don't have a library card, and stealing is wrong.

Well, there you go. I got what I came here for. I dust imaginary crumbs from my pants, and try to figure out what to do next. I have to go back to Seattle, buy a car, pay my deposit on my downtown apartment, and sign the lease. Busy, busy. My little trip to Port Townsend has come to an interesting end. Tomorrow, I'll say goodbye to little Port Townsend and go back to where the Muggles live.

Tomorrow comes, and instead of getting in my rental and driving to the ferry, I walk once more down Main Street. I turn right in the direction of the water. I walk toward a beautiful, old brick building with aquamarine doors. This was the clam cannery someone mentioned. Someone purchased it a few years back and lived on the upper floor. The dock surrounding the cannery is open to public. A few couples stand with their backs to the water taking selfies and kissing. I wait until they are gone to venture closer to the water, my eyes searching for the glossy bodies of seals. It is breathtaking, this place. I desperately want to stay here. *So why not stay?* a voice in my head asks me. It is not my voice. It's the reckless dream voice that told me to take art classes, and pottery classes, and move to Washington. I tell the voice to shut up—I've listened to it too much lately—then I make my way toward my hotel. I'll leave tomorrow morning. Bright and early. I cross the street and turn back to look at the cannery one last time. That's when the door opens.

She looks nothing like her pictures in the yearbook. I only recognize her because of the unique structure of her face. High cheekbones and full lips. She's wearing a lavender dress, simple. On anyone else it would look like a sack. To wear something that simple, you had to be stunning. *God, Kit.* I seriously want to face palm on his behalf. She has a trail of lavender flowers tattooed down her outer thigh. The Greer of my mind disintegrates into a pile of camp T-shirts, leaving behind this lean, pert breasted beauty with silvery hair and bright strawberry lips. Her right arm is tattooed from wrist to shoulder, with what looks like vines and lilacs. She's like a canvas for expensive art. Kit's Greer can make straight girls gay. I know this because I consider it. I watch as she opens the lid to the giant dumpster behind the building and tosses her trash bag inside. She stops on the way back to the cannery to crouch down and talk to a little boy in red shorts who is walking with his mother, then she holds open a door for an elderly woman trying to fit her walker into the tight doorway of a gift shop. And finally, to top off all of her fun, spunky kindness, she high-fives a bum who looks genuinely happy to see her. When at last she disappears back into the cannery, I am hungry for KFC. I wander into an art gallery. I have never viewed art as something you do on weekends. Something you do outside of extra-curricular credit. The smell of paint pulls me through the door. It's the smell of my stolen nights at painting class. They are acrylic on canvas; Neptune taught me that. The artist is the same for most of the gallery—local I take it. The paintings are of water. But, not the way water is usually painted, with land stationed around it. There is just water, as viewed from above. There are ripples, sometimes disturbed by only a leaf or a feather. Mostly just water. I don't know that I can say these paintings make me feel things that are good. But perhaps art isn't supposed to make you feel good, but just to make you feel. Does it cure the numb? I don't know. A woman greets me; she is lean and tall, her hair tied in a bun on top of her head. I tell her I just moved here and wandered in. She is aloof but friendly. She asks what I did before I came, and if I need a job. I think about the accounting job my mother lined up for me in Seattle, and I automatically say yes. I don't want to go back to Seattle. I want to stay here. The woman's name is Eldine, and she owns the gallery, which features the work of local artists. "People come from all over America to buy her work," she says, nodding to the paintings of water.

"What's her name?" I ask.

I suddenly get psychic. I know what she's going to say before she says it.

"Greer Warren. She lives in the old cannery along the waterfront."

I feel my head spin. This keeps getting better and better. I can't call this fate because I came here looking, but it's still weird how things are manifesting. I look back at Greer's paintings and wonder if they're about Kit. The ripples she caused in their lives. The effects of her choices. Kit, the writer, was engaged to Greer, the painter. How perfect. How beautiful. I can picture him living his life in the cannery, being full of art and happiness, and bullshit. They'd have a candy jar filled with Kit Kats, and he'd trace her thigh lilacs with his Kit Kat stained tongue. This is exactly the reason Kit looks awkward in Florida. He was from a place where giant bubbles blew down Main Street, and artists lived in old clam canneries. The magic of this town clung to him.

"A few of us business owners around town could use help with our books," she says to me. "Part time accounting?"

"Sure," I say. *What are you doing? What are you doing?*

"You can work some hours here at the gallery if you like. I could use the help."

And so I wander into a gallery, lost, and leave it found. I have a job in this little town of magic. I get to stay. I stop outside the cannery and look up at its high windows. Somewhere behind the Coke bottle panes is an ashen-haired pixie who Kit loved. I want to know her. Is that wrong? There are so many things wrong about me.

If only Della could see her predecessor. She'd freak out and ask Kit a hundred times if he thought she was prettier than Greer. Kit would have to lie. Della has always been unparalleled in her beauty, but Greer is not even human; she's ethereal. I turn my back to the cannery and walk back down Main Street, the air whipping my skirt around my legs. I am in so way over my head. I'm not so sure the Sorting Hat would put me in Ravenclaw anymore. I am Slytherin. I take a selfie, Port Townsend outlined behind me. I call it, crazyperson.

23
#CRAIGANDHISLIST

When procuring a place of residence, most people take to Craigslist. I find Craigslist creepy. Who is Craig? Why did he make a list? I prefer the newspaper, or community boards. I find the nearest grocery store and check out their board. Two enthusiastic teenage girls have made babysitting fliers. *Trustworthy! Fun! Reliable!* Each word is written on a pompom, each letter in a different colored marker. I respect their handmade signs. Babysitters who rely on the computer for everything should not be trusted. All the children I've had can tell you that. I lift the corner of their paper to study what's underneath. There's a guy looking for a girl roommate. *Clean guy looking for girl roommate who likes to do dishes. No pets.* To me this says: *Needy, incompetent male with control issues. Looking for a wife.* "Ew, dude," I say. I pass it up and find another pinned to the top left corner. It's buried underneath a community garage sale flier, printed on lilac paper. I pull out the pin holding it to the board so I can read it.

Likes to take long walks on the beach-but not with you!
Looking for an independent FEMALE roommate to share my space.
I don't want a sister. I don't want a friend. Just a roommate.

I laugh when I read it. The only thing she's given is an e-mail address. I should put it back, but instead, I fold the paper into a small square and slip it into my back pocket, glancing around to make sure no one has seen me. Fuck them, I need a place to live. I

give the whole grocery store a dirty look, then turn to march out …
and walk into a wall. It's a beautiful thing to be humbled.

Her e-mail address is Gswizzle@gmail.com. She says that we can
meet at a teashop on Main Street. *How will I know it's you?* I send
back. This is creepy; she could be a he. Maybe I should have
trusted Craig and his list.

You'll know, she sends back. I don't trust bitches that easily, but
what choice do I have? I arrive at the coffee shop an hour early to
scope out the place. I realize that I veer toward dramatic, but this
place is maybe a little too perfect. I order a scone and they hand me
a dollop of cream and jam. Too perfect. I take it, frowning, and
find a seat to wait for my tea. The tea comes in a delicate glass
mug—too perfect. I sip suspiciously from my corner, licking the
cream from my lips. I am turning on Port Townsend. Distrusting
and sour. And then she walks in. Her. The purple fairy, with her
lush silver hair tied back in a ponytail. *Hell no!*

Greer matches her flier. I take it out of my pocket and smooth
it on the table as she glances around the tearoom, smiling at those
she knows, looking for … me. I hold up the flier like an idiot. Her
eyes light up when she sees me, and she waves with both hands. I
want her to trip over a chair leg or something, but she's graceful,
and she slips through small spaces like a lithe, little minx.

"Helena?" she asks. I stand up, and she hugs me—throws her
arms around my neck like we're old friends. I try to stiffen and pull
away, but I'm weak, and I really need a hug. Also, she smells like
spices: nutmeg and cinnamon and clove.

"How brave," she says, still holding on to me. "To move all
this way alone."

I don't feel brave. I almost miss my chair when I sit back
down, but Greer doesn't seem to notice. "I've only ever lived
here," she says. "I'm too chicken to leave."

Ohmygodohmygodohmygod. I like her. I smile weakly and pick up
my tea, which has gone cold. She's painted flowers all over her
skin, and dyed her hair gray, and she's still talking about being a
chicken, and how brave I am.

Hello, I'm beige bitch, I want to say.

"Tell me about yourself," she says finally, leaning forward. She has gray eyes. They match her hair and add to the overall ethereal look. It's very intimidating to sit across from a real life fairy and know you have nothing interesting to tell her about your life. Well ... maybe something a little bit interesting, like, *my best friend dates your ex fiancé*.

"I ... I just want to ... find myself." It's a horribly cheesy thing to say, but Greer is nodding, like finding yourself is something to be taken seriously, rather than the words spoken by a lost girl.

"You've come to the right place," she tells me. "Not just Port Townsend, but Washington. It's God's country. Something about this place heals people." I take hope in her words. There's nothing about me that is broken or disparaged. I am not the unfortunate heroine in a romance novel. My parents are not divorced, and my heart has never truly been broken. I am an overly simple girl who got an itch. I do not tell Greer that my itch came from a dream about her ruggedly handsome ex-fiancé, nor do I tell her that in my mind the line between Harry Potter and real life is blurry, if not non-existent. I rub the hem of my beige top between my fingers and listen to Greer's lyrical voice talk about all of Port Townsend's hidden gems: the cinema, built in 1907, which had an old fashioned popcorn maker, and only showed three movies at a time. She told me about old, Mr. Rugamiester, who went to a movie every single Saturday and sat in the same seat, in the same theater, wearing the same navy blue corduroy sports coat. "He doesn't care what is playing in theater number three, or how many times he's seen it. He's there for the three o'clock show with his bag of popcorn."

"But there has to be a reason." I lean forward despite myself, pulled in by old, Mr. Rugamiester and his bag of popcorn. Greer's eyes never leave my face; she's laughing at my reaction, her knees pulled up underneath her, a cup of tea in her hand. It feels like old friends having lunch. "There isn't always," she says. She reaches out and her slim white hand covers mine, just for a moment. "There isn't always," she assures me. And then her hand is gone. I ponder her words, wondering if she's right. I believe in math, and I believe in answers, and I believe if you keep looking, you'll find one. Maybe it was just a dream. It *was* just a dream. But this is real, and I am here now. There is a single white female feel to this moment. I most certainly am a creep, because I know who this woman is, yet she does not know who I am.

"Greer," I say, once the talk of Mr. Rugamiester has finished. "I think I know someone you may know. I'm not sure if you're the same person, but he says there's only one Greer in Port Townsend."

Greer sets her teacup on the table and unfolds her legs so that she's leaning toward me with her elbows resting on her knees.

I can't look at her when I say it. I'm afraid she'll think I orchestrated this whole thing. "Kit Isley," I say. "Do you know him?"

Her face betrays nothing but happiness. She nods, and smiles, and asks how I know Kit.

"He's dating my friend," I tell her. "I don't know him very well; they hadn't been dating for too long before I left."

"How is Kit?" she asks. "He just up and left us for sunny Florida."

"He seems to be well. He wears a lot of flannel," I blurt. Greer laughs.

"Well, Helena. I'd love to have you, if you still want the room."

I'm a bit shocked. We moved past the fact that I know her ex-fiancé like it was no big deal. She doesn't even further question me on the matter. We exchange cell phone numbers, and Greer hands me a folder that has all of the information about the cannery, the rules, and a lease to sign and return to her. She says since we sort of know each other, she'll waive the deposit. When we part ways outside of the teashop, she hugs me, and my face gets lost in her silver hair. "See you tomorrow," she says, and then adds, "roommate."

I haven't even seen the place, but I'm so happy. I didn't do the expected thing—the Helena thing. I veered off and took my own road. This is a big, old deal. I'm learning magic.

24
#ARTiSWAR

The historic Clam Cannery building on the Quincy Street waterfront is a 6,482 square foot two-story brick building, which dates back to 1873. Greer is waiting outside for me when I pull up in my rental car.

"Wow, nice car," she says. I blush.

"It's just a rental. It's not very big inside. I actually really need to return it to Seattle and buy a car."

"You don't need a car here," she says. "And you can always use mine."

"Thanks."

The kindness makes me feel awkward. I'm usually the one dishing it out. I follow her inside, and it takes a minute for my eyes to adjust.

"Whoa," I say.

Greer ducks her head, kind of shy about it. There's lots of space, exposed beams, and concrete flooring. Is it just me, or does it smell like saltwater in here?

"I don't do anything with this part. I was thinking about opening it up to the community. Letting them use it for meetings and stuff." I follow her up the stairs and into the living area. To my relief, I see that it's much cozier up here. A small kitchen with three green barstools sits under mellow light. She's addicted to candles, and the color purple, and candles that are the color purple. Not that it's a new observation. I eye her tattoos and look away quickly when she turns to face me.

"The kitchen and living room," she says. "I know, I know. I just love the color." The kitchen/dining area leads into a hallway with two bedrooms. Greer opens the door on the left and I press back a smile when I see the large windows and skylight.

"Wow," I say, stepping inside. "This is dreamy."

"It's all yours." Greer smiles. There's a queen bed and two nightstands. I'm going to fill the shit out of those nightstands: papers, gum, bobby pins.

When I spin around I see a large oak dresser and the door to my own bathroom.

"The closet is in the bathroom," she tells me. "I'm next door. Please don't greet me in the morning."

I can't picture her being anything but perky and friendly, but *mmkay*.

She doesn't show me her bedroom. Is it purple? Or does it break all the rules and is blue? Are there giant Kit posters, or giant teddy bears? She leads me into the reading room, which is surprisingly filled with paint supplies.

"Why isn't it called the painting room?" I ask.

Greer looks confused. "I don't know." There's not much to talk about after that because her paintings are beautiful. Truly it's not fair to be as beautiful as Greer, and also have this much talent. I get lost in all the water, the ripples. There are so many patterns and variations. Some of the paintings have more transparent water than others. You can see the smooth white rocks beneath the surface, or a little minnow.

"Wow, Greer. There's so much hidden meaning in these. They're beautiful." She ducks her head, bashful. I like that about her. Humble artists always genuinely impress me. She looks really uncomfortable, so I ask to see the rest. When she's done giving me the tour, she helps me carry my suitcases inside, and I write her a check.

"Why do you paint ripples?" She's on her way to the fridge. Her steps falter. It's slight, but heavy.

Her back is to me when she answers, and I don't know her well enough to hear a change in her voice.

"Cause and effect," she says. When she turns around she has a bottle of water in her hand. She unscrews the cap and takes a sip. "We think we can control our lives, but our lives control us. And everything that touches our lives controls us. People have less power than they think they do. It's just the reactions we control."

She says it with such conviction. I partially believe it.

"So we are all just sitting waiting for things to cause ripples?" I ask.

What caused me to have that dream? It certainly wasn't me. Yet that dream rippled my life. Caused me to change everything.

"I think so," she says.

"But we have power to choose the reaction. That means something." I'm getting upset, and I don't know why.

Greer shrugs. "Does it? Or are past experiences controlling our choices? It's a scary thought, I know."

"I like math," I blurt.

Greer laughs.

"I don't like to think that I have no choice," I say. "It may be true, but it frightens me."

"That's why we make art, Helena," Greer says. "Art is the war against what we do not choose to feel. It's the battle of color, words, sound, and shape, and it rages for or against love."

God, Kit, you're so fucking stupid. Della?

I want Greer to tell me all the things. Like I need to know who I am, and why I'm not good at painting. And I'd like to know the meaning of life, because I think she has the answer.

She asks me if I'm hungry, and I lie and say yes, even though I just ate. I watch her make Panini in a fancy press. She squeezes oranges by hand and hands me a cup of juice. It's sweet and pulpy. No one has ever squeezed oranges for me before, except maybe the guy at Jamba Juice.

I learn more from Greer in those two minutes than I've learned from anyone in the history of ever.

"I'd like for you to teach me everything you know about life," I say. "Are you willing to do this?"

She spins around and flicks an orange at me. It hits me in the forehead.

"I know nothing about life," she laughs.

"Okay, but I'm trying to find myself."

Greer grins. "That, my dear, is the scariest thing you're ever going to do."

"Why is that?"

"Because you might not like what you find."

25
#MARROWSTONE

I move in with my small collection of belongings: mostly clothes, and shoes, and photos. My bedroom has a view of the water, and for the first six weeks, I wake up each morning frightened that this new life will be taken from me like the other one I fell in love with. I have nightmares about having to leave Port Townsend and the cannery. Each dream ends with the Range Rover sinking into the water behind the ferry. During the day I work in the gallery, helping Eldine with the books, the sales, and shipping pieces to customers from other states and countries. I like it; it's peaceful work, and Eldine mostly keeps to herself. Some days Greer meets me for lunch, and other days I carry my sandwich to the harbor where I wander around reading the names of the boats until it's time to go back. Nights, I work on my art—all of which is terrible. *You can't force it*, Greer tells me when I throw a paintbrush across the room. I'm not really good at anything, but I want to be. That's enough to keep my hands and mind moving between paints, and clays, and words. What I refuse to do is anything that I did before. It takes discipline to accomplish this, as humans are addicted to the familiar. I don't eat my usual cereal; I don't drink a soy latte with Splenda. I don't watch reality TV, or read romance novels to fill my life with all the things I'm missing. I do not text Kit. Except that one time. But mostly I do not text Kit. And then one day he texts me, after the longest stretch we've ever gone without speaking. I am taking a walk along the dock, taking pictures of the boats, when his name appears on my screen. I'm nervous to open the text. Silly.

Or maybe not, since I don't want him to know I'm living in the cannery with Greer.

> K: *You can't just move to my home and not speak to me anymore.*

> *Why not?*

> K: *So, you really aren't speaking to me?*

> *No! I didn't say that.*

> K: *Where are you living?*

Ugh. Yuck. It's none of his business anyway. I don't have to answer. In fact, I won't.

> *I have a roommate. It's Greer. I rent a room from her.*

I bite my nails while I wait for his text bubble to pop up, but it never does. God, it's like I have no self-control. No will power. I think about texting *PSYCH!* But I don't do things like that either. Oh my God, I'm supposed to be doing things differently.

> I text: *psych*

> And then: *Just kidding. About the psych. Not Greer. I really live with her.*

> And then: *She's so great. I don't even care what you think.*

> And then: *Are you mad at me?*

I almost have no nails left by the time his bubble pops up, but that's cool because everyone has fingernails, and I like to be different.

> K: *You're manic.*

> I swear to God, I'm so sad about my nails. I was trying to grow them. I study my hands before typing: *No. Not at all*

He sends a picture. I recognize it as being part of the bar at Tavern on Hyde. The picture is of a glass of wine sitting on a beverage napkin. I smile.

> K: *I feel like you need it*

> *Yeah. I wish*

> K: *The good news is everywhere has wine! A friend of mine owns a winery over on Marrowstone. You should go check it out.*

He sends me the address, and tells me it's called Marrowstone Vineyards.

I mention the winery to Greer that night, hoping she'll want to go with me. I sit on the only available stool in the reading room and watch her paint.

"Who told you about that place?" She puts down her brush. Her voice is defensive.

"Ummm, I just heard there's wine. And I like wine. Are you okay?"

She clears her throat. "Yeah, sure. It's just … that place has a lot of memories. My friends and I used to sneak on the property when we were younger, get high, and drink."

I've never actually met any of her friends. Don't get me wrong—Greer is a popular girl. When you have silver hair, and only wear one color, people will start to notice you. She never has people over, and though she knows everyone, there's never been someone she's seemed truly intimate with.

"So…"

"Sure," she says. "It'll be fun. Do you want to go tonight?" I wasn't expecting to go tonight, but I shrug, and Greer goes to her room to get ready.

Ten minutes later she walks out wearing all black. Like, I've never seen Greer in anything but shades of purple. It scares me.

"Everything else is dirty," she says when she sees my face. "Let's go."

I follow her out, wishing I had changed out of my work clothes. I'm such an underachiever it's depressing. *Beige bitch.*

We listen to oldies as we curve the roads to Marrowstone. It's unusually dry outside, but the clouds are dark and heavy—an ominous warning of the days to come. It's like Greer reads my mind.

"Today is the last day before the rain comes. Enjoy it."

I'll enjoy the rain, but I don't say so. It's considered blasphemy in Washington to not enjoy the rainless summer while you have it. The winery sits on the water where you can watch the cruise ships pass on their way to the ocean. We pull up to a building and hop out of the car into the dirt. A vineyard sits beyond the building; already harvested of grapes, it's just a dusty shadow of vines and leaves. To my left is a large house, which watches both the water and the winery from a collection of sharp rectangular windows. You can see the remnants of fruit on the ground around the trees: apples, cherries, pears, and plums—shriveled, their juices soaked into the dirt. Greer seems to be frozen on the spot as she looks toward the house.

"What is it?" I ask. "You look like you've seen a—"

"I-I'm fine. Let's drink wine. Can we? Do you want to? Let's go." She marches up to the door of the winery. Did we exchange personalities on the ride over? I'm confused. She springs for a bottle and carries it outside to sit on the patio.

"Okay, seriously, Greer. What's wrong with you?" I take the bottle from her and use the corkscrew to open it.

She points to the house.

"I cheated on my boyfriend," she says. "Right there, next to that house." I don't look; I'd rather watch her face right now. Was this the place of downfall? The end of Kit and Greer?

"We didn't have to come," I say, wondering why Kit would suggest this place. *Stupid fuck*. It's like he was trying to get ... *revenge!* OMG!

"Greer," I say. "Let's go."

"No," she says firmly. "It's just a place."

"Tell me about it then," I say. "Was it Kit?"

Her head turns so hard I'm afraid her little neck is going to break.

"How do you...?"

"A guess," I say.

Greer is staring at her wine glass, glassy-eyed. All of a sudden she smiles.

"That was a long time ago."

"I'm sorry," I tell her.

"It's cool," she says. "I got you; it's the ripples."

I can't tell if she's covering her true feelings, but she just included me in her art—and I like that.

"I was just young," she says. "I abandon before I can be abandoned. Sometimes that's been a good thing, but with Kit, it wasn't. I really hurt him. I'm not as reckless anymore. But I haven't dated in a long time. I'm on strike."

"My boyfriend cheated on me," I tell her. "Before I came here. He got a girl in his office pregnant."

"Fuck him," Greer says. "That's awful."

"Yeah," I say. "Fuck him, and fuck love." We clink glasses, and she looks genuinely happy after that. Maybe coming here wasn't so bad after all. Therapeutic. I look toward the angular roof of the house and wonder who lives there. How many secret things has that house seen? I want to live in a house that's seen things. I want to live.

26
#DONTFEARTHEANIMALS

You'll never find a better place to be depressed than Washington State. There are thousands of places you can go to stare at beautiful scenery and feel deeply sorry for yourself. Most days, the sky will even weep with you. And thank God for that—for the absence of light. The setting of a perfect melodrama. Greer offers to take me to all of the best places to be depressed.

"Have you ever been depressed?" I ask her.

"Well, there was this one time…" she says, winking at me. For an artist, her personality lacks the ups and downs, the moodiness.

She makes a list in purple sharpie, and we check off places one by one. It's all a trick; I know this. She's trying to wake me up, and I do wake up. The air, the wind, the water, the mountains—they all wake up my senses. My heart is asleep. We are at Hurricane Ridge one afternoon when Della texts to say she thinks Kit is going to propose to her. I turn off my phone and lie back on the narrow wall we're sitting on until I am looking up at the gray sky.

"What is it, Helena?" Greer asks, crouching next to me. "You're only melodramatic like this when something is really wrong. Is it Kit who makes you like this?"

I can't lie to her after everything she's done for me. I try to turn my face away, but she grabs my chin with her long, smooth fingers and studies my face, frowning.

"Della thinks he's going to propose," I say. And then, "It's no big deal."

"Shit," she says. And then, "Shit." Again. "What are you going to do?"

"Oh, you know … nothing."

Greer laughs. "You should at least tell him."

"Hell no. Tell him what?"

She doesn't say anything; she's thinking. I pull out clumps of grass as I wait for her evaluation. "Don't hurt the grass, Helena. We need everything on our side from here on out, especially the earth. Tell me about that dream you had. The one you said started all of your troubles."

I dust my hands on my pants. "No. You'll think I'm crazy."

Greer sighs. I'm trying the pixie's patience.

"You're his ex," I hiss. "I'm the psycho who's in love with him. Forgive me for not wanting to talk about my inappropriate feelings with the woman who chased him out of town."

"Ahh, Helena!" She spreads her arms out, and the wind whips the tassels on her purple jacket. "The best kind of love is the love that isn't supposed to happen."

I chew my nails, spitting them out the side of my mouth.

Greer slaps my hands then motions for me to start talking.

I tell her about my dream as we sit on a wall on top of Hurricane Ridge. I'm terribly embarrassed by it. When I'm done, she's quiet.

"When Kit was a little boy, he had this recurring dream." She shakes her silver hair at the mountains, smiling some long ago smile. "It was about lions. A pride of them. They'd come for him, only him. Pace the empty streets of Port Townsend looking for him. He'd hide, but no matter where he hid, they'd always find him. He was terrified. He said he could smell their rancid breath, feel them ripping into his body with their teeth, and he'd wake up screaming."

I grimace.

"So, we went to see this 'witch.'" She makes air quotes around the word 'witch,' and smiles at me. "She had this new age store, sold dream catchers and whatnot. She doesn't have the store anymore, but she lives near the winery on Marrowstone. People still go to her. Anyway, she told us that Kit needed a talisman to chase away the dreams. First, she gave us a dream catcher. Of course it didn't work. So we went back to her the following week. She gave us these stones next—said that Kit was to put them under his pillow and they'd trap the dream."

Greer hands me a bottle of water from the cooler. She opens and sips her own, and I notice that her lips leave a strawberry pink mark on her bottle.

"When the stones didn't work we went back, and when the tonic didn't work we went back, and so on and so on. Finally, when we went to her for the fiftieth time, she sat us both down. She told us that something in Kit's life was causing him to have the dream, and we could stop it together."

I feel uncomfortable now. I know so little about Kit's life, and she knows so much. It makes me feel like I have no ground for this thing I feel for him.

"What did you do?" I ask.

"Kit said that sometimes he was aware that he was dreaming, and it was still frightening, but less so because he knew he'd wake up. So we talked about him fighting back during those aware dreams. Hurting the lions before they could hurt him. He was skeptical, but he said he'd try. A week later he came running up to me at school, said he'd done what I'd told him. He'd ripped the lions' jaws open with his bare hands. Fought them off."

"Did he have the dream again?" I ask.

"Yes," Greer said. "But, less and less frequently. Sometimes he still had it before he left PT. But he conquered some sort of subconscious fear, and he wasn't afraid of it anymore."

"Ah," I say.

Now that the story is over, I'm not sure why she told it to me. And then it clicks. The night Kit and I took a walk through my apartment complex. My asking him about having a Greer-inspired tattoo. 'Don't fear the animals.' That was hers. I feel sick with jealousy. So much more meaning than a flower, or cross, or even her name. It is their history. Their bond. And what right do I have to be jealous? He isn't even mine. I am not in the chain of girlfriends; Della is.

"He's going to be in Santa Fe next weekend," Greer says.

"What? How do you know?"

"His cousin's wedding. I'm invited, and I'd love it if you came along as my date."

I shake my head. "No. I can't. Della will—"

"Della will not be there," Greer tells me. "Her mother's birthday or some shit like that."

I feel guilty that I forgot about her mom's upcoming birthday. I used to be very close to her family.

"Either way, it's not right. I can't do that. They're a family, her and Kit."

"Not until they're married," Greer says. "And we have ample time to stop that from happening."

"It's wrong," I say.

Greer shrugs. "Suit yourself." She stands up and stretches, her purple shirt bright against the green backdrop. "Let's go hike," she says. "Stop the talk about Kit and Della, yes?"

I stand up, too, and follow her. We make it half way up the hill before we stop. And then we decide that we'd rather go get hot chocolate. Or chocolate. Or not hike.

A day later, an e-mail arrives in my inbox. It's from Greer. I open it to find an airplane ticket to Santa Fe.

"What is this?" I call to ask her.

"You're my date, remember?"

"I don't think I ever agreed to this. In fact, I'm sure I didn't."

"Don't be such a coward, Helena. You have to fight for what you want. Hasn't anybody ever told you that?"

No one ever had, and I didn't feel good about fighting for something that someone else had already laid claim to. I think of ways to get out of it all week, but in the end I pack a small carry-on and pretend I'm doing this for Greer. All I have to take with is a beige dress; in fact, most of my clothes are beige, and cream, and white. Creamy colors aren't offended by Florida's heat. But now I live in Washington, and I'm just some beige bitch with too many pairs of cutoff shorts.

We land in Santa Fe mid-afternoon, and our cab drives us through the antique streets of the city, and my eyes hang large. It looks like another place. Most of America looks like America, but Santa Fe looks like Santa Fe. I love it, and I'm scared of it. I ask Greer about this cousin of Kit's who is getting married, and she tells me her name is Rhea and she's marrying a guy named Dirt.

"He's an artist. He makes pottery from sacred dirt."

"Is that why he named himself Dirt?" I ask.

"His name was already Dirt; he went on a search for himself, and then incorporated his name into his art."

I want to laugh, but I realize it's the accountant side of me that wants to make fun of Dirt's journey. As someone who is inartistic and trying very hard, I will respect Dirt's creative vision. Maybe I will learn from it.

We check into our funky hotel, with its uneven concrete floors and rickety furniture. Greer tells me it's actually really expensive to stay here because it's all about the authentic experience.

"It was a Spanish mission in the 1800s. You're sleeping in the same room conquistadors stayed in!" she says brightly.

I look around at the patchy walls, and the bloody toe I got from the cracked floor, and feel lucky to live in the 21st century.

"Freshen up," Greer says. "We can hit the town."

I am fresh. But I change, put a new band-aid on my toe, and put on lipstick.

"Uh uh," Greer says, when I walk out of my bedroom. "We aren't going to a Mommy-and-Me group."

She digs around in her suitcase and produces a sleeveless black dress with tassels running from under the arm to the hem.

"That's not your style at all," I laugh. "I can't believe you bought that."

"You're right. I brought it for you. It's your style." She tosses it at me.

"Greer, I have never in my life worn something like this. It's not my style."

"Just because you haven't worn it doesn't mean it's not your style. Some people are too reserved and stuck in their ways to really know what suits them."

Okay. I have nothing to lose, so I put on the dress. All of a sudden I have breasts and an ass.

"Yikes," she says. "You're so ugly. Maybe you should take that off."

I make a face at her. I'm not stupid. I'm a fast learner.

We go to a fancy bar. We drink fancy wine. We dance to eighties music. My hair is askew, tumbling and stuck to my face. And when I sway, so do my tassels. So I sway. God, this is fun. Della never wanted to dance because it made her sweaty. Greer is dancing so hard I can see the sweat running down her neck.

And then Kit walks in. And I don't stop swaying. I blow him a kiss, and dance with Greer, and watch him watch me. My heart is aching just from the sight of him. I've never wanted something so bad in my life. He looks different, but I know that's probably not true. My eyes are different. In my eyes, Kit grows more beautiful every time I see him.

"He didn't know I was coming?" I ask Greer.

"On the contrary," Greer says. "He asked me to bring you."

27
#MYBESTFRIENDSWEDDING

"Hey, lonely heart. Wanna go for a walk?" That's the first thing he says to me after all this time. Months and months. *Wanna go for a walk?* Kit and his walks.

I really, really want to go for a walk, because this bar is hot, and there are too many people, and I need to breathe clean air. All of these things come secondary to the fact that it's him I want to walk near.

I lead the way out of the bar, my shoulders still moving to the music. I hear Kit's laughter behind me. It curls up and around my heart and causes it to beat faster—a heart jockey. He thinks I'm funny. I guess he always has. I'm not really funny, just very awkward. As we make our way out, I think about the fact that he's leaving his friends behind—people he hasn't seen in ages—to go on a walk with me, the weekend of his cousin's wedding.

The New Mexico air doesn't taste the same as the Florida air. When it hits us in the face I don't flinch. It smells dry and earthy. I think of Dirt, and giggle. When Kit and I are far enough away from the music, I look at him out of the corner of my eye and grin. He sort of looks the same. Maybe tanner. I bet Della's been dragging him to the beach. I do a little jig next to a fountain while Kit quietly watches me. If I didn't know him, I would think that it looks like he has a million things to say. And he probably does; he just never says them.

I stumble forward, clumsily, and sit next to him, swinging my legs back and forth.

"Hey," I say.

"Hey."

"Why do you have that look on your face?"

"What look?" he asks. "This is just my face."

"Your face has a look. Like you're anxious or something."

"I am."

I jump up. "I'm so hyper right now. Hold that thought while I run around the fountain."

Kit laughs so hard he almost falls over, craning his neck all the way around to watch me.

"I forgot how weird you are," he says when I sit back down. "You're a dead language, you know that? No one is like you, and you are like no one."

It's a nice compliment, probably more than my brain can handle right now.

"So, why are you anxious?" I reach into the fountain and cup some water in my hand, letting it run down the back of my neck.

"I'm waiting for the inevitable question."

Am I that predictable?

"So," I say. "Are you in love?" I make jazz hands, and he grabs my wrists, but then quickly drops them.

"Yes."

This time, no hesitation. No dancing eyes. No avoiding the question. My stomach drops, and my heart grows old and saggy. I couldn't run around the fountain even if I tried. Why did I even feel happy enough to do it in the first place?

"Word," I say. And then, "Wow."

Kit has thick, black lashes. They almost make him too pretty, but the square shape of his jaw rescues his masculinity—giving all of the fine features a square, hard canvas. When he looks at you, though, through those lashes, it's like he's conveying something important with his eyes. He doesn't know the effect he has on women. I've watched the silent swooning, the way he makes women stumble over their words, and causes their faces to fill up with color.

"May I use your phone, please?" I ask. Kit hands me his phone without hesitation. I open the camera, turn it to selfie mode, and snap a picture of myself.

"What are you doing?" Kit asks.

"What does it look like I'm doing? Taking a picture of myself."

"I know that. But why?"

He watches as I text the picture to myself. I left my phone back in the hotel room, but now I wish I'd brought it. I could send an SOS to Greer.

"I take pictures of myself as I experience big moments in life. I name them and keep them in an album." He makes a face and shakes his head. His eyes are dancing, though—thinking, thinking, thinking.

"What will you name the moment you just experienced?"

I look at the picture I just took: spiral curls stick straight out from the sides of my head, my topknot is crooked, and mascara decorates the underside of my eyes like black bruises. I look a little hopeless, a little angry.

"Fuck love," I tell him. I'm glaring at him defiantly. He draws back like I've hit him, the smile turning into a wince.

"Fuck love," I say again. Kit doesn't understand. He's shaking his head like love doesn't deserve cruel words. I want to find Greer, get out of this place. Get away from Kit, who takes a year to acquire love, and a year to destroy my heart.

"Helena," he says. "It's not like that."

"Have you seen Greer yet? Long lost love Greer? Are you out of love with her? It only took you a year to fall in love with Della, and—"

"Stop it," he says.

I have tears now. Stupid, repulsive tears.

"I'm in love with you!" I yell, and immediately regret it. Why would a person feel the need to yell something like that at the top of their lungs?

The silence is all consuming. It's a thing of pain. It draws out, and across, and over—like a dull-bladed knife. A confession so bare. The shock on his face, I can't stand to see it. It's embarrassing. I turn to go. A step or two, and then I take off running. My hair comes loose and streams out behind me. It makes my escape heavier than it already is.

He doesn't call out to me like men do in the movies. My footsteps are the only ones I hear. There is no chase, no romance. And in that moment I think of the dumbest thing, a line from *My Best Friend's Wedding*. '*You're chasing him, but who's chasing you?*'

I don't go to the bar. I go back to the hotel and pack my things. A shirt here, a shirt there—tossed into my duffel. I rush through it all, trying not to think about what just happened. How I burned my relationship with both Kit and Della in that one irresponsible moment. I splash water on my face, and run outside to meet my cab. And, as I get to the airport, I realize that I'm a runner. Life gets hot and I pack my things and leave. It's new, but so is being an adult. I'm learning about myself. But, hey! I did what I came to do. So I'm an accomplished runner. Greer has been blowing up my phone for the last three hours. I wonder if she saw me leave the bar with Kit. If she found him when she couldn't find me. Did he feel all of the old things when he saw her, or is his heart firmly grounded in Della now? I text and tell her that I'm going home.

Greer texts me back: *He's on his way there.*

I look around, panicked. I'm already through security. He can't get to me. And why would he want to? I'm already so embarrassed. I said the unsayable thing to my best friend's boyfriend. I clutch my duffel to my chest and count backward from a thousand. I'm a lot falling apart. A lot hurting. I feel like a failure and a flake. And then we board, and I order a drink without a mixer. And I know I'm wearing a slutty dress, and my hair is a mess, and people are looking at me. But they can't see my heart. If they could see my heart, they'd understand why my mascara is smudged.

28
#SQUASH

It's fall, on a sidewalk, in a town I love. It's a month after the wedding. My embarrassment has mostly congealed, though I've spent a lot of time *not* thinking about what I said to Kit. This month I am a writer. I document my days in a series of blog posts I never actually publish. The blog is called Fuck Love. I'm not sure what the purpose of it is, except to journal my feelings, and also it feels good. You don't have to publicly fail with writing like you do with watercolors, or clay birds, or sketching a tree. Private failure is much more comfortable. I am mentally planning a blog post called: I Didn't Get to Fuck My Love-when I hear my name being called. I turn around to search the sidewalk. And then he's there-the love I didn't get to fuck- the cold wind lifting his hair, his smile lifting me. My heart is vigorous and angry. It's not agreeing with the rest of my body, which is turning toward him. *No, no, no,* it beats.

"My God! Kit! What are you doing here?"

"Hey, lonely heart."

An ache burns in my chest as my heart succumbs to him.

I fall into his hug, pressing my face against his leather jacket. He smells like gasoline. "I'm so homesick," I say. "I'm so glad to see you."

"I was homesick, too," he says. He brings two gloved hands to my face and looks in my eyes. "Among other things."

I suddenly feel it; our awkward last encounter comes creeping back to me. I look away, and he lets me go.

We're on a stage now, and it feels awkward. There are other humans flowing around us. For a minute it was just Kit and I.

"So," I say.

"So," he says.

My heart is racing. I wonder where Greer is. Does she know he's here? Is he here for her?

"Is Della…?"

"No," he says. "I came on my own. Want to go for a walk?"

I laugh and shake my head. "God. Yeah … sure."

We walk up Main Street past shoppers and mothers pushing strollers. I try to catch someone's eyes. I want to relay, using telepathy, that I am with the man I love and can't have. A car hits a puddle, and I have to jump out of the way to avoid the spray. I jump sideways and knock a little old lady to the ground. Kit and I rush to help her up, and I start to cry because I'm worried that I broke her hip.

"Oh, honey. I've already done that. I'm made of metal." She taps her hip and her knee, and also her skull, which makes me really worried. She lets us fuss over her for a few minutes, seeming to enjoy the attention, then tells us we're a really cute couple, and we should go spend the rest of the afternoon kissing. I flush at the thought, but Kit just laughs and plays along. With our new friend—whose name is Gloria—watching us, Kit grabs my hand and leads me away.

"I didn't want to disappoint her," he tells me. "I did it for Gloria."

"Gloria can't see us anymore," I say. "So why are you still holding my hand?"

He smirks at me, but still doesn't let go. We pass an ice cream shop, and he looks at me.

"It's too cold for ice cream," I say. But I really want one, and he knows it.

"Says who?"

I don't know. My mom? Society? Fuck it.

"Get me apricot brandy," I say. I don't crowd into the warmth of the shop; I stay on the sidewalk where I wait for him.

"Are you … here for Greer?" I ask when he hands me a cone.

He looks confused. A drop of ice cream lands on his hand. "Why would I be here for Greer?"

I wipe away the ice cream on his hand with my napkin.

"Because she was the one. Great love, true love, young love, first love—"

"Thanks, Helena. I get the picture. And no, I'm not here for Greer."

"Oh," I say.

We walk in silence for a little bit. The ice cream becomes my enemy. He was holding my hand five minutes ago, but now he is holding ice cream.

"Why are you here then?" I blurt.

"I told you. I was homesick. I needed to come back and do some soul searching."

"Oh. But—"

"Helena!"

"No more questions," I say. I make the motion of zipping my lips, after which Kit's eyes drag to my mouth, and I blush.

"We're taking a break," he says. "Things got…"

"What?"

I don't want to seem like an eager beaver here, but I am. Also, I know how these things go. How couples fall in and out of a relationship, but always seem to get back together in the end. When Neil cheated on me, I tried to find ways to mentally justify getting back together with him. If I could save the relationship, it wouldn't seem like I just lost years of my life with the wrong person. Salvage what's left to cover my mistakes.

"I don't know," he finally says. "Things went wrong. Even if you have something strong, jealousy will destroy it."

I bite back all the words, all the questions. I am familiar with Della's jealousy. More familiar with the insecurity that strikes like a match against anything that threatens her.

"Where are you staying?" I ask.

"I have a place here," he says.

I look at him out of the corner of my eye. I didn't know.

"Like, you just keep it here. In case…"

"It belonged to my uncle. When he died he left it to me."

"Oh." I clear my throat. There's so much I don't know, and that makes me sad. "And how long will you be staying?"

He looks at me then, and suddenly I know that people are what you truly need to be afraid of. People with eyes that communicate. People who can hurt you so hard you'd wish you were never born.

"It all depends."

I trip on a crack in the sidewalk, and Kit reaches out to steady me.

"On what?"

While I wait for him to answer, I notice the length and curl of his lashes, the downward tilt of full lips. I look away, try to focus on something else: a soggy half-eaten hot dog on the sidewalk, a woman's mismatched socks peeking out from her tennis shoes. Things that don't make me dizzy.

"On how my truth is received."

I'm about to ask him to further expound, when he says he has to go.

"I have to meet my mom for lunch. She's trying to get me to move back."

"Oh," I say. I like his mom already. "Moms usually know what's best for you."

"Oh yeah?"

"No," I say. "If she's anything like my mom, you probably shouldn't listen to her."

He laughs. "See you soon, Helena."

Soon after, I hear from Della. Della, who I haven't heard from in months. She texts to say that they broke up after a fight they had. When I don't answer her texts right away she calls me.

"Is he there, Helena? Do you know?"

I catch sight of my own face in the mirror when I answer her; I look like a disgusted human. I don't want to be in the middle of whatever they have going on. I don't want to betray one for the other.

"You should call him," I say. "Remember he's disappeared before."

"I have called him. Oh my God, Helena, I call every five minutes. He just said he needed some time away. Like, I don't know how to do anything. I don't even know how to pay my mortgage."

I can hear the tears, the snot, the Della who sits in a robe and eats chocolate and frets. I feel guilty for not being there for her, but no, I am not everyone's crutch. I am learning to walk on my own; they need to learn, too.

"You can figure things out until he comes back," I say. "Your mom will help you."

There's a long pause before she says, "Have you seen him?"

"Yes," I say. "Not that long ago. Walking down the street. He was going to see his mom."

"Did he say anything? About me?"

"Not really. Just that you were on a break."

Della starts to cry. I hold the phone away from my ear and chew vigorously on my lip. I am feeling two things: pity, which is truly a nasty, condescending thing to feel for someone, and opportunistic. I don't want her to have him back. I don't want her to convince him she can be different. I know she can't.

"It'll be okay," I tell her. "If he needs time to figure things out, you have to give that to him. Don't call every five minutes either. Try to spend some time ... thinking." After we hang up, she sends a text to thank me, and also to beg me to call with anything I hear. I want to tell her I'm not her personal gossip girl. I feel sick. Sick for Della, sick for myself. A little bit sick for Kit, but not much. He deserves to suffer.

June texts to tell me she saw Neil's baby at the grocery store, and its head looks like a squash.

Is it a boy or girl? I ask.

J: It's a squash!

News of Neil's baby looking like something you can find in the produce section of the grocery store should make me happy. I feel nothing. I don't care to revel in infant ugliness. I don't care to think about Neil at all. What does that mean? Have I moved on from my hurt? And is squash a fruit or a vegetable?

29
#MENTELLLÏES

I am just getting off work when I get a text from Kit. It's a photo of a staircase covered in bright red leaves. I know it. I've passed by on occasion. I walk without really thinking about it, and when I get there, my steps falter. I find Kit Isley, sitting on the bottom stair, his head dipped toward the ground. He's wearing a peacoat, and there's gel in his hair. The leaves stir around him, the soft trembling of mottled red. A little tornado at his feet. I sigh. It's okay to have an appreciation for something beautiful, so long as you know your place. I wish I could take a photo of him sitting among the crimson leaves. And why can't I? I take out my phone and snap a picture that I can already tell will be blurry.

"Hey," he says.

"Hey yourself."

He stands up, hands in pocket. "You hungry?"

"Someone once told me I'm always hungry." I smile. Kit smiles back, but it doesn't reach his eyes. I wonder if he spoke to Della. Nothing like a good dose of Della to wipe you clear of joy. *That was mean*, I think, *but also true.*

We fall into step. He seems to know where he's going so I let him lead. I've come to think of these streets as mine, but they are really Kit's. I just followed his shadow here.

"You know," he says. "I always thought you were beautiful, but this weather suits you. Wild hair and winter coats."

"That's a compliment only a writer could give," I say. I can't even look at him. I want to throw myself off the side of a building, or in front of a moving car. I'm fidgety all of a sudden, adjusting my purse, and hair, and face.

"Helena…?"

"Yeah…? What?"

He grins, knowingly. He makes me feel so transparent. It's so vulnerable to be under his gaze, emotionally naked.

"Shut up," I say. "You don't know me."

"Maybe. But I don't think anyone can."

"What does that mean?" I'm ready to be offended. So ready. Ready like Freddy. Ready like—

"You're not easy to know. That's not a bad thing, so stop looking at me like that."

"This is just my face," I say. "It's how I always look." I've caught glimpses of myself in the mirror before, when I'm in emotional turmoil. All the lines in my face popping out, my eyes frightened.

He laughs hard. I like making him laugh. I really do.

"So, obviously compliments make me super uncomfortable. I'm not hard to know. I'm really simple. I don't even know who I am yet."

"Helena!" Kit says. "I'd be worried if you said you did know yourself. Did you know that Albert Einstein never wore socks?"

"Huh?"

"He had a complex mind. Never stopped thinking, but socks complicated his life. So he just didn't wear them."

I think about the homeless dude in Seattle, the one who liked the socks I wasn't wearing. I'm not sure why I'm thinking of that. Or why Kit is talking about socks. Oh my God, focus Helena. I shake my head, hoping to jolt my brain back to working order.

"Where are we going?"

"To eat," he says.

"Yes, I know that. But where?"

"Trust."

Lanzo's of the Lanzo family. These people know food. I didn't trust him. I grumble all the way there, and then look over the menu suspiciously. It's called being hangry. Kit smiles at me the whole time, even when I eat all of the bread. His eyes are on me as I take my first bite. His own food left untouched until he knows that I like mine.

"Oh, good, Holy Mother of—"

"Shh," he says. "They're Catholics."

"Zeus," I finish.

He still hasn't touched his food. He sips his wine, watching me.

"Aren't you going to eat?" I ask.

"I already ate."

"So why are we having dinner?"

"So you can eat," he says.

I slide his plate to my side of the table. "Kit, I know you have something to say. So go ahead and say it. Because I'm stress eating right now, and I'd really like to stop."

I can feel the spaghetti slapping at my cheeks, but I'm not wiping shit away until he tells me why we're here. Or why he's here. Or...

He slides a napkin across the table. At first I think he's telling me to wipe my face, but then I start choking. I can't read the words because my eyes are watering. Our server comes over to ask if I'm all right. Kit nods calmly, his eyes still on me. He's not smiling. I'm supposed to stop coughing. I cough a little more to buy myself time.

I had a dream. Don't marry Della

"Where did you get that?" I ask. Though I know where. *Such an idiot, Helena.*

"You know where," he says.

"I was drunk."

"You were. But I know you. You're extra honest when you're drunk."

He calls the server over. "Another glass of wine for the lady," he says.

I laugh.

"You're so dumb."

"At the wedding—" he says.

"No, no, no, no, no," I interrupt. I want to stand up and leave, but the server is right there with my wine, blocking my path.

"Helena, shut up and listen."

"Okay." I take my wine and go to town on it.

"I shouldn't have let you run off like that. I was a little in shock."

"Oh my God, it's so hot in here," I say, ignoring him. I look around, fanning myself.

"I'm in love with you, Helena. I should have told you then, but I'm telling you now. I'm sorry."

He's sorry?

"You're sorry for being in love with me?"

"I'm sorry for not telling you. Focus."

"Did you break up with Della?"

"Della and I broke up, yes."

"Because…"

"Because I'm in love with you."

There's a ringing in my ears. "I think maybe there's something wrong with the wine. I'm allergic."

"You're allergic to emotion," Kit says.

"I have to go," I tell him, standing up. "Wait. Does she know? Did you tell her that thing you just told me?"

It's the first time he looks away. "No."

"So you're secretly in love with me? And you came here to tell me. And if I don't reciprocate, then you can go back to Della? No harm, no foul."

"No. It's not like that. I don't want to hurt her."

"Are you still in love with Greer, too?"

"Oh my God. No, I'm not in love with Greer." He jumps up and pulls me back down to my chair. I don't think I've ever been more scared in my life. Or angry.

"Helena—"

"Stop saying my name."

"Why?"

"It gives me butterflies, and I don't trust you or your butterflies."

His lips pinch together like he's finding all of this very funny. "You're not supposed to admit I give you butterflies."

He takes out his phone and starts texting. I'm about to ask him who texts at a time like this, but then I see his name pop up on my screen.

We'll try this, he says.

Okay

K: Do you remember the day you taught me how to make eggs?

Yes…

I look up at him. His head is bent over his screen, and he's grinning.

K: I went home and started writing. An hour with you and I felt like the inspiration I'd been waiting for my whole life hit me all at once.

Why didn't you tell me?

K: Why would I? You were my girlfriend's best friend. And you were with Neil. I took it for what it was. You were my muse.

I'm grinding my teeth so hard I can hear the cracking. Kit pauses texting to nudge my glass of wine toward me.

K: Helena, I love you. I'm in love with you. Say something…

Men tell lies

And then I stand up and walk out before he can stop me.

30
#CORKED

I don't know where to go. I press the heels of my hands into my eye sockets and breathe in the sharp, piney air. I feel compressed. I'm folding my emotions like a piece of paper—a tiny square, into a tiny square, into a tiny square. When they're folded up enough I can leave them in a corner of my mind somewhere, to be forgotten. That's how I deal, isn't it? And sometimes, on a day like today, I imagine that my brain is littered with hundreds of bastard feelings I won't claim.

I'm on the sidewalk looking left to right, ready to sprint. I forgot my coat inside the restaurant, which is unfortunate because it's cold. I'm afraid he's going to come after me, and I'm also afraid he's not. I'm not sure what's worse at this point? I have to get out of here so I can think. I duck my head and stick my phone in my back pocket as I head for the docks. It's late for Port Townsend. I'm dizzy from the wine; my limbs feel loose like the spaghetti I was eating. Most of the shops that sit along Main have closed for the night. A few stragglers walk the sidewalk with their dogs, already bundled up for the cooler weather. I clutch my arms around myself, and try to smile as I pass them. I'm in a hurry, and they move out of the way for me.

The walk to the marina is ten minutes; the run is six. I'm not wearing the right shoes, and my feet are aching. I stop when I reach the Belle, my favorite. She's rogue among the other boats—handcrafted and hardworking with rustic milled logs. She makes all the other boats look like they're trying too hard.

My wine cork is in my hand. I spin it around my thumb over and over as I look at the water. I don't even know how it got there. It always finds its way into my hands when I'm distressed. It's so stupid, holding onto a little piece of cork like it's a security blanket. I lift my fist above my head, with only a moment's hesitation before I throw it into the water. And then I start to cry because I really love my wine cork. Fuck that. I pull off my shoes and straighten my topknot. There's no point to straightening it, but it feels like I should, like a boxer cracking his neck before he dances into the ring. I'm about to dive in when someone grabs me from behind.

"Helena! Don't be crazy." Kit drags me back from the edge of the dock. I struggle to get away from him.

"I want my wine cork," I say. I realize how crazy that sounds. I do. But I can barely see it anymore, just a tiny smudge on the surface of all that ink. Kit doesn't look at me like I'm crazy. He ducks his head and narrows his eyes, pointing to the wine cork, which is drifting farther and farther away.

"That?"

"Yes," I say.

He pulls off his jacket and shoes, never taking his eyes from the spot in the water.

"Oh my God! Kit, no! It's just a wine cork." I wait until he's already lowering himself into the water to say it, though. I don't want him to change his mind. When he pulls himself back onto the dock, water is running into his eyes, and he's shivering. If he gets pneumonia and dies, it's going to be my fault. And then I'll hate my wine cork. But I'll still have it.

"We need to get you dry," I tell him. I look back toward the cannery. Greer will be home. I'm thinking of Greer. Seeing her. Her seeing him. Him seeing her. Us all together. So bizarre. Also, I don't want to share Kit.

"Let's get out of here," he says. "Come on." He helps me pull on my coat. I stick my cork in my pocket, but it just feels like a thing now. The action overpowered the thing. What Kit did…

We walk the few blocks to his condo. I'm surprised when he stops in front of one of my favorite buildings and takes out a key. It's the sky blue building with ornate cream trim. So close to the cannery I'm surprised Greer's never mentioned it. We take an elevator that smells like fresh paint. Kit is dripping all over the floor, leaving puddles. I glance at him sympathetically, and he laughs.

"I'm fine. I'd do it again just to show you I'd do it."

Mother of all holy fucks.

I get the hazy eye lightheadedness that comes with a really good kiss.

I follow him out of the elevator to his unit and wait anxiously as he opens the door. I'm fretting. I care about what Greer will think, and Della too. And my mother. And Kit's mother. I'm about to make an excuse not to follow him in when he turns around and grins at me. I don't even remember what I was thinking a second ago. Kit's condo is bare, except for a leather sofa and some boxes stacked in a corner, the tape still sealing their mouths shut. Everything is new and freshly painted; the wood floors gleam, newly polished. There is heavy wainscoting on the walls—squares within squares. Kit disappears into the bedroom to change his clothes, and I wander over to the window to look down at Port Townsend. The rain is really coming now. I like the way it makes everything shine. I'd been on a vacation with my parents to Arizona once—the typical family pilgrimage to the Grand Canyon. The towns on the drive through all looked the same to me, dusty and matted. I wanted to raise a giant bowl of water over the whole state and rinse it off.

"What do you think?" Kit asks. I jump, turning around. He's wearing a gray pullover and jeans.

"Nice," I say. "Actually, pretty dreamy." I turn away so he can't see my smile.

"Me or the condo?"

My smile turns to a frown. It's not fair that he always catches me.

"Both," I sigh. When I turn around he's staring at me. He looks sleepy and sexy.

He nods. "My uncle loved it. He restored the whole place. He owned the building and left each of his nephews a unit when he died."

"How did he die?"

"Pancreatic cancer. He was forty-five."

I sit on the couch, and he goes to the kitchen to make coffee. While it brews he builds a fire, and without asking me to move first, he pushes the sofa across the floor until it's in front of the fire. I like how he just does things. Without my permission. He just knows himself. I deeply envy that.

"How'd you know to go to the docks?" I ask.

"You post pictures there all the time. It's your go-to place."

"Am I that transparent? God, don't answer that."

He sits down next to me. "Some people pay attention."

Then he puts his hand palm up on his leg and looks at me like he expects me to hold it. I do. God, he's so bossy. I'm mortified at myself, truly.

"Listen," he says. "You can pretend that never happened at the restaurant. I'm sorry if me telling you that hurt you. That wasn't my intent."

"How'd you know about my dream?"

He squeezes my hand, his eyebrows drawing together.

"You just said you had one, and I imagined what mine would look like."

"That's impossible. The things you wrote were things I actually dreamt about."

Kit shrugs. "Can't we share the same dream?"

I swallow hard and look away. "I don't know."

He squeezes my knee knowingly. "I'll get the coffee while you deal with your overload of emotions."

"Two sugars," I call after him.

It's funny, but also not. How does he know that stuff?

And that's how we end the night. Sitting on the sofa in front of the fire, drinking coffee and listening to the sound of each other's voices. Afterward, Kit walks me back to the cannery and gives me a hug goodbye. Della has been blowing up my phone: twelve texts and four missed calls. I feel guilt creep into my belly. *They're not together*, I tell myself. But that's lousy reasoning. A slippery slope. I've known her since we were kids. My loyalty is supposed to be with Della; chicks before dicks. Is that even realistic? Humans seek connection above all else, and we are willing to destroy things to attain it. I decide not to answer Della. Not until I've had time to process what Kit said. I put my phone on silent and crawl into bed a guilty woman.

31
#DONOTTOUCH

I'm locking up the gallery the following night, struggling not to drop my purse or the bags of trash I'm holding, when I get a text from Kit. His text tone is set to a train whistle. Every time I hear the whistle I look around in alarm for its source. It makes me laugh, though I'm always mildly embarrassed at myself. Kit has sent a picture. I let everything drop to the sidewalk, suddenly unconcerned. The picture is of his building, the creams and blues outlined in front of a malevolent gray sky. Did he just take this? It feels like a booty call, even though I've never given him booty. What does it make me if I go?

I take my time walking down Main Street, stopping to glance in store windows while carefully examining the quality of my heart. My heart is in deep conflict with my mind. I feel weak and foolish. Selfish. Disloyal. I feel like the kind of girl other girls talk about. I stop at the corner, a choice to make. I can continue on to the cannery, or I can cross the street and visit with Kit Isley.

He is waiting downstairs to let me into the building. We exchange only a look as I step inside. I can smell him right away—gasoline and pine. He's wearing a dark blue athletic shirt with yellow trim around the collar.

"How did you know I'd come?"

"I didn't. I was hoping."

Hoping. I spend most days fighting my feelings for him, making up my mind to never see him again. By evening, I fold like wet paper. My will is soggy, and my morals smudged.

Upstairs, he has a fire going, and I can smell something delicious.

"You cooked!" I exclaim.

"Something I caught with my own hands."

"Mmmhmmm. I've heard that before." I stand outside the kitchen to check out his setup, but he grabs the tops of my arms and steers me away.

"Give me a minute," he says. "It's almost ready."

"How do you know I'm even hungry?" I ask, because it seems like the thing to ask now.

"You're always hungry."

He's right.

A few minutes later he carries out two plates and sets them on TV trays that still have price tags hanging on them. He goes back to the kitchen for the wine.

"You have skills," I tell him. He grins as he pours my wine and hands it to me.

"That's from Marrowstone Vineyards," I say. "Demise of your relationship. Thanks for telling me about that, by the way. She almost had a mental breakdown when we went."

Kit shrugs. "You can remember the bad things about a place, or you can remember the good. Sometimes they're tied together. That makes it even more interesting."

"Word," I say, as we clink glasses.

He won't let me clean up the mess. He stacks the plates in the kitchen and comes to stand at the window with me. Port Townsend is covered in fog. It's rolling down the streets, eating up the visibility. I can feel him next to me. It's corny to think you can feel a person, especially if it's clear across the country like we were before. But I felt him. And now that he's next to me, I am overpowered by how intense it is to be next to him.

"This feels wrong," I say quietly.

"Why?"

"You know why." I turn to look at him.

"It doesn't feel wrong to me," he says. "It feels right." He mimics my action and turns to me, so we're facing each other.

"What does it feel like?"

Kit Isley is a full foot taller than me, so when I look at him, and we're this close, I have to tilt my head back.

"Do you remember the first time we met?" he asks.

Yeah, I sort of do. Don't I? A couple months back, before they became serious. I remember waiting outside of Della's apartment. They were late. Everyone was supposed to meet at her place for pizza and the game. She was introducing us to her new boyfriend. He came up the stairs before her, carrying the pizza boxes, wearing a Seahawks cap. He immediately made my hair feel frizzy. Just by existing. Because he was beautiful.

He'd said my name right away, like he knew me.

How'd you know?

You're just like Della described you.

How had I forgotten that? All these months of obsession, and I'd forgotten that he knew me right away.

"Yeah, I remember," I say, softly. "The night we watched the Seahawks play ... at her apartment."

Kit's eyes are soft and sleepy as he looks at me. "No," he says. "No, that wasn't it. Think again."

My head jerks back. "No, that was it. I remember."

The corners of his lips turn up slowly. "We'd already met. You just don't remember."

"Before that night?"

He nods. I search my mind, flipping through memories. My eyes are fixated on the dip in his throat that sits above his clavicle. Had I run into them somewhere before I officially met him as her boyfriend? On a date perhaps? I come up with nothing. I lift my eyes back to his face and shake my head.

"It was at a bar," he said. "You were drunk."

"When?" Being in a bar as a college student was pretty common. It was also common to be drunk and not remember half the events of the night.

"Six months before we were officially introduced."

"And you remembered me?"

He nods, and I want to stretch up on my tiptoes and taste his mouth.

"What bar?"

"Mandarin Hide."

Mandarin Hide. Did I remember going there? The bartenders wore suspenders and waistcoats, like what Kit wore at—

"Your suspenders," I say.

He nods. "I had them from Mandarin. I just carried them over to the new place."

I'd ordered Tito's Blind Pig because I liked the name. Della drank sidecars next to me. But she wasn't *talking* to me. No, she was talking to some guy who approached her, which wasn't unusual at all. Whenever we went out together, I expected to spend half the night amusing myself while Della amused herself with boys. On that night, a fresh-faced man in a suit approached her. She'd turned her back on me to flirt with him, and all of a sudden I was alone at a bar. I remember ordering another drink. The bartender was nice. He made me another Pig and then brought me a Redbull and set it down in front of me.

What's that for? I'd asked.

He'd smiled and pointed at Della's back. *It's going to be a long night.* I drank it, grateful and felt a weird connection with him.

"That was you. The bartender who gave me the Redbull."

"You remembered?"

"I wasn't that drunk," I tell him. "And you were nice. But you had a—"

"Beard," he finishes.

"Yeah. Holy shit." I turn away from him and look out the window. I swore to myself that I'd never forget that night. In my alcohol haze, I'd seen Della so clearly, how willing she was to turn her back on me for a stranger. How a stranger who gave me a Redbull saw it too and showed compassion. I'd felt seen.

What's your name? he'd asked me. And then he'd repeated it. *Helena, that's beautiful.*

"So, that's the bar where you met Della?"

He looks away. "Yeah," he says. "She came back a few times after that. We started talking."

"That's why you remembered my name. That day outside of Della's apartment."

"Yes."

"Wow."

I lick my lips. My mouth is dry. I suddenly wish I had a Tito's Blind Pig to wash out my nerves.

"Do you have any alcohol?" I ask. "Like something hard. To shoot."

"I have a bottle of tequila," he says.

"Perfect. Bring the whole thing."

He leaves for the kitchen, and I contemplate slipping out the front door. How long would it take for the elevator? Would he come after me? Of course he would. And I'd get all wet for nothing while trying to run away. I decide to stay dry.

Kit carries out a bowl of limes with the bottle, and a little shaker of salt. We sit in front of the fireplace and do three shots apiece, the bottle of tequila and bowl of limes between us. Passing the salt back and forth, there is more eye contact than I'd normally be comfortable with. I have the urge to look away, change the subject, laugh hysterically. But the tequila gives me courage, and I don't break eye contact with him. We sit in the light of the fire since the kitchen light cannot reach us, and Kit has yet to buy lamps. Outside, the rain and wind have picked up, a soft susurration of the Pacific Northwest. It's a night of fire and water, metaphorically and physically. The *shush-ah shush-ah* of tires cutting through puddles in the street below. The fire flicking light across Kit's forehead and lips, warming his skin. I want to touch him so much my hands are shaking. I'm in emotional purgatory, the up and the down, the right and the wrong. I'm trying, I'm trying, I'm trying not to…

touch

him

32
#BADASSTOBATHTUB

Kit touches me. He reaches out with a tanned finger and runs it along my cheekbone. I shiver involuntarily.

"When the light hits you right here, you look…"

"What?" I ask. I'm all coiled up on the inside. Waiting for him to give me permission to spring.

He sighs and looks away.

"Do you really want me to say it? When I try to tell you things you get upset."

"Because I'm not sure what you're doing or what you want," I tell him.

"We're hanging out and getting to know each other."

"Like pals?" I ask.

"Absolutely."

"Really? No funny business."

"I don't know what funny business is. I can ask my grandma; she says that sometimes."

I sniff. Kit shakes his head. "I'm okay with just being near you for now."

How can words like that not exercise your heart? I breathe through my nose. All the things I'm feeling are so wrong, but I don't know how to stop them. Maybe I shouldn't be beige.

"Because you're such a disciplined person?" I ask quickly. "And you can keep things strictly buddy-buddy?"

Kit cocks his head and looks at me through narrowed eyes.

"Yes, yes I can."

"Would you like to put that to the test?" My throat is dry, but I say it anyway.

Kit's light eyes are watching me carefully. The beauty of them gives me courage—the desire to own those eyes.

"What did you have in mind?" he asks.

"Go sit on the couch and close your eyes."

"Are you serious?"

"Kit," I say, pointing to my face. "This is my serious face. Now, do you want to do this or not?"

He does what I ask, walking over to the couch, and then closing his eyes. Now that he's not looking at me I can freak out a little. I fill my cheeks with air, bulge my eyes out, and mouth the word *fuck,* before I take a step forward.

Hey, hey Helena, gotta finish what you started.

I climb onto his lap until I'm straddling him. He doesn't open his eyes, but they stretch in surprise behind his eyelids.

"Don't open," I say. "Or you lose."

His hands immediately come up to my waist. "I'm not sure if there's a way to lose when there's a woman straddling you," he says.

"Shh," I tell him. My cheeks are so hot you could probably fry an egg on them.

I look at his hair, then his eyes, then his lips. His hands are holding my hips; this is probably the most physical contact I've ever had with him. If he were to open his eyes and see my face, this would all fall apart. Correction: I would fall apart. I'm barely able to concentrate. God, what is he? A human oven? I clear my throat and lean toward his ear.

"Whatever you do, Kit Isley," I say softly, "do not kiss me."

I want to laugh at the way his Adam's apple suddenly bobs in his throat. This is crazy.

You're such a fucking badass, Helena, I tell myself. *You could fucking house small rodents in your topknot. Besides the point.*

I focus and lean toward his face. The luxury is that I don't have to close my eyes, and I can look at him all I want. I can touch him if I want, to; these are my rules. Bringing my hand up, I trace the line from his ear to the slight cleft in his chin. He gets goosebumps;

they scatter across his tanned forearms. Encouraged, I lean forward more and kiss the corner of his mouth. Very softly. Very slowly. I breathe him in as I do it, and his body stiffens. "Be disciplined, Kit," I whisper. "You *cannot* kiss me." My eyes flutter when I pull away slightly to move to the other side of his mouth. This is harder than I thought. It's making me dizzy. I kiss him again, and I can feel him swallow. I move to his lower lip next, taking it between my lips and tugging a little. Then I pull back and look at him. The crease between his eyebrows is deep. A slash of concentration. He's working hard. I wrap my hands around the back of his head and tilt his head up as I come up on my knees. His hands are on the back of my thighs--*hot, hot, hot*. Then I lower my mouth to his, brushing my open mouth against his, pulling away, brushing, nip, pull back. I use my tongue to taunt him, licking just along the inside of his lips.

This is my first real experience with sexual tension, and I can barely catch my breath. *God*, he tastes like he looks. I kiss him full on, just press my mouth against his. The deep sigh just slips out.

I suddenly feel his hand on the back of my neck. *Fucking oven hands!*

And that's my last thought. He traps me at his mouth, pulls me flat onto his lap, and kisses me so deeply that I whimper into his mouth. Lank, drunk, dizzy, glassy-eyed: my body is so ready for anything he wants to do to it that I feel ashamed. I pull away from his mouth and his hands, and stumble off his lap. I back up as far as the room will let me go, bumping into the wall. I want to hug the wall, or for the wall to hug me.

"Fuck that," I say in his general direction. "You have no discipline." My shirt is hanging off my shoulder, and my topknot is sloping left. He leans over, still sitting on the couch, and puts his face in his hands.

"That's not true. I'd like a do-over."

I cackle, and reach up to cover my mouth, trapping the rest of my laugh behind my hand. Kit leans back when he hears my laugh, and smiles.

"Come here, Helena," he says. He reaches his hand toward me. I go to him. Maybe I run. Probably not, though, because that's not cool.

I spring onto his lap as he's standing up, and he catches me, hands around my butt. Then he lays me down very gently on the couch, before lowering himself on top of me. We kiss like that for a long time. Slow kisses with my hands in his silky, black hair. It feels like my dream—so familiar—but neither of us pushes forward. It's enough to feel his weight, and taste his mouth, and know that he's ready, pressed between my thighs. I never knew that I was capable of kissing someone for that long. I didn't even know I liked kissing. Maybe I didn't like things enough because I was doing them with the wrong person. The only reason we stop kissing is because someone is knocking on Kit's door. He rolls off me, and then pulls me to my feet. We both stand in the middle of his living room, completely disoriented.

"You should answer that," I say.

"Okay, so you hear it too? I wasn't sure if it was my heart."

So cheesy, but I can't help but love it. I point him to the door. "I'll um … go to the bathroom."

"Why?" he asks.

"Because. I don't know. I feel like I shouldn't be here."

Kit scratches the back of his head. "Okay. We can talk about that later. Do you think they're denting my door knocking that hard?"

I laugh and shove him forward. "Go!" I say.

I rinse my face in the sink and try to straighten my hair. I'm not really thinking about the person at the door until her voice catches me. Greer. I immediately look for a window to climb out of. I'm willing to fall to my death to not be here right now. Kit's bathroom windows are sealed. I sit in the bathtub and try to cover my ears. *It's not my business, it's not my business, it's not my business.*

But it is. A little bit at least.

"Why didn't you tell me you were coming back?" she asks. *Yeah, I want to know that too.* I pick up his green soap and smell it.

"I didn't know I had to," I hear Kit say. "Listen, can we do this another time?"

Greer's voice gets snippy. I've never heard her be that snippy with anyone.

"I'm dismissed, huh?"

"Greer, it's not like that. You just came charging up here and put a dent in my door with your fist."

"Fine," I hear her say. "I just wanted to tell you that while you were gone, Roberta died. I didn't want to text it."

"For real? You could have told me."

I can't stop sniffing the soap. Like, I'm just holding it below my nose, and I'm sitting in a bathtub, and I'm a psycho.

"Well, now I did."

"How?" Kit asks.

"She was run over."

Oh God, I hope they're talking about a dog. If I had my wine cork, this thing with the soap wouldn't be happening. They talk for another minute, and then I hear the door close. Kit calls to me from the living room. When I don't come out right away he knocks on the door.

"You okay?"

"Who's Roberta?"

He tries the knob.

"She was our dog. Wanna talk about it?"

"What kind of dog was she?"

"A poodle."

I put down the soap. "You had a poodle named Roberta?"

"I'm a cool guy." I climb out of Kit's bath and open the door.

"I feel weird about being here. You have a girlfriend who happens to be my friend, and I live with your old girlfriend, and I'm way too saturated in this situation to be making out with you."

"I'm sorry I've put you in a difficult position," he says. "But I'm not sorry I kissed you. Or you kissed me. I'm not sorry."

"You said that." I try to bite my lip to keep from smiling.

"I'm not sorry. I just need you to know," he says, again. "I'm no—"

I jump at him and press my hand over his mouth. He laughs and kisses the inside of my palm.

"I have to go," I say. "It was nice kissing you."

He hugs me tightly before I leave, and kisses me on the temple. "Let me find you. Don't run."

I walk home very slowly.

Four missed calls and eight texts from Della. What the hell am I doing?

33
#PLACES

Each night, right before I lock up the gallery, my screen will light up to notify me that I have a text. *Kit*, my notification will say. I become flustered when his name appears. I spend a few moments not looking at my phone and distracting myself with other things—an empty stapler, a painting I've seen every day for months will have a new speck of paint to observe, writing down that we need more trash bags. During this time, an ache will start in my chest and build like a bad case of heartburn. Except it's not heartburn; it's Kit burn. When I finally run out of things to do, and make my way over to my phone, I know what I will see. Each night he sends a picture of a different place in Port Townsend; one day it's a statue of Galatea, the sea goddess, and the next what looks like an old, rusted elevator shaft the color of a robin's egg. He sends one of the Rose Theatre, and on another day a grimy restaurant that serves the best hash brown casserole I've ever eaten. The old boat/bike sculptor—a hippie "fuck you" to conformity—sits on Main Street, a beautifully, scrappy eyesore. He sent me there yesterday. Though she's in plain view, he wanted me to find her. Pay attention only to her on that particular day. I love it. Each night after my picture comes, I put on my coat, lock the gallery doors for the evening, and find the place where Kit is waiting. It's a treasure hunt for Kit. And all that other stuff. That's the essence of him. I wonder if Della appreciates that part of his nature, or if it goes unseen.

On one particular day, Kit sends me a picture of a courtyard of brown brick. It is grown over with fluorescent green moss, the floor a thick carpet of red leaves. It takes me thirty minutes to find it, though it was only two blocks away.

"You bastard," I say, when I round the corner and see him standing against a wall, leaning ever so casually. "It's hidden. That was hard!"

"Nothing worth finding is actually easy to find," he says. "I know this from experience." I pretend to not hear him and stop to look around. The beauty overtakes me. Of the courtyard, and him. And him in the courtyard. He's wearing a plaid hoodie and ripped jeans, standing amongst all those leaves. It's not an image I'll easily get out of my mind.

"Why did you want to show me this?" I ask, though I already know. He's teaching me Port Townsend.

"It's a favorite place. A hiding spot."

We don't stay there. We walk back to his condo where he gives me a mug of mulled wine, heady with clove and oranges. Pulling me back against his chest, I sit between his legs on the couch, facing the window.

"Helena," he says, into my ear. "You've been giving me a lot of attention lately. I like it."

"Because you're so starved for attention?" I laugh. Even as we walked toward his condo earlier, women turned around to look at him as he passed them.

"I want *your* attention," he says. I close my eyes, glad he can't see my face. I watch a couple of kids walk tightrope on a wall across the street.

"Why?"

"Helena, look at me."

"Ugh."

I look at him.

"I don't have a good reason, except something about me responds to something about you."

I know the feeling.

"I don't know what you're talking about," I say.

"Yes," he says, watching my lips. "You do."

He's right.

No one knows about the time we spend together, not even Greer. Especially not Greer. One morning, when we are in the kitchen, she asks me where all the light in my eyes comes from.

"Port Townsend," I tell her. She looks at me over the rim of her coffee cup. "It's Kit," she says.

"What? No. Who?" I spill my yogurt.

I glance at her while I wipe up the mess. Her face is neutral, but I can feel something radiating off her.

"Yes," I say.

"I saw your purse at his apartment. The day I came pounding on his door."

"Oh," is all I can think to say. My face is burning.

"Did he come back here for you?"

I've wondered the same, though it feels indulgent to do so. This is his home. Coming to his home has nothing to do with me. As much as I'd like to believe otherwise.

"Greer. I don't know why Kit is here," I say, standing up. "They broke up, and I think he needed to come home for a bit."

She nods, slowly. "Makes sense. But you know what I think? You're going to get hurt."

I know that. I do.

"I can't get hurt if my heart's not in it."

"You're a very, very poor liar, Helena."

I know that too.

We don't talk about it any more. Greer leaves without a goodbye, and I get ready to go to work. She was right. I needed to stop this now. I take out my phone and delete Kit's number. There. Now I couldn't text him first. Such a stupid thing, but I feel mildly triumphant. For the moment. I walk to work, formulating a plan. I'll text Della, listen to her, comfort her. I'll reaffirm our friendship. Chicks before dicks. I will be the friend she needs me to be, and put my feelings for Kit aside. There! I make it down the block, and turn left when I reach the Conservatory. I see him about twenty steps ahead, walking right toward me. His head is bent over his phone. I have time to turn around and run. Maybe running isn't the best option. I go inside the Conservatory. It's my favorite store, but today it will just serve as my hiding spot. I move past the shelves of red coral and fur throws, and head to the back of the store. There's a piece of art I like to look at, hanging on the far wall. An octopus, legs furled, ink shooting from its mouth.

"I'll always find you. Even when you run."

"That's not creepy at all," I say, not turning around. I'm cool as a cucumber, but my heart is violent in its pumping. "I was just doing my morning exercise routine."

"I see that," he says. "Running away from me." I glance at him out of the corner of my eye.

"That's a very self-absorbed thing to say."

"Hey, wanna go for a walk?"

"Nope. I have to work."

"I'll walk you to work."

I shrug.

Kit walks with his hands buried in his pockets. There is no wind today, but I clutch my purse like it's going to blow away anyway. Something to do with all my tension. When we reach the gallery doors, we stop, and I dangle the keys from my fingertip, shaking them a little. Just to let him know. This is it. *Peace out! I'm jingling my keys at you!*

"Thank you for walking me to work," I say stiffly. I jingle the keys louder, and they slip off my finger. Kit bends down to retrieve them, and when I look at him, he's on one knee in front of me. He lifts my hand from my side and slips the ring of the keychain back onto my finger. It's not on my ring finger, and for that I'm mildly grateful. There would be the issue of not being able to conceal a swoon. He's already on his knees, looking me in the eyes. And he doesn't break eye contact with me when he stands up either.

"I have to go," I say.

I turn, insert key into lock, all robotic. I see him come up behind me in the reflection on the window. His voice is close to my ear. I imagine I can feel his breath, but it's probably just a blow of wind. I imagine myself pushing the door open and walking inside—the gallery swallowing me and pressing Kit out. The gallery would have to press him out, because I can't. *I can't, I can't, I can't.*

"Don't push me out, Helena. I'm not ready to go."

And what can you do in that moment but close your eyes as tightly as you can and try to control the trembling in your limbs. I turn around, the stupid girl that I am, and let him kiss me. He holds my face like he wants to keep me from pulling away. He doesn't have anything to worry about. All my attention is…

His phone rings. That's what ends our kiss. I am left pressed to the glass doors of the gallery. I can feel Greer's warnings staring at my back—ripples upon ripples in blues and greens and blacks. I am blurry eyed, my chest aching from … what? Longing? I watch him answer his phone, our eyes connected, then a look of surprise takes over his face.

"Whose number is this?" His voice is hard. I wouldn't like to be on the other side of that voice. I come out of my daze a little bit. I don't need the gallery to hold me up anymore. I right myself, straightening my hair, which was mussed underneath Kit's hands.

I have an uneasiness. It's building by the second. And then Kit's eyes find mine. He's quiet as he listens, but I can see it on his face. I already know, before he hangs up the phone and slips it back into his pocket. We are over before we even start.

"It was Della," he says. There's a pause. "She's pregnant."

34
#JUSTADREAM

Not five minutes after she called Kit, Della posts a sonogram picture to Instagram. A perfectly timed scheme by a perfectly insecure girl. *Helluva way to go about this, Dells.* She captioned it: *my little been.* Been. As in I've **been** there. IF ONLY THERE'D BEEN SOMEONE TO PROOF THIS CAPTION. Her hashtag crushes me: #eightweeks. Right before he came back to PT. *Oh my God,* I feel so sick.

You'll be okay, I tell myself. *This isn't even a big deal.* I hung out with him, like, what? Five times? Fifty-five times? I married him once, and we had a baby, but he doesn't know that. Plus, I've been through this before. A guy. A woman who is not me. A baby. But, what Neil did does not compare to this. Neil betrayed me, sure. But Neil and I were together because we were young, and it made sense. Had we really had a connection? Ha! No. Our connection was circumstantial. We went to the same school, had the same friends. We watched the same things on television because our friends were watching, and we needed something to talk about.

Kit hit me out of nowhere. I had a dream that made me take a closer look at a guy I was otherwise ignoring. And from that dream I discovered a connection. I don't even think about the dream anymore. For the last eight weeks I've been living it.

But I don't think about that as I answer calls, pack some pieces up for shipment, and deposit checks. I feel like all of my insides have been taken out and replaced with stuffing that has made me stiff, and numb, and mechanical. I do not get my usual text from Kit when it's time to lock up and go home, so I stay later than usual. I remind myself of my granny, who moves from room to room, managing to look busy without really doing anything.

Kit is probably on his way back to Florida by now, a plastic cup of shitty wine in his hand. To think of him being so far away causes the muscles in my heart to stretch painfully. This isn't okay. I am not okay. There is no one on the street when I leave. It's eerily quiet; the only sound is of the rain and the distant hum of a generator. It's a cold night; the wind has been touching the tops of the snowy mountains and blowing our way. I shrink deeper into my coat and look toward the cannery. I don't want to be there. Or here. Or anywhere. I walk toward the harbor, my steps determined. Deep in my pocket, my wine cork sits clutched in my fist. I'm not feeling quite as numb as I was before. The shock has worn off and filled with something sharper. I think it's called realization. *Ha!* The Belle is not in her slip. It's the first time I've found her spot empty. I stand on the dock, shivering and wondering what to do next.

"Helena."

I'll always find you.

"Don't bother," I say without turning around. He comes to stand next to me, and we stare at the water together. I can see my breath.

"I thought you would have left by now."

He looks down at his feet, and I hear him sigh. "I fly back tomorrow."

"Ah."

More silence.

"A baby. You must be very excited."

"Don't, Helena. This is … I didn't plan for this. I have to go talk to her, take care of things."

"You have to go take care of your family," I say, turning to face him. "That's the right thing. I mean, what were we even doing here, Kit?"

He makes a face, starts to say something, then looks away, grinding his teeth. "We were doing something good. My intentions were to get to know you. To really get to know you," he says.

"We weren't doing something good. It just felt good. I betrayed Della. What was I? Your little distraction before you settled down?"

He's bouncing on his heels, shaking his head like he can't believe what *I'm* saying.

"You know that's not true. We have something, Helena. In another life, it would have been a beautiful something."

That hurts. God, does it. I've seen that life. He doesn't even know what he's talking about. In his mind, I'm just some possibility that could have been, but in my mind, he's the only possibility.

I step close to him, close enough to see the stubble on his cheeks. I reach up to touch it, and it scrapes against the tender side of my hand. Kit closes his eyes. "There's a house uptown on Washington; we live there together in that life," I say softly. "Everything is green, green, green in our backyard. We have two children, a boy and a girl. She looks like you," I say. "But she acts like me." I caress his cheek because I know it's the last time I'm going to get to do it. Kit's eyes are open and storming. I run my teeth across my bottom lip before I continue. "In the summer, we make love outside, against the big wooden table that still holds our dinner dishes. And we talk about all the places we want to make love." I lick the tears from my lip where they are pooling. Running in a straight line down my cheeks, a leaky faucet. "And we're so happy, Kit. It's like a dream every day." I reach up on my tiptoes and kiss him softly on the lips, letting him taste my tears. He's staring at me so hard I want to crack. "But, it's just a dream, isn't it?"

Before I move away, I touch the crease between his eyes. He hasn't said a word, but his mouth is puckered into this angry frown. He has less right to say things now. I understand.

"Here," I say. I hold out my fist, and he lifts his hand. I drop the wine cork into his palm. "Will you do me a favor?"

He's looking at the cork; I can see the confusion on his face. There are a hundred things going on behind his eyes. I point to the water.

"Throw it in," I say.

"Is this the … why?"

"Just do it," I plead, closing my eyes. "Please."

He's struggling. He wants to say more, but he turns to the water and lifts his arm above his head. I can only see it for a second before it disappears into the dark.

There. I breathe a sigh of relief.

"Goodbye, Kit," I say.

35
#LEFTTOBURN

There are days—many of them. I can't tell you what happened on those days: who I met, who I spoke to, what I ate. I definitely can't recall the details of my thoughts, only that my dread jangled around the quiet corners of my mind until I couldn't keep it sectioned off from anything. It soaked into work, and into home. Into my dealings with customers, and my phone calls with my parents. I was dreading life without him, and that was a sad, sad thing.

Numbness. That came next. After weeks of feeling pain so potently, it was a welcome relief. *It is what it is,* I tell myself. And I feel so proud that I made it to the point of nothingness.

But, then it comes back. *Fucker.* I don't expect that. I wake up one morning with the sun streaming through my window. The sun, for God's sake. Isn't this the land of no sun? I roll over onto my stomach and pull a pillow over my head. And that's when it happens. Everything comes rushing back—the intensity of what I feel for him, the dream right down to the ridiculous Pottery Barn couch, and the way he left with a big fat *sorry.* I can see the sinews in his neck pulled taut when I close my eyes. The full lower lip that falls into a pout when he's thinking about something. I know his smell—not of his cologne—but his actual skin. I think of the day in his closet when he caught me smelling his shirt. God, that seems like forever ago. I am so devastated. So utterly devastated.

I tell Phyllis. It's an accident, really. I'm browsing through knitted hats that look like doilies when she suddenly smiles at me from behind the register. I start to cry right away. It's not even normal crying—it's an ugly cry.

"Hurt of this magnitude is like menopause," Phyllis tells me. I've just wiped my nose with one of the hats. She takes it from me and hands me a tissue. "Comes in hot flashes. Just when you feel like you can't take it anymore, it passes for a bit. But it comes back, boy does it."

I nod, but Phyllis is wrong. It never passes, and it never pauses. It's like a fist clutched around my heart, squeezing all day long. The only thing that eases the pressure is when I'm working. You can distract a mind for a little bit, but when the heart and mind work together, they're cruel. Phyllis sends me off with the hat I used to wipe my nose—as a gift. It takes me a few days to notice the glances. People in town seem to know. I'm in the Conservatory picking up something to send to my mom for her birthday when the owner touches my hand. I look up, startled. I'm hardly ever touched nowadays. I almost cry because everything makes me cry.

"Just so you know," she says, "we were all rooting for you."

I blink away the tears. I can't speak. I don't know whether or not to thank her, so I grab my purchase and nod at her before walking quickly from the store. When I mention it to Greer later that evening, she frowns at me.

"Did you really think that no one knew? This is a small town, Helena. When a golden boy like Kit follows a girl around town with a bottle of wine in his hand, people get excited."

"He wasn't … he didn't…"

Greer rolls her eyes. "He's clearly in love with you. Too bad he knocked that girl up."

Her words take my breath away. Kit … in love with me? No. That is laughable. I do laugh a little bit. I haven't heard from Kit or Della in weeks. As far as I know, they are painting their nursery some puke shade of gender neutral. I'll just be over here in magic town licking my wounds. Drinking my wine. Slowly dying inside. Being melodramatic. Clinging to a dream I had once that changed everything I thought I wanted. I miss him so bad. I am too afraid to look at pictures. Too afraid to remember the way he sucked on my lips like they were candy. It is all a slippery slope. Me sitting in the dark with wine dribbling down my chin. Hating Della for touching him. Hating him for letting her. Where does it end? It doesn't. That's why you have to put it away.

News of the Della/Kit wedding comes five months later via Instagram (surprise, surprise!), where Della posts a picture of her freshly manicured hand with the caption: *He put a ring on it!*

Also, their baby's lungs are developed, and she can open and close her eyes. We know it's a *her* because Della hasn't stopped announcing it ... also on her Instagram.

I feel sick. Also, stupid caption. #realoriginaldells

I also feel sick because I'm so mean-hearted. #imsorry

Della will not get married until she's had her baby and is back to a size two. I feel comforted by this. It's not imminent, and I have time to adjust. As for Kit: fuck you, you fuck! I make to delete his number from my phone again, then I start to type a text. I want to send him something angry and mean. *Coward! Fool!* But I can't find the words to express how I'm feeling. How am I feeling? I touch the patch of skin that rests over my heart, massaging it. It aches right there. I almost had something, and now I'll never know it. I'll never know what I want most. I do text him.

Fuck you, Kit.

It doesn't take him long to respond: *Helena...*

The text bubble appears and disappears. I wait, but it doesn't come. I feel disregarded. Used. And then my phone rings. A chill runs through me when I see his name. I answer.

I don't say a word, though he knows I'm there because he says my name.

"Helena..." I can hear him breathing into the receiver. Harsh breath. I cover my mouth with my free hand so he can't hear me crying.

"Helena," he says my name again. "I'm so sorry. Please believe me."

We sit in the middle of that for a few seconds. My heart shakes off the day's numbness and begins to ache.

"It's not what I wanted. I wanted you. I can't run away from this. This child is part of me."

His voice breaks, and I wonder where he is. In the storage room at work? In his car? At the home they'll share with their child? I can't hear anything aside from the roughness of his voice as he speaks those words.

"I know," I say.

"I'm a coward," he says. "I've wanted to talk to you every day since I left, and I haven't known what to say."

"There really isn't anything to say, is there, Kit?"

"There is. That I'm sorry. That I had no right to pursue you and then hurt you. That it wasn't easy for me to walk away. I ignited something in your heart, and then left you to burn on your own. Forgive me, Helena. I wanted to protect you from the world's cruelty, not become it."

I can't. I bend over, wrapping my arms around my belly. There isn't a way to stop the grief. I'm going to have to let it take its course. I need his words to seal the wound.

"Thank you," I say softly.

And then I hang up.

36
#BADNEWS

I wake up. My phone is ringing. I fumble for the light, knocking things off the nightstand—my water bottle and my watch hit the floor. I reach for my phone.

Kit

I sit up, swiping hair from my face. I can't find my ear! Where is my ear? My topknot has fallen to the side of my head and is covering my ear like a giant fur earmuff.

"Hello?" My voice is thick, filled with sleep. I look for my bottle of water, but it rolled under the bed.

"Helena…"

I get chills at the sound of his voice. When someone calls you in the middle of the night it's never a good thing.

"Yes, what's wrong?" I'm suddenly wide awake, standing up and walking over to the window.

"It's Della," he says. I hear a lot of words after that. I can barely make sense of them before he's said something else that has me reeling. But the thing that stands out most is, "We don't know if she's going to make it."

I go to them—all three of them. After stuffing clothes into a bag, grabbing deodorant and contact solution, I wake Greer to drive me to Seattle. I take the first flight, and don't sleep a second of it. I clutch my hands between my knees and bounce my feet on the floor until my seatmate asks me to stop. I can't throw the feeling that this is all my fault. It's illogical, but if I'd been there, maybe…

Kit meets me at the airport, standing at the bottom of the escalator with red-rimmed eyes and hair longer than I've ever seen it. I run, throwing myself into his open arms, and we stand like that, holding each other. I try not to cry, but the way his shoulders sag around me. *God.* I lose it. People must look as they walk by, but we don't notice.

"Is that all you brought?" he asks of my duffel. He won't look at me when he pulls way. I wipe away my tears and nod. We head for the car in silence. I want to ask him a million things: *How did this happen? What can they do for her? What are you feeling? What are you thinking? How is the baby?*

We climb into his truck. I notice the carseat in the back, and my stomach clenches. I quickly turn back around. I don't want to think about that.

It's not until we are on the freeway, rain pounding down from a charcoal sky that he tells me what happened.

"She had an amniotic fluid embolism." He says this, carefully; I imagine just like the doctors said it to him. "The amniotic fluid got into her bloodstream during the birth. It made her blood unable to clot, so during labor she started bleeding out. Disseminated intravascular coagulation. After Annie was born, they rushed Della out and wouldn't tell me anything."

Annie, I think. So sweet.

"They made us wait forever. God, that was the longest day of my life. They wouldn't let me see her or the baby. The doctor finally came out and told us her kidneys shut down, and her lungs filled with fluid. They put her in a medically-induced coma to allow her body to heal."

My reaction is mostly internal; I don't want to freak out in front of Kit and make things worse. I clutch the edge of my seat with both hands as he speaks. *God, Della. She almost died. We could have lost her. And I wasn't here.*

"Is she…?" My voice cuts—breaks—whatever you want to call it.

"We don't know." He pauses, and out of the corner of my eye I see his hand swipe at his cheek. "They asked us if she was religious. Told us to have a priest come."

I wrap my arms around my stomach and lean forward until my head touches the dash. This was not the sort of thing that happened in real life; this was a special on television, a soap opera.

The fact that it was happening to my best friend seemed inconceivable. Couldn't be. I'd get to the hospital and she'd be fine, sitting up in bed holding Annie, her hair perfect and shiny, styled to perfection so everyone could walk in and say, '*Oh my God! I can't believe you just had a baby!*'

"The baby?" I ask Kit. "Annie?"

"She's fine," he says. "Perfect."

"There's something else," he says.

God, what else could there be?

"They had to give her an emergency hysterectomy."

I get a cold shiver. It runs all the way through my body and out my fingertips. Della was from a big, Italian family. Her mother was only able to have three children before the doctor told her another would kill her. Since as far back as I can remember, Della's mother had been prepping Della to have the large family she herself had always wanted. Her older brother, Tony, was a bachelor. He had no intention of settling down, and her sister, Gia, was a lesbian. No one in the family would speak to Gia, who lived in New York with her partner and their three rescue dogs. *She doesn't even get pedigrees,* Della had said once about Gia's dogs. *She just takes all the mutts.* It was an unspoken thing that Della would be the one to carry the large family torch. This was going to crush her. If she woke up.

Since it's a Saturday, the hospital is crowded. Visiting families, children holding tightly to parents' hands. I have to remind myself that not everyone is here for something sad. Babies have been born, kidney stones have been removed, lives have been saved. Kit grabs my hand and leads me through hallways and up elevators until we are on the fifth floor. Everything on this floor is hushed, somber. I try to ignore the thoughts of panic that enter my mind, but they are loud. *They put her here to die, and they told her Catholic family to bring a priest.*

We walk past the nurses' station to a room at the end of the corridor. I am breathing through my mouth, afraid of what the smells will make me feel. *Beggiro* is written on the white board outside the door. I brace myself, hold my breath, clench both fists.

The door pushes open, and my eyes focus on the hospital bed. It's strung across with lines: red ones, white ones, all connecting to machinery that stands like sentries beside her. They are loud, protesting her medical condition with beeps, and clicks, and humming. Her mother sits in a chair to her right; her brother is asleep on a cot. I am embraced, spoken to through tears and random Italian words I've come to know well over the years. It is only when they are through with me that I approach the bed and get a look at my best friend. My hand goes to my mouth, and I stifle a cry. This is not Della. It's not.

She is swollen, bruised; her face is a dull beige, like cooked pasta. I want to brush her hair away from her face-why has no one done that? It hangs limp and dirty. When I turn around, Kit is standing by the door, head bowed as if looking at her hurts him. I touch her hands, which are folded across her stomach, the remnants of pink nail polish still there. They are cold, so I pull a blanket up to cover them. How would anyone know if she were cold when she can't say it? I want to say something to her. Tell her to wake up and meet her baby girl, but I am crippled by shock.

I feel a hand on my back—Della's mother, Annette. "Go see Annie," she says. "It'll be good for you. Della will be here when you get back. Come sit with her tomorrow."

I nod, wiping my nose on my sleeve. Kit drives me to their little house in Ft. Lauderdale. Keith Sweat is playing on the radio. *'But I gotta be strong, you did me wrong.'* I suddenly have a terrible headache. Della's cousin, Geri, is watching Annie, he tells me. I don't tell him that Geri does recreational coke five days a week, or that she did a stint in rehab for heroin. She is reading a tabloid magazine on the couch when we arrive. She lifts a finger to her lips to tell us that Annie is sleeping. She hugs me warmly, and I can smell the alcohol on her breath. I've always been cool with Geri. But I'm not cool with her drinking on baby watch. Not with any baby, but especially not with this baby. I have the urge to tell her to leave and not come back. Instead, I excuse myself to the bathroom. It's strange to see the baby things strewn about Della's space: swings, bassinets, soft pink blankets. When I come out of the bathroom Geri is gone. Kit stands in the doorway to the living room, hands in pockets. He's not looking at me; he's not looking at anything.

"Kit," I say. He jumps a little, and then shakes his head like he's coming out of a dream.

"Do you want to meet Annie?" he asks softly.

"Yeah, I do."

He leads me to the back bedroom. The house smells of fresh paint, and before he opens the door to Annie's nursery, I already know Della's had the room painted pink. It's bright, not the soft color I was expecting. I stand there for a minute, blinking at the color before my eyes focus on the crib against the wall. It's black. I can hear rustling from inside it, like she's just deciding to wake up. Kit stands next to the crib and waits for me to come over. It feels … weird. My feet sink into the carpet. My hands are stupidly clutched together. I see her hair first, poking out from her swaddling. It's troll hair, a tuft of black against creamy white skin. Her eyes are open, glassy like newborns usually are. Her mouth opens to let out a cry, and I'm surprised by how soft and gentle it is. I pick her up. I can't help myself. She's the most perfect thing I've ever seen.

"Annie," I say. "I'm your Aunt Helena." I sniff her head, and then I kiss it. I carry her to the changing table and unwrap her. I want to see the rest—the little bird legs, and the perfect tiny fingers and toes. I'm so engrossed that I forget Kit is in the room.

"I'm sorry," I say. "Did you want to do this?"

I feel so bad. I just jumped in without asking. Kit smiles, shakes his head. "Go ahead," he says. "You should get to know each other."

That's all he has to say. I'm a bonafide baby lover. Kit goes to get her bottle while I change her diaper. Halfway through I start to cry. Della. She hasn't even held her little girl. This all feels like my fault. I have to stay to help them. At least until Della gets well. I have to do the right thing by all of them. Especially after everything I've done.

Kit and I take turns with Annie for the rest of the night. I'd take all of the shifts and let him sleep, but Kit says waking up with her makes him feel like he's doing something, and he *needs* to feel like he's doing something or he'll go crazy. I sleep in the office across from Annie's nursery, and each time she wakes up and I hear her little cries, I want to rush into the room. When it's Kit's turn I roll onto my side so I can hear them. He sings to her. It's so tender it makes me feel the same way Christmas does, like there's so much good and so much hope. It feels so wrong that I'm getting to hear what Della should be hearing. It's like I'm eavesdropping on someone else's life.

Della's brother comes to take care of Annie the following day. He brings us paper cups of coffee and mushroom frittata that Annette made. We clutch our coffee and make small talk until Kit suggests we beat the traffic and go. I don't like leaving Annie with Tony; in high school he smoked a lot of pot and lit things on fire. It's been seven years, but he doesn't seem like the responsible choice. I mention it to Kit when we're in the car.

"How old did you say he was when he did that?"

"Sixteen," I say.

"I think he may be past that stage," he offers. "It's been ten years."

"He's hairy," I say. "If he tries to kiss her, it'll scratch her face."

"What exactly do you have against Tony?" He turns onto the freeway, and I start to panic. Once we're on the I-95 we're going to be stuck in traffic, unable to get off if something happens.

"I don't have anything against him; I just don't want him to be the one watching Annie." I unbuckle my seat belt. I don't know what I'm planning to do … maybe jump out of the moving car and run back. Surely I'm not crazy enough to—

"What are you doing?" Kit says. "Put your belt back on."

"One of us has to be with her," I say. "You or me. The other can go to the hospital. We can work in shifts."

"You're serious?" he asks. "You do realize Tony is Annie's blood?"

"I don't care. Take me back."

He doesn't say anything. He gets off at the first exit and takes a different way back to the house. Tony doesn't look surprised to see us; he seems relieved when we tell him that he can go.

"See that," I wave my finger in Kit's face. "A non-excited babysitter is a non-attentive babysitter."

He grabs my finger, and I laugh.

"You want to go first, or you want me to go?" he asks.

I look at Annie, who is asleep in her swing, and bite my lip.

"You stay," he says, smiling. "You can go to the hospital tomorrow when some of your anxiety has eased up."

I nod.

I watch as he walks down the driveway to his truck, and before he gets in, he looks back at me and raises his hand to wave.

It's only then that I remember how much I love him.

37
#CHILIPEPPER

I've never taken care of a tiny human before. It's all movement: running to get this, running to get that. Washing things, washing the tiny human, never washing yourself. It's a labor during which you are given very little time to think about you. You. You who are still heartbroken. You who are managing your feelings even as you wrap, and wipe, and feed. Feelings you have no right to have. You do not think about these feelings or put a name to them. Live, live, live. Wipe, love, sleep. They all help me, but somewhere in the first week it becomes clear that I am Annie's caretaker. *Helena knows what she needs; Helena knows what type of formula she eats; Helena, where are the diapers? Helena, she's fussy; Helena…*

It's all true. Annie and I have a system. I figure out that if you rub her back counterclockwise twice, then pat up from her lower back to between her shoulder blades, those difficult burps will be worked out. She has a protein allergy. I notice the bumps on her skin and take her to the pediatrician Della chose, an Iranian woman named Dr. Mikhail. She is stern and gives me the stink eye the whole time.

"Most new mothers are nervous and hovering. You must have done this before."

"I'm not her mother," I say. "Should I hover more? I trust you, should I not trust you? Do you think I'm too trusting?" I walk to the table where she is examining Annie, and I pick her up. Dr. Mikhail gives me another searing look and takes the baby back from me and returns her to the table.

"My mistake. Maybe I should prescribe something for your mania."

Annie has to be on special formula. When Kit gets home from the hospital, we all go to Target so we can pick some up. He grabs a pack of diapers, and I stop him. "I don't like those," I say. "They leak." He stands back with a smile and lets me choose.

"Don't look at me like that," I tell him.

"Like what, Helena?" he asks. "Like I'm really impressed with you? I can't help it."

I am flustered. I drop the pack of diapers, and we both bend to pick it up. I concede, and we stand up at the same time; he clutches the diapers under his arm, his eyes never leaving my face. Then Annie starts to cry, and we both go to her. I do not concede. I elbow him out the way to take her out of her carseat. He's grinning the whole time.

"Kit! What?"

He drops his head. "Nothing," he says, looking at me through his lashes. "You're just really good at this. I'm so thankful you're here."

I blush. I feel it creep hot, up my neck and to my cheeks.

"Ew, stop. Let's go," I tell him. At the register, two people tell me that my baby is beautiful, and I look great. Kit just keeps smiling.

Kit divides his time between Annie and Della. I get the in-between. I think about the old days a lot. When we drank cheap beer in dirty dive bars, and spoke excitedly about the days when we would be grown-ups. All the big plans, and they did not include your boyfriend getting another woman pregnant, or having a broken heart, or taking care of your best friend's baby while she is in a coma. No one tells you that it hurts this much to be a grown-up. That people are so complicated they end up hurting each other to self preserve. I look at Annie, and I'm frightened for her already. I don't want the world to get her. I hold her close and cry sometimes, my tears sprinkling the back of her onesie as she sleeps on my shoulder.

When Annie is a few weeks old I start leaving the house with her on a regular basis. We go on walks; we go to the market to buy diapers. I read all of Della's books on how to stimulate her, what to expect from each week of development. I lose so much weight in those weeks that Kit starts bringing me cupcakes and cheesecakes. People in the store tell me I look fantastic for a new mother. How did I do it?

"I eat cheesecake and cupcakes," I say. I collect their dirty looks. Mind your business, people. One Wednesday, Kit doesn't leave for work, or the hospital. I peek at him from the kitchen where I am washing bottles, as he plays with Annie on the living room floor. I wait for him to leave; I almost want him to so I can get started with my day. But he doesn't.

"Why are you here?" I ask suspiciously.

"Well, it's my house. And this is my baby. Is that okay?"

I make a face at him, and he laughs.

"I thought I'd take the day off. Take you guys somewhere." He touches the tip of his finger to Annie's nose, and I am hit with a wave of dread. I don't want to go anywhere with him. I can't.

"Why don't you go? I'll pack the diaper bag for you." I move toward the bag to stuff it with diapers, and formula. I am the diaper bag pro.

"No," he says. "You need to get out. You're stuck here all day. Go get dressed."

I look down at myself: sweatpants and a tank top. I smell like throw up and baby lotion.

"All right."

I don't have clean clothes. I borrow something from Della's closet. A pair of jeans and a cerulean top. I don't have time to dry my hair, so I wind it up in a knot. Before we leave, I take the whiskey out of the cabinet and take a shot. I need something to clip my edge. I do not need this to feel like a family outing. We are not a family. Annie is not my baby. I'm going to hate every second of this day. I know it with certainty. HATE. Horrible, awful, fake family time.

He loads the carseat into the back of his truck, and holds the door open for me while I climb in. It's obnoxious how he plays the right music and switches the station at the right time. He drives for the length of my buzz, and by the time we pull up in the dirt lot of some place I don't recognize, I am wishing I snuck the bottle of whiskey into the diaper bag.

"Where are we?"

"It's a farm!" he says. "We can pick our own oranges and have them squeezed into juice. And there are goats."

"Goats?" I ask. "We're spending our day with goats?"

"Don't be lame, Helena. Goats are awesome."

I don't like goats. And I want whiskey to go with my orange juice. Within five minutes, we're strolling to the farm entrance. Kit has Annie in a carrier strapped to his chest. It's like the most beautiful thing I've ever seen. Fuck the goats. They give us baskets and send us to the grove. I'm worried that an orange will fall on Annie's head so I hover around Kit until he figures out what I'm doing.

"Get out of here," he says. "Pick some fruit. I got her." He pushes me toward a tree.

So I pick fruit and watch them out of the corner of my eye. A man in overalls, who smells of peanut butter and has a braid in his hair, hauls our oranges inside the barn to be juiced. We are sent to see the goats. There are twelve of them. All with 'M' names. I take photos of Kit feeding the goats. And then he makes me feed them, and he tells me he won't leave until I touch one and mean it. I try to mean it. I try so hard that Melanie the goat jumps on me, resting her two muddy hoofs on my chest.

"Kit!" I yell. "Get her off me!"

Kit shoos Melanie away, and I give him a dirty look. That was funny, and I'm having fun. We go to the barn next where they give us two giant glasses of orange juice full of pulp. We sit on red rocking chairs, and watch the orange grove simmer under the sun, while Kit feeds Annie. I offer to do it, but he tells me to relax.

"What color would you say these chairs are?" I ask him. He raises an eyebrow.

"Red?"

"Yes, but what type of red? Think a box of crayons."

He folds his lips in as he thinks.

"Chili pepper red."

"Yes," I say. "Exactly." I'm thinking of the crayon he handed me in my dream. The one that was blue.

When we leave I can't think of a profound moment in our day. There were goats, and laughter, and chili pepper red rocking chairs. There was a diaper blow out, an orange juice stain on my shirt, and a small disagreement on how to strap Annie into her chair. There was an illusion of a family. A lie. A temporary thing that would later break my heart. But, for now, my heart is in Kit's truck, beating wildly in my chest, aching-with all of the love I have for these two.

Della wakes up the next day.

38
#CAROUSEL

She is mostly confused. She asks if she can stay at my apartment for a while after she leaves the hospital so that I can take care of her.

"I don't live here anymore, Dells," I say gently. "Remember? I live in Washington now. But I can stay at your house with you."

"Kit is from Washington," she says. "Have you met him?"

"Yes. Do you need more water?"

I stroke her hands, and brush the tangles from her hair. She moans and closes her eyes like it's the best thing she's ever felt. She mostly wants me in the room with her, insisting that Kit be the one to leave when she needs something. Kit and her mom take a step back, placing my seat next to her bed, urging me to be the one to answer her questions.

"Do I tell her about Annie?" I ask.

"Let's give her some time to catch up," her doctor tells me. "Her brain is adjusting. We don't want to overload her."

So, I tell her about Washington. The deepness of the Sound, the rolling hills in Seattle that burn the hell out of your glutes when you walk up them. I describe the champagne bar that serves you strawberries coated in rhinestone sugar. I tell her about the homeless guy who gave me a cigarette and complimented my imaginary socks. And what it feels like to stand on the top deck of the ferry with the silvery air licking your face and neck until you close your eyes at the intimacy of it. When I am done telling her, there are tears in her eyes, and she reaches up to touch my cheek with her pale hand.

"I'm so glad you're so brave," she says. "I wish we all could be that brave." I look away, tears in my own eyes. Brave, I am not. And then she says something that makes me lose it.

"You remind me so much of Kit, Helena."

I stand up, excusing myself to the restroom. When I turn around, Kit is in the doorway watching me. I never heard him come in. I wonder how much he heard, and then I don't have to wonder because as I walk past him he grabs my hand and squeezes.

It's soon after that when she remembers we aren't on the best terms. It comes when Kit and her doctor tell her about Annie, and the emergency hysterectomy. I stand against a wall in the back of the room, my head down and my hands clasped at my waist. I've never felt so exposed, or hated myself as much. I feel her eyes move past the doctor and Kit and focus on me. I've been holding her baby, feeding her baby, loving on her baby while she wastes away in this hospital room. All that's left to come is her resentment. But I'm ready for it, and I don't blame her.

"Where is my baby?" she asks, tears in her voice.

"They're bringing her now," Kit says gently. She starts to sob, and I mean *really* sob. I can't take it. I leave the room and run downstairs. In the lobby, I all but collide with Della's mom, who is carrying Annie toward the elevator. Annie smiles instantly when she sees me and starts kicking her legs. I can't deal with this right now. I give her mom a weak smile and head in the opposite direction. It hurts. I want to hold her. She's my Annie. She's not my Annie.

Kit comes home around ten o'clock. He doesn't have the baby with him.

"Her grandmother took her for the night," he tells me. "I wanted to have the chance to talk to you."

I sink into the couch, tucking my legs underneath me. I am prepared. My heart armored. He leans against the wall, folding his arms across his chest. He won't look at me, which is never a good sign.

"You don't have to give me some speech. I get it. I was looking at flights right before you walked in the door." All of my fear turned to anger. Why had I done this? Why had he let me? I should have just come to see Della, stayed a few days, and left. Now, I know every curve of that little girl's face, and I won't ever be able to forget.

"What are you talking about?" he says.

"Me leaving," I shoot back. "Now that Della is awake."

Kit looks at his feet and shakes his head. "Helena, that's not what I was going to say at all. I'm asking you to stay. For a little bit longer at least. Until Della is well enough herself. I know that's unfair, but I'm asking you anyway."

I open and close my mouth in shock. Before Kit walked in the door, I was on my second vodka. Just vodka, not vodka with something. Now, I am paying the price, steeped in thoughts that are doggy paddling around my brain uselessly.

"You want me to what now?"

"Stay. I know it's a lot to ask."

I turn my face away; my eyes hunt for my glass of vodka. Had there been anything left? Just ice cubes maybe, swirling around in their own sweat.

"She doesn't want me here, Kit. I saw her face."

"Ahhh, Helena. Come on now. She just woke up from a coma and remembered she had a baby. We had to tell her that she couldn't have any more."

I cover my face with my hands. I'm glad I wasn't there for that part.

"You know," I say. "I'm surprised by you sometimes. I really am."

His lips pull tight as he gazes at me through his heavy lashes.

"You seem to see everything and nothing at all."

I stand up, taking my time. Making sure he sees how casually angry I am. I'm wearing leather leggings I found in Della's box of Goodwill donations. They swish as I cross the room toward him. Kit tenses up, and I enjoy it, being unpredictable.

"I'll stay for Annie," I say, as I walk past him and into my room.

Life is but a carousel of four seasons. Unpredictable for the most part. Happy. Unhappy. Content. Searching. Mess up the order, and they still rebound at one point or another. I've learned that revolution can be inward or outward. A move across the country to gain perspective. A change of heart and mind to gain sanity. But the point is to revolt when the season changes. If only to quench your thirst, revolt.

39
#COUPLESBEDTiME

Della sits limp in her wheelchair, her hands curled into balls in her lap. She is most angry with her hands, she tells me, because they keep her from holding Annie. I've yet to hear her complain about the fact she's stuck in a wheelchair all day, her thin legs even thinner. And she's never mentioned the bruises that run from her stomach to below her knees in angry slaps of blue and purple. Her hands, though…

Twice, I've caught her sitting on them, trying to use her body weight to straighten out her fingers. She cried so hard when it didn't work she started to choke. I thought I was going to have to call Kit home from work to calm her down. I hear her ask her home nurse about it later, looking embarrassed but altogether determined.

"A body isn't like a piece of paper; you can't put something heavy on it and expect it to straighten out. Give it time to heal," the nurse tells her. I flinch at the callousness, and try to pretend that I'm not listening. At night, after Kit leaves for work, and I am in charge, I rub hands with sesame oil. Her skin is dry and brittle like old wood. She closes her eyes and moans as I straighten out her fingers, massaging the joints and tugging on them gently, trying to will them back to normal. It's not only her body that is different; her spirit is as well. Upbeat Della, a cheerleader, an optimist, a singing in the rain type of girl is gone. Now she is a barren girl. A bent girl. Sullen, silent, her eyes gone from a high gloss to a dull matte. Kit and I whisper about it at night and try to think of ways to bring her back. I arrange for her stylist to come to the house to wash and trim her hair. At first she seems excited, but then after a few hours she changes her mind. It takes Kit to convince her that it would be good for her. On the day that Joe is scheduled to come, Della is even quieter than usual. When I ask if she wants to hold Annie she shakes her head no. Joe rings the bell early and brings Della her usual coffee and a bouquet of bright pink peonies. I hug him and make a face when he asks how she is. "I'll take care of her Boo Boo," he says. Joe Bae is straight; we want him to be gay, but he's very straight. He's always had a thing for Della, which is why he's willing to make house calls. Today I am very thankful that he's straight. "Flirt extra," I whisper. "See if you can get her to smile." He winks at me and wanders off to find her. Everything is going well until twenty minutes later when she catches sight of herself in the mirror. She begins to cry and asks Joe to cover the mirror with a towel. She begs Joe to cut her hair short, and when I argue, she asks me to leave. Joe makes a frightened face as I'm closing the door. He doesn't know what to do. When they emerge an hour later, Della has a pixie cut. I am genuinely afraid for my life. Kit is going to kill me. Joe makes a *shut the hell up* face at me, and I try to smile and be positive. "It's so different and fun! Would you like some cottage cheese and pineapple?"

"I don't care what you think," Della snaps, when she sees the look on my face. "You didn't smell it after…"

She's right. I didn't. Her mother washed her when she woke up from the coma. She told Kit and I that it took three shampoos to get the smell out of her hair. When Kit gets home from work, he doesn't miss a beat, smiling and touching the chopped pieces on her head like they're the prettiest thing he's ever seen. Della beams, looking relieved. I hide in the kitchen, washing the same bottles over and over until he comes to find me. I wait for him to be mad, but he's talking about dinner.

"You're not angry with me?" I ask. "For letting her chop off all her hair?"

"No." He lights the burners on the stove, a doughnut held between his lips. "She's happy. If she's happy, I'm happy."

"Okay," I say.

"Okay," he says. "Breakfast for dinner?"

Twice a day I make her smoothies filled with promises. Websites sell me on information: super fruits will brighten your skin; kale will make your hair grow. Flaxseed and Omega-3 will take away your blues. Drinking my magical smoothies is the only thing she does with enthusiasm, sucking the very last drops from her straw, and then almost immediately reaching a hand up to feel her hair. She always looks crestfallen for a minute when she realizes she's had it chopped off, then she gets that determined look on her face. Annie and I watch it all with optimism.

"She'll get back to normal soon," I tell Annie on our afternoon walk. "Then you'll get to meet your real mom." Annie gurgles and chews on her foot, her troll hair blowing gently in the wind. I feel guilty for telling Annie that the Della she knows isn't her real mom. Maybe this is just who Della is now, and that is okay. She'll love her mom the same no matter what. On our next walk, I lecture Annie about accepting people for who they are, and not trying to make them something you want them to be. Annie cries all the way home, and I tell her not to be selfish.

The only time Della doesn't look sad is when Kit is home. If I were to be honest, it's probably the only time I don't feel sad. Square-shouldered, full of smiles, he comes in carrying flowers, or diapers, or takeout, and the relief is drawn across our faces. When he walks in the door, he kicks off his shoes and bellows, '*Lucy I'm home!*' in a truly horrible Cuban accent. When Annie hears his voice, her arms and legs start pumping frantically until he comes to pick her up, after which she's not at all interested in the rest of us. It all makes me tearful—the emotion—the fact that I always feel like I'm intruding on their moments. Also, I'm jealous, because I will never own these moments. Not with Kit and Annie anyway. They're not mine. I hate the dream that made me think they would be. I'm lost in all of these ugly thoughts until Kit puts on his records. When the music is loud, and his little family—plus one—is greeted, he goes into the kitchen to make dinner, holding Annie in one arm, and stirring with the other. Tonight, I try not to watch him sing to her as he sprinkles something green into a pot and replaces the lid. She's so small in his arms, so peaceful. I lust for Della's life.

"Sometimes, when you look at Annie, you look really stressed out," I tell Kit as we wash the dinner dishes. His eyes are focused on the water, but he grins. I'm not sure why we wash the dishes this way when there's a dishwasher. Maybe it's because it gives us a little more time in the kitchen.

"You're too observant for your own good, you know that?"

"What are you thinking when you look at her like that?"

He hands me a plate without looking at me.

"I don't know. I worry a lot about how I'm going to protect her."

"From what? Guys like you?"

He glances at me. "Well, yeah. I know what guys think. I'm researching all-girl schools."

I cackle as I put the dish in the cabinet. "If you raise her right she won't be easily wooed," I tell him.

"Are you easily wooed?" He pulls out the plug and turns to look at me, leaning against the sink.

I shrug. " I guess not. I've only really had one boyfriend, and it took me years to trust him enough to date him."

"So, you don't give your heart away easily?"

"If at all." I avoid his eyes. I'm not sure where he's going with this, and talking about myself feels like sitting in the gyno's chair.

"Are you saying you weren't in love with Neil?"

I lean on the counter opposite him and dry my hands on a dishtowel. It should be an easy question to answer, especially since it's been turned over in my mind hundreds of times. "I wasn't as devastated as I should have been. I've seen my friends go through breakups, and I didn't feel that. I was hurt, I was sad, but I didn't feel like I lost the love of my life. Is that … you know … it's like…?" My mouth is dry. I grab a glass from the cabinet, but Kit is blocking the sink. He holds out his hand, half-grinning, and I give him the glass. Instead of filling it with water, he reaches for the cabinet and pulls out a bottle of tequila.

"I thought you were a wine guy," I say. He ignores me, screwing the cap off the bottle and pouring a shot. I can taste it, even though it's in his mouth. It's the way he sucks in his cheeks after he swallows.

"He wasn't the love of your life," Kit says, pouring another shot and handing me the glass.

"Oh yeah? You knew us for what? Five minutes?"

When Kit is dipping deep into his own mind, he looks you right in the eye. It feels like he's trying to find himself in your eyes. I've seen people squirm under his looks. I take my shot just so I can look away.

"I know you," he says softly.

I know you; I walked with you once upon a dream...

"What? No. What do you know?" I hold the back of my hand against my mouth to stifle my laughter. Tequila doesn't work that fast. I'm buzzing on something else.

Behind Kit is the kitchen window. I can see cars drive past, their lights illuminating him each time they pass, and I realize that at some point during our dish duty, it became night. We never bothered to turn on the lights, and we make no move to now, though we probably should.

"I think it's hard for you to fall in love because you like control, and you can't control what another person does or feels, so you keep all your cards."

I'd gasp, except he can't possibly be right. Can he? Also, gasping is for damsels, and I'm a gangster.

"Word," I say. "Maybe, if I had something more to go on other than love…"

"Like what?" Kit asks. "A dream?"

I don't gasp, but I hear my intake of breath. The refrigerator hums, ice drops into the tray in the freezer, a motorcycle drives by. I hold out the glass for another shot. There's the clink of the bottle on the glass rim as he pours, never taking his eyes off mine.

"Have you ever had a dream like that?" I ask, licking the tequila from my lips. "One that was so real you couldn't let it go?" Something passes across Kit's eyes.

"Yeah, sure," he says. I'm about to ask the inevitable *What about?* when Della's voice calls from the bedroom. It's rare that she will ever go to bed without Kit tucked in safely beside her. Most nights he complains about not being tired.

"Couples' bedtime," I grin.

"I hate you," he grimaces. "Are you going to watch that stupid show tonight?"

"That stupid show you keep sneaking out of your bedroom to watch with me? Yes."

He narrows his eyes and grins.

"You better go, you've been summoned."

He takes one last shot before he leaves the kitchen. When he's in the doorway, he turns around.

"I want her to be like you."

"What?" I'm distracted, tidying up the last of the kitchen. I glance at him over my shoulder.

"My daughter," he says. "I want her to be like you."

I feel many things at once, but at forefront is hurt. I can still see Brandy in my mind, and yet I wouldn't do a thing to change Annie's existence.

"Then you should have had her with me," I say.

Kit blinks hard, once, twice, then he's gone.

I store the bottle of tequila, and rinse the glass in the sink, before putting it away in the cabinet to erase evidence of our night.

40
#SUCKS

Kit graduates with his master's. He doesn't tell me, and the only reason I find out is because his parents send a card, which I find in the trash under an egg carton. *Congratulations, Son!*

"Why didn't you tell me?" I ask him, holding up the card. The Congratulations is smeared and bubbled from egg yolk. I hear the accusation in my voice, and I flinch. I sound like a nagging wife. `

He glances at me from where he stirs something in a pot, and grins.

"With everything that's going on, I just didn't think about it."

"That's bullshit," I tell him. "It's a big deal."

He shrugs. "It kind of pales in comparison."

"No," I say. "It's something to celebrate and be happy about in the midst of all the bad."

"Hush, lonely heart. Pass me the paprika."

He hasn't called me that in a very long time. I get tingles all over.

"I didn't have wrapping paper, I'm sorry." I push a package across the counter. He stops stirring to look at it, then glances up at me.

"Did you wrap that in a diaper?"

I nod. Kit laughs, drying his hands on a dishtowel. He leans against the stove and holds the diaper-wrapped present in his hands, looking it over.

"You didn't even need tape this way," he says.

"It's really quite genius," I tell him. He keeps his eyes on me as he lifts the diaper tabs, smirking until my stomach flips. I know that grin. Nights wandering around Port Townsend, a bottle of wine in his hand. His nose was always red from the cold … smirking, smirking. Tonight I am in the kitchen with the Kit of Port Townsend. Lately, it's been Kit the dad, Kit the worried fiancé. Tonight, he feels like my Kit. And I've missed him so much.

He opens the diaper wrapping and inside is three things: a blue crayon, a wine cork, and a sketchbook. When he looks at me it's not with confusion. His jaw works as he touches each one and then sets the crayon and cork down to open the sketchbook. I watch, my heart racing.

"You did these?"

"Yeah," I say softly. "Remember the—"

"Book I bought you. Yeah, I do," he says. He nods slowly, and then some more like he forgets he's doing it.

"You made me a coloring book." His voice is raspy. I look away.

The pictures are a story, sketched in ink. I labored over each one for months. It was the story of the dream, and it hurt to make it.

"Helena…"

"I just want you to know that aside from any degree you get, or what job you get, or any accomplishment you make in life, you changed mine. You have that thing about you that changes other people."

I don't stay to hear what he says.

When Annie is five months old, Della takes her first steps. It's a big deal in her recovery, those jittery five steps. While her mother totters across the hardwood, Annie watches from her blanket on the floor. She rolled over for the first time that very morning. Kit, Della, and I all happened to be in the room, and our reaction was so loud and spontaneous that Annie burst into frightened tears. Now, daughter and best friend watch from the corner of the room as Della's therapist urges her forward. At first, I think she's going to fall over; her legs are so frail and thin they don't look like they can hold up anything. But, she makes it across the room, her face glowing in triumph. Perhaps my imagination, but does she glance at me in victory? Her hair is just past her ears now, and she's put on a little of the weight she lost. She looks so much better. I like to think that my presence here is helping her recovery—and in a way it is—but the truth is, she wants me gone. That's why she's working as hard as she is. I would happily go, except Kit got a job at marketing firm, and there is no one to take care of Annie during the day. Della has suggested I take my leave and get back to my own life, but Kit won't have it. "Annie knows Helena," he says. "I'm not going to have some stranger watching her." He says it so firmly, neither of us argues. Later, when Della is giving Annie a bath, I corner Kit in the yard as he's taking out the trash.

"I have to go, Kit. She's almost well enough."

His eyes come alive with something, but he looks at a passing car to cover it up. "I know you eventually have to get back to your own life, I do. But stay a little while longer." When I cock my head at him, he says, "Please, Helena."

"Why?" I ask. "She doesn't want me here."

"I do," he says. He clears his throat, and then repeats himself. "I want you here."

I don't know what to say to that.

"Annie loves you," he says, like it's explanation enough.

"Yes," I say cautiously. "And I love Annie. But, I'm not her mother; Della is. And I'm not your girlfriend; Della is. And I can't stay here and play house with you. It's hurting me. It's going to hurt me to leave. I just want to get it over with."

I didn't intend on saying all of that, but I'm sort of relieved. Kit suddenly spins toward the street. Both hands go to his head, where he grips his hair until it's standing straight up. I can't see his face. Just the tensed up rear side of him.

When he turns back around, he's angry. I've seen many things in Kit's eyes—fear, wonder, play. I have never seen emotions boil. Irises hot and sharp and full of color. They're zoned in on me, pounding out anger in between blinks. I back up a step.

"Go back where?" he says. "To my hometown? To Greer's cannery? Why are you even there, Helena? Want to tell me that?"

I smooth down my hair. "Sure, Kit. I'll tell you. I moved to Port Townsend because I fell in love with my best friend's boyfriend. I wanted to get as far away from the both of you as I could, while also being as close to you as I could. Does that make sense, or does it sound too crazy?" He's blinking fast, so I keep going. "Because when I say it to myself it sounds crazy. And here I am, taking care of your baby, falling in love with your baby, which, by the way, she's so much better than both of you. Your girlfriend is a narcissistic bitch, and you're an indecisive coward. Congrats on creating a little human that's perfect. So, I'll go home now, back to Washington, which you left, and I chose. And you stay here with the woman you chose. And I'll keep loving all of you, despite the fact you're all idiots. And Kit, take care of my little girl. If you fuck her up, I'm going to fuck you up. Now move your car so I can leave."

I fully expect him to do as I say. Hands on hips, I wait. After all, I am angry, and yelling—channeling my inner Professor McGonagall like a bad bitch. Kit doesn't leave. *Son of a bitch.* All Florida does is make my hair frizzy, and my brain crazy. I have to get out of here.

"Would you stop just standing there with your pretty hair blowing in the wind, and say something," I yell. Kit's eyes are focused over my left shoulder.

"My God," I whisper, closing my eyes. *Of course this would happen, of course.* I turn around to face my former best friend. Former, as of five months, or five seconds, ago. I don't even know anymore. She's leaning against the side of Kit's truck, her chest heaving. It must have taken everything she had to walk out here on her own. My impulse is to go to her, help her back inside, but the look on her face keeps me where I am. It feels like a standoff, no one really knowing how to break the silence. *It should be me,* I think. *I'm the one who screwed up.*

I feel the air move as Kit rushes to her. She lets him pick her up, never taking her eyes from mine. I can see the betrayal, the hurt. This sucks so badly.

"Della…" her name drops from my lips too late; they're already inside. I don't know what to do. I can't leave because Kit's car is still in the way. What have I done? I shouldn't have come back. Kit comes out a few minutes later, his head bowed, hands in pockets.

"She wants to speak to you," he says. "She's in the living room."

I nod.

"I'm so sorry, Kit. I shouldn't have—"

"No," he says. "You should have. Just go speak to her. I need to take a walk." He walks past me, down the street, and my stomach rolls with sick. I just admitted to being in love with my best friend's guy. Out loud. To him, and unknowingly her.

I take my time going in. This whole situation has been boiling for months. I knew it was coming, but I still feel wholly unprepared. Della is sitting in her pink armchair when I walk in, like a queen. She's always made me feel small, and I'm tired of it. She doesn't look at me. No one wants to look at me. That's how the truth works. If you avoid looking at it, you can pretend it's not there.

"You're not even as pretty as me."

That's the first thing she says to me.

"I'm having a really hard time believing you just said that to me," I say. "Can you say it again, just so I can confirm to my own mind what a bitch you are?"

"You came here to steal my family."

I shake my head. It's sort of a slow shake because I'm trying to mentally catch up to the fact that my best friend of ten years just told me I wasn't as pretty as her, followed by one of the most insane accusations ever.

"I came here to help you. To help you with Annie until you got better."

"You're a liar," she says. "I've seen the way you are with him. You came here hoping something would happen to me so that you could have Kit and Annie. I'm not going to let you take my family. She's my baby, and I don't want you near her. Do you hear me?"

At twenty-five years old, I'd assumed I'd felt hurt before. But then Della takes Annie from me in one bitter sentence, and I am so grief-stricken I immediately sit on the couch. Annie has made my heart a delicate thing. Before, my heart cared about the things that were important to me, but it forsook me for Annie. A mute drummer, it constricts and aches in my chest until I reach a palm up to touch the place above it. There's nothing I can do to change her mind. And do I blame her? Just this morning, Annie cried and squirmed to get out of her mother's arms to come to me. I have no rights. I have no reason to feel angry. I am the bitch, not Della.

"I want you out of my house by tonight." She starts to leave the room, when the monitor on the counter says that Annie is waking up. "He's mine, Helena." And then she's gone.

41
#LIFINIT

Since I didn't bring much, it takes only a few minutes to gather my things and throw them in my bag. There's a flight leaving in two hours if I hurry. I text Greer and ask if she can pick me up at the airport. It's a long drive for her, but I don't know who else to ask.

She texts back right away: *Thank God you're coming back. I'll be there.*

I leave Della's car keys on the counter, along with the spare house keys, and step outside to call a cab. Kit is leaning against his truck.

"You don't have to leave tonight," he says softly.

"That's not what Della said," I say. My throat is burning, and my eyes are burning. I am humiliated, heart tired. In the two minutes I stand outside, I have five mosquito bites.

"She doesn't mean it. She almost died, Helena. She's been in a wheelchair for five months."

"You're dumb," I tell him. "She's defending her own. She means it. I would mean it too. You can't tone down what just happened. It's fucked up."

"You're right," he says. Then he looks up at me suddenly. I can see the light of determination in his eyes, and I know that what he's going to say next is going to be hard to hear.

"Don't go. We can make this work. Just give me some time to get her situated."

"No. She needs you. You chose her. You have to stay. I'm okay." All these words come tumbling out of me. Lies and excuses.

"She won't always need me. She doesn't need to be with someone who loves another woman. I did the wrong thing. It's you I wanted; it's you who I came to find. I should have told Della the truth."

It all hurts too much. Don't make someone burn, and then try to douse the flames with the things you should have done. Those regrets are gasoline not water. I have to make him stop. This is madness.

"Annie," I say softly. And that name holds enough weight to slow us both down.

His lips tighten, and he shakes his head from side to side. *How dare you bring her into this.* But I have to. She's what matters.

"She is my daughter regardless of who I give my heart to. What type of message am I giving her by not choosing to be happy?"

It's cruel, but I say it anyway. "You made your bed, Kit. Now lie in it."

He opens the passenger side door to his truck. "In," he says. I make to argue, but then I decide I don't have the energy. I climb in, hugging my bag to my chest.

"Kit," I say. "I didn't get to say goodbye to Annie." I try to keep my voice even, but it cracks on her name. Kit nods, then strides toward the house. I didn't expect him to do that. I can't imagine Della allowing it, but a minute later he emerges carrying Annie, who is covered in sweet potatoes, and I smile. He passes her to me, and I let her stand up on my thighs while holding her hands. I can feel Della seething from behind her poplin curtains. Kit will probably return to a fight, and for that I feel bad.

"I love you, Annie," I tell her. Her knees are stiff and fat as she stands as straight as she can, wobbling left to right. The wind tickles her tuft of troll hair as she looks around the truck. I kiss her cheeks, even though they're covered in bright orange goo, and she smiles and grabs my hair with a sticky fist. "Be good and be kind," I tell her. "No matter how pretty you grow up to be."

I hand her back to her father, holding the back of my hand over my mouth. Kit presses his lips together as he carries her back inside. When he returns, he has sweet potato all over the front of his shirt and along his arms.

"She left her mark on both of us," I say, holding up my hair. He laughs, and it breaks the tightness between us.

It's not until we are inside of the airport that he speaks to me again.

"Helena," he says.

"You don't have to say anything," I say quickly. "Seriously, it's all good." I mess with my ticket, compulsively folding and unfolding, pretending to search in my purse for something that isn't there.

"It's not all good. Stop telling me what to do."

I hold up my hands. "Go ahead then," I tell him. "I'm all ears, Kit Isley." He glares at me for saying his name like that, but I don't care.

We stand near security, my duffel at my feet. Families have to part to pass us; an older couple turns around to give us a dirty look.

"You're gonna take five minutes to get your shoes off and into a tray. Plenty of time to pay me back," I say to them. Kit covers his mouth and turns away.

"What?" I say. "They are."

He grabs my wrist and pulls me out of the traffic.

"Don't be rude to the middle-agers," he says. "They didn't even have microwaves when they were young, and that's really, really sad."

"Look, that's not my fault," I say, pointedly. "We lived without iPhone 6+. Sometimes life is hard."

He grabs my shoulders and shakes me. "Stop making jokes. I'm trying to be serious."

"Mmkay." I rub my temples and squint up at the ceiling lights. Anything to not look at him. The hypocrite.

"Helena, I know you hate this stuff, but just bear with me for a minute. You rushed here with that small bag five months ago. You came to be with us when we needed you, and you took care of my little girl. There's no one I'd trust her with more than you. I'll never forget that."

I clear my throat. "You're welcome," I say, shuffling my feet.

"I haven't said thank you yet," Kit says.

"And you don't need to," I rush. "I really should get going." I grab my bag and head for the end of the line, but Kit grabs my wrist and pulls me back. I have a Ginger Rogers moment where I am suddenly full of grace and flair, and then I land against his chest with an *Ooomph.*

He pulls me into such a tight hug that for a minute I lose my breath. I'm stiff at first, my face pressed against his shoulder, but he's hugging me, and I really need to be hugged. It's all just too much. I start sobbing. That's not the surprising part; I'm a crier. The surprising part is that Kit is crying too. I wrap my arms around him, and we cry together as the people, who didn't have microwaves and iPhone 6+ when they were young, walk past us. Before he lets go, he presses his lips to my ear. "Thank you, Helena. I love you." I'm dropped from his arms, and all of a sudden I'm watching his back disappear into the crowd. It's a good day for hurting. I get the feeling that all of that was Kit's way of saying goodbye for good. I could let that be it. Take my goodbye and be on my way for the rest of my life. But, I'm angry. Angry at the things Della said. She gave me a value today, stuck a price tag on my forehead that said: *not as pretty as me!* I wonder how long that value tag has been there, and if perhaps all of her friends were chosen by being not as pretty as her. I don't even remember why we were best friends. Had she been different? Had I been blind?

I board my plane, squeezing through the center aisle to get to my seat. I've never felt like this before. Usually I swallow my feelings, deal with them in the privacy of my own mind. I just gave up five months of my life to help someone who said I wasn't as pretty as she was. What the fuck was that? I scoot into my seat, which is in the very back of the plane, and take a selfie. All of my selfies look shocked, sad, confused, or insanely happy. This is the very first angry selfie. It sits right next to FUCK LOVE. So, I call it FUCK BEST FRIENDS. At this rate I won't believe in anything by the end of the year. Except maybe Greer, who is waiting for me at the airport, wearing a purple tutu and holding a unicorn balloon.

I hug her so tightly she yelps, then I take my balloon and plan out my future.

42
#iLLSHOWTHEMiMPRETTY

Fuck love, fuck Florida, Fuck Kit Isley and his prettier-than-me girlfriend.

.

43
#ROSECOLOREDGLASSES

Greer doesn't like Della. She tells me this as we stand on the top deck of the ferry, drinking apple juice from paper cups and watching the sun set in shades of pinks and purples.

"How dare she," she says. "Why is he with someone like that?" Greer sounds genuinely bitter. She's spitting out one-liners aimed at Kit and Della, and it's almost making me smile.

"You've never met her," I point out. "She's not all bad."

"Oh sure," she says. "But how many girls have we met just like her? They're everywhere. They make reality shows about them now."

"True," I say. "But she was my best friend. I didn't see her that way."

"You don't see a lot of shit, Helena. You have a blind soul." I pour my apple juice into the Sound.

"Hey! What's that supposed to mean?" I try to keep the offense out of my voice, but Greer knows me too well. She kneads my neck like she can rub away the insult.

"Had … *had* a blind soul. It's waking up—to art, people … men."

"Yeah? It's kind of painful," I say. "Like being dropped into ice water."

"That's the nature of the truth, though. What's fun about being dropped into ice water? That's why half the world walks around wearing rose-colored glasses, watching comedies and reading romance books."

I look at her out of the corner of my eye. I like comedies and romance.

"If you're such a realist, why do you dress the way you do?" I ask her. "You dress like a fairy, wearing the same color every day."

"I dress the way I want the world to look. I'm living out my fantasy visually. But I'm not sheltering myself mentally."

I always sulk for a few minutes after she makes sense. It's not fair that she's so pretty and so wise. And if I were dressing the way I wanted the world to look, it would be a beige bitch world. I'm wearing a tan hoodie because I suck, and because my soul is visually impaired.

"They don't do it on purpose, you know."

"Who?" I ask. The wind is whipping her hair around. Strands of gray keep getting stuck to her purple lips. She reaches up to pull them away with lavender nails. I back up slowly as she speaks, trying to be inconspicuous.

"The people who blind themselves to the truth. They're just trying to survive."

I'm distracted for a minute, my finger suspended over the camera button on my phone. "Who wants to survive without truth?"

Greer shrugs, and her shirt slips off her slender shoulder. *Perfect.* "Maybe people who have had too much of it. Or people who have had too little. Or people who are too shallow to appreciate its hard edges."

I take the picture, then lower my phone to look at her. Greer is the truth. Right now, she's the truth to me. The one person who cares enough to let me know that I still have on my blindfold. If I were one of the three, I'd be the shallow one. My life hasn't been an extreme of any kind. My childhood typically dysfunctional, but typically functional. I've been so very underexposed that I turned into a beige bitch. What happened to pink? In third grade, I liked pink.

"Greer," I say. "Do you still love Kit?"

I don't know where that comes from. Greer has never even hinted at still having feelings for Kit. But how many times has she told me that art begins to flow from a source of hurt?

"Art is the blood that comes from a wound. You can't let it scab; let it keep bleeding. Let it bleed until you have enough blood to paint with."

Her face changes with my question. There is a shift in her eyebrows, a dulling of her eyes.

"The truth, Greer," I say. I'm holding my breath. The answer to that question is so fragile I'm afraid the air from my lungs will break it. She turns to face me, holding the hair back from her face with both hands. The tattoos on the underside of her arms are visible against her white skin. BE THOU on one side, YOUR ART, on the other.

"Yes," she says. "I am."

I look away from Greer and back out at the water. Kit, the pied piper of love. How many others were there? Girls at work? Girls in his graduate program? I laugh at my own stupidity, but the wind catches the sound and carries it away.

"Oh shit," I say, dropping my head into my hands. This was really messed up.

When we climb back into her car, we've yet to say anything else to each other. A line I have never seen before appeared between Greer's eyes after her confession, and has yet to smooth away. I sit slouched in the passenger seat, my mouth dry, and a heaviness weighing across my chest. Her car smells like leather and lemons. I breathe it in as we follow the line of cars off the ferry. I remember the pictures I took and scroll through them to distract myself. There is a picture of her surrounded by the pastel sunset. It's so vibrant. The light catches the top of her exposed shoulder, where there is a hint of a tattoo. It's beautiful. I post it to Instagram— because it's probably one of the best pictures I've ever taken— hoping Kit sees it. *Look what I have of yours. It's purple!*

I caption it with Greer's words. *Who wants to hide from the truth? Maybe people who have had too much of it. Or people who have had too little. Or people who are too shallow to appreciate its hard edges. #TRUTH*

The ride from the Kingston ferry to Port Townsend is about an hour, depending on how fast you're driving. During that hour, the photo of Greer gets three thousand likes, and my Instagram gets a thousand new follows. I track the likes to two blogs who reposted the picture, crediting me, each blog having over thirty thousand followers. I read through the comments on the photo, blushing at the things they say both about Greer, and the mysterious photographer. Kit is not one of those likes. He liked someone else's picture a few minutes after I posted the picture of Greer, so I know he saw it.

"Whoa," Greer says, when she opens her Instagram. "That's a great picture."

"A fluke," I say. "I've never taken anything as good as that before."

She puts the car in park outside of the cannery. "So, maybe today is the start of great pictures. Make sure your next one is better."

I purse my lips. "Okay."

I make to open my door, but Greer grabs my hand and squeezes it.

"I've moved on, Helena," she says. "You can love someone your whole life and not know why. You can even live with it. This doesn't change our friendship."

I smile tightly. "Of course it doesn't. Because he's not mine. If he were, you wouldn't be okay with me."

"That's not true," she says. "I want him to be happy."

"That's easy to say until the person you love is happy with someone else. Girls always choose men, and men always choose the wrong girls. It's an endless cycle." I wonder if she was helping herself or helping me when she forced me to go to the wedding with her.

This time, she doesn't try to stop me when I get out of the car. The beige bitch can say things that make sense too.

44
#STRANGER

There's a lot of rebuilding to do after your heart breaks. For instance, you have to rearrange your perspective. What is important now that I have no desire to eat, drink, work, play, love, sleep, talk, or think? Healing. You have to focus on the minuscule, stupid things that make you happy every day. Like taking out your box of socks and touching each one. Posting beautifully depressing pictures of Port Townsend to Instagram, which generate thousands of likes. I get paid by third party advertisers to wear this and post that. I'm just a beige bitch with something to say. Wine makes me happy. Every night I drink an entire bottle and stare at my favorite wall. I even like the way it feels when I wake up to a headache, my stomach rolling from a hangover. It gives me something to focus on other than the melancholy of my heart. My mood changes by the hour, which makes me feel like a crazy person. Like yesterday, when I stood looking at the water and didn't think about drowning myself, I felt proud. But two hours later I held a bag of rat poison in my hands and wondered if it was delicious. Greer tells me I have to take back my power.

"What power?" I ask her.

She screws her face up in deep thought before she finally says, "Do you know how in *Pirates of the Caribbean* when Calypso…"

I've never met anyone who delivers Disney analogies with such a punch. I get it. I think. It makes me laugh in any case.

I'm different. Kit showed me things, so I focus on that—the things I've learned rather than the things I'm not getting to experience. I've noticed that people don't really look you in the eye, because their eyes are somewhere else. Pointed inward. I make it a point to look everyone in the eye so they know I'm seeing them. That's how Kit made me feel—seen. I want to see people. I've also noticed that the more you see people the more they want to trust you with their secrets. Phyllis tells me that she gave a baby boy up for adoption when she was fifteen. A customer tells me that she collects rocks the color of her ex-boyfriend's eyes, and that her husband thinks her rock gardens are just a love of minerals. A stranger tells me that she was raped two weeks ago. It goes on and on. When you care, people can feel it. And then, in my new position as town secret carrier, I realize that Kit made me a better person.

Contrast is important in life. We understand what light is because we can compare it with what we know is dark. Sweet is made sweeter after we eat something bitter. It's the very same with sadness. And it's important to experience sadness, to embrace it in order to truly know happiness. I was just a flat line until he came along. And maybe now I'm hurting. But isn't that what love is supposed to do? Make you feel, make you brave, make you look at yourself more carefully?

A month after Kit's swift departure back to Florida, a package arrives for me at the cannery with his return address scratched in the upper left corner. I weigh it in my hands, and let my fingers explore through the envelope. Pages. Pages, and pages, and pages. I don't open it, because I know what it is. The words that he wanted to say. That we didn't have time to say. I have those words too. I'm not ready. For weeks, I carry it in my purse just to feel the weight of it on my shoulder. Unopened. A little bit ignored. I'm afraid to touch those pages. They could tell a very different story than the one I'm expecting, but Kit's approach and appearance in PT makes me believe.

One day, shortly after Christmas, I walk to a bar on Water Street—called Sirens. There is still tinsel draped across the back of the bar. One side of it has come loose of the tape and loops down lower than the rest. It depresses me. I slide onto a barstool and order whiskey straight up, turning my back on the droopy tinsel. The bartender slides the glass over without meeting my eyes. *Seasonal depression. Yeah, me too, buddy.* I take a sip and flinch. Drinking is a good plan. You want to ignore your inner pain and pour fermented corn down your throat so you can ignore your pain some more. It'll burn harder than your heart.

"Bad day?" A man's voice—chalky, rich. He's sitting directly across from me on the other side of the bar. He's in the darkest corner, which makes it hard for him to be seen. I wonder if he planned it that way.

"Did the whiskey give it away?" My voice is raspy. I lick my lips and look away. The last thing I feel like doing is bullshitting with a stranger in a bar.

"Plenty of women drink whiskey straight up. You just look like you took a sip of battery acid."

I laugh.

I turn to him, despite myself. "Yeah. It was a really bad day. But, they're mostly like that." I spin my glass on the counter and narrow my eyes on the shadows, trying to see his face. His voice is young, but his presence is old. Maybe he's a ghost. I make the sign of the cross under the table. I'm not even Catholic.

"A man," he says. "And a broken heart."

"That's fairly obvious," I say. "What else causes a woman to walk into a bar at three o' clock on a weekday and drink battery acid?"

Now it's his turn to laugh. *Young—definitely young.*

"Tell me," he says. And that's all he says. I like that. It's like he just expects you to spill all of your secrets, and I'm sure many do.

"Tell me," I say. "Why you're drinking alone in the darkest corner of the bar, trying to pry the hurt out of strangers."

For a minute he's quiet, and I think I've imagined the whole conversation. I take another sip of whiskey, determined to keep my face still as I watch the place where he sits. *A ghost!*

"Because that's what I do," he finally says.

I'm surprised he answered, though it's a cheap, noncommittal answer.

"What's the point of making conversation if you're going to be guarded and give me rehearsed answers?"

I can feel his smile. Is that even possible? It's like the air carries everything he does and lets you know.

"Okay," he says slowly. I hear him set down his glass. "I'm a predator. I wait for women to tell me what they want, and then I convince them that I can give it to them."

I laugh. "I already know you're a man. Tell me something new."

He shifts on his stool and light hits his face. For a moment I see a beard and a very sharp blue eye. My heart races.

"What's your name?" he asks. I blink at the terseness in his voice.

"Helena," I say. "And you're right. I do have a broken heart. And I don't drink whiskey. What's your name?"

"Muslim," he says. He waits like he expects something from me. When I don't respond, he says, "Tell me about this man you love, Helena."

The man I love? I suck in my cheeks and stare at the place where he's sitting like I can see him.

"Tell me about all the women you didn't, Muslim."

He slides his glass back and forth across the bar top, considering me.

"It's your power move," I tell him. "Getting women to tell you their truths while you hide all of yours. Is that right?"

"Perhaps." I hear the catch in his voice.

"What causes you to want that power?"

He laughs. It's a deep, throaty laugh.

"The lack or distortion of something usually causes a deep need for it," he answers. "Wouldn't you think?"

"Unless you're a sociopath. Then you just crave things because you were born with the need. Are you a sociopath, Muslim?"

"My truth for yours," he says. His voice slays me. It makes me feel lightheaded with all of that richness. A grating finery. I want to kiss him based on his voice alone.

"All right," I say slowly. I turn my body toward him because I'm really getting into this. "He's my former best friend's fiancé. They have a baby." I tell him the story of Della's time in the hospital, and of my time with Kit and Annie. When I'm finished, there's a flash of light as he lifts his glass to his mouth and takes a sip.

"Yes, I am," he says. It takes a minute for me to realize he's answering my question and is not commenting on what I told him. "I find out what makes people tick, and then I use it against them."

"And when you say people, you mean women?"

"Yes," he says.

I am a little stunned.

"Don't you … don't you feel bad about that?"

"I am a sociopath, remember?"

"But you're not supposed to admit that," I say quietly.

And then he says, "Does he feel the same way about you that you feel about him?"

"I don't know," I say. "He feels something."

"So why aren't you doing anything about it?"

I am taken by surprise, though I probably shouldn't be, considering he just admitted to being a sociopath.

"What is there to do? He's with someone else. They have a baby."

"You have something of his," he says. At first I shake my head; I have nothing of Kit's. I wish I did. Then I feel the ache in my shoulder. There is a manuscript in my purse, the envelope wrinkled and soft. How does he know? I get chills.

"I do. A book he wrote. I haven't opened the envelope to read it."

I expect him at least to recoil about that one. Instead, I see his shoulder lift and fall in a shrug.

"Did he write it to reach you?" he asks.

"Good question. I don't know. Maybe to say goodbye." My eyes focus on the tinsel. It doesn't look so bad. I don't know why I was so jazzed about it.

"You'll never know unless you read it. Then you can decide what to do." His voice is a little melancholy. I'm just noticing. Rich and sad.

"There's nothing to do. He's moved on. I told him to go."

Where is the bartender? My drink is done. I need saving from this man who is trying to bend my thoughts.

"You're going to tell me that all is fair in love and war," I say. "And that's just not true."

He laughs. It's a throaty laugh. Not insincere, but not completely honest either.

"There is only war in love," he says. "If anyone tells you otherwise, they're lying. The constant fight to keep love relevant, while growing and changing as a human, is the battle. You fight for them, fight to keep them, fight to love them. Do you fight for yourself, or do you fight for the relationship? What can't you live without? There's your answer."

I listen. He speaks with conviction, and whether or not I believe him, I am compelled to weigh his words. I see him stand up, and I am given a brief glimpse of his face as he slides a bill out of his wallet and drops it on the bar. He is even younger than I thought, handsome, with a neatly trimmed beard. He walks toward me, and I tense. It's the roll of his shoulders—a man who moves like a lion. I don't want to know who he is, but I do. He feels dangerous, like a man with an agenda. I've barely had time to register the agenda part when he's looming over me, and I have to look up at him. The sunlight from the windows glints in my eyes. I clutch the edges of my stool like a child.

"We are only given one life. You want to waste it waging war against yourself, go right ahead."

He reaches out and touches a thumb to the space between my eyes, then leans down to speak close to my ear. "Or you can fight for what you want," he says softly. His breath blows up strands of my hair. "What are you scared of, Helena?"

I've never said it out loud. Never confessed to a friend, but here I am confessing to a stranger.

"I'm scared of what they'll really think of me. If I embrace who I know I am."

I am trembling. My confession saps the strength, the whiskey, right out of me.

He smiles like he was waiting for this all along. He has warm skin; I can feel the heat radiating off him. God, this man probably never cold.

"Let people feel the weight of who you really are, and let them fucking deal with it."

I am breathless—my mouth open and my eyes glazed. An orgasm for the truth.

He drops a piece of paper on the bar next to my empty glass and walks out the door.

The spot on my forehead where he touched me is tingling. I reach up and rub it. The weight of who I am. It isn't my responsibility to deal with it. It is theirs. Muslim is right. I am, what I am, what I am. Stay or leave.

His words settle over me. I narrow my eyes against them. I don't have to believe. I don't. But I do. And that's when things change. Can change wash over you in a matter of seconds? It just takes the right moment, the right words, the aligning of brain and heart. I will fight.

45
#HOOKED

Muslim Black is staying in Manresa Castle. I hear it's haunted to high hell—dead women tortured by love and all of that bullshit. You can't even die and escape a broken heart. Depressing. Haunting or not, there's something about Muslim that tells me he won't mind a few ghosts. I don't call him right away. I carry the slip of paper in my pocket. It feels like a live thing. *It's just your curiosity*, I remind myself. Did he creep me out, or was I attracted to him? Maybe it was both. What does that say about me anyway? When I do finally call him, he answers the phone saying my name. The voice that encumbers enough rasp and spice to make every hair on your body stand on end. And then it says your name. The E's are breathy, the last letter strong. It's his own way, and no one has ever said it like that before.

"Hello, Helena."

"How'd you know it was me?" My heart pounds, and I have to bend over at the waist and hide my face between my knees until it's time to talk again.

"I don't give people this number."

"You gave me the number."

"I can't hear you…"

I sit up and say it again.

"You're not people," he says.

I wonder if he's lying on the hotel bed or walking around the room.

"Who am I?"

I hear him shifting the phone around. Perhaps changing positions. Is he weighing how best to answer me? I don't want to be part of his game; that's not why I called. When he answers me, his voice is rich, back to normal. "You're Helena. Isn't that enough?"

I sniff. "Don't do that," I say. "Try to make me feel special so you can hook me."

He's quiet for a moment, and then he says, "Okay."

"Can you teach me how to do what you do?"

"Which is what?"

I don't want to play that game. I want him to read my mind like before. Not make me beg.

"Never mind." I start to hang up the phone when I hear him say, "No, no, no! Wait. Helena…" Did his facade falter? I'm curious. Which is the only reason I bring the phone back to my ear. I don't have time to be sorry for calling, because then he's telling me what I want to hear.

"Yes. Yes, I'll teach you."

To get what you want, but to still be suspicious—it's a grimy feeling. Like you're doing something wrong. And I am, aren't I? I decide to check Muslim's motives, not mine.

"Why?" I ask.

"Because you asked me to." And then, "Would you like to meet for dinner?"

I agree to meet him at Alchemy the next night. I suggested somewhere light and warm with lilac walls that reminded me of Greer, but Muslim wanted Alchemy.

"I like the name," he said, before we settled on six o' clock.

I dress all in black, but when I look at myself in the mirror, I look deranged and frightened. So, I change into a beige sweater and ripped blue jeans that Greer says make me look like a sexpot. My topknot is extra large and in charge as I walk down to Alchemy at 5:55. I do not feel in charge, and that is the point of Muslim Black, I suppose. Am I really doing this to get Kit back? Or am I in some sort of grieving, fascinated rebound phase? *Who cares?* I tell myself. *Just do what you need to. Whatever that is.* Before I walk in the door to Alchemy, I take a selfie, titled: Hooked.

Muslim is already sitting at the table, a drink next to his hand, the glass sweating. I'm glad I'm not the only one sweating. Wait, Kit. How long has it been since I've thought about Kit? When he sees me, he stands up. He's not a city boy. That's something my dad does, and he does it because his dad made him.

"Seems you're never without one," I say, slinging my purse over the back of my chair. He waits for me to sit down, and then takes his own seat.

"Says the girl who drinks whiskey at three o'clock on a weekday, while picking up sociopathic men."

What can I even say to that?

I lick my lips and order a nice, feminine glass of wine to go with my mirth.

Muslim watches everything I do with interest. When I laugh and joke around with our server, he watches us with a small smile, his eyes traveling from her to me. When I drop a butterball on my lap, and then five minutes later almost knock my glass of wine over, he laughs and shakes his head. If he hadn't admitted all of those things about himself earlier, I'd think he was enamored with me. It's all part of his ruse. I respect that—in the kind of way you respect a rattlesnake. It has me on edge, biting the inside of my cheeks. I'm waiting for him to strike, poison me. But he's surprisingly normal, natural, charismatic. *Oh my God, he's so good at this.*

"I have to tell you something," he says, when our meals arrive. "I came tonight because I wanted to have dinner with you. There's not a thing I can show you about yourself, or teach you, that you don't already know."

I laugh. I'm on my third glass of wine, and everything feels funny.

"I'm a mess," I say.

"A lovely mess."

"What does that mean?" I eye him over my plate, wanting and not wanting. He makes me feel like someone else. Someone dangerous and sexy.

"You're just raw, and yourself, and beautiful. You don't need anything from anyone, unless it's the kind of love that chooses you first, always."

"Chooses me over who? His baby? His fiancée?" I shake my head dismissively. "He can't do that. I need to convince him."

Muslim reaches across the table and touches the top of my hand as I reach for my wine glass. The spot starts to tingle right away.

"You shouldn't have to convince anyone to choose you. There is no real choice in love."

He settles back in his seat, and I stay frozen, the stem of the glass still between my fingertips.

"It shouldn't just be people he chooses you over. But himself as well."

"So maybe you should be coaching me on how to move on and not give a fuck," I say finally. "Because that's not going to happen."

"Have you ever tried to walk away from something you love?" he asks me.

"Kit Isley is the first thing I've truly loved," I tell him. "I haven't walked away yet."

"There is no walking away." He dips the bread they brought us into the oil they brought us. When he touches his mouth with it, it leaves a glistening mark on his lips. Something to kiss away. *God!* What is wrong with me? It's like I'm in heat.

"Trying to walk away from something you love is like trying to drown yourself. You want to, but it's unnatural to not crave air. Your body demands it; your mind says you need it. Eventually you break to the surface, gasping and unable to deny yourself that basic need of air. Of love. Of fierce desire."

I am so enraptured I barely notice my water being filled in light of my soul being filled. Muslim is giving me answers.

"How many women have you slept with?" I ask.

It's not okay to ask strangers personal questions. My mother taught me this. Do not ask them their age, or their weight, or how many people they've slept with. My mother never told me that, but I can imagine it's high up on the no-no list.

"I wouldn't be able to tell you," he says. "How many have you slept with?"

I think about Roger in high school. Sweet, pimply-faced Roger. I liked him for five minutes before we graduated. Hey, he got my virginity.

"Two," I tell him. "You shouldn't ask people such personal questions, you know?"

"I know."

He pushes his glass around with his fingertips. Furtive, little pushes like he just needs something to do with his hands. His incisors, I notice, are longer than the rest of his teeth. When he's thinking, he rubs the tip of his tongue across their points.

"You remind me of a vampire," I say. "In more than one way."

Muslim laughs for the first time. It's a quiet laugh. It reaches his eyes more than it reaches my ears.

"I like you," he says.

"I can tell."

"Do you like me?"

"I don't know."

I could be mistaken, but this seems to make him happier.

"Maybe I do like you," I say. "I wouldn't really know because I'm not sure if you're showing me who you really are."

"My, my, my Helena Conway. You certainly say whatever you're thinking."

"If only we could both be so lucky," I shoot back. Muslim laughs, looks away, laughs some more. When he turns back to me, he's licking his lips.

"Want to get out of here, Helena?"

I have a moment of hesitation before I nod.

46
#BEIGEBITCH

"How are you going to do this?" Greer asks. She has a notepad and a stack of purple permanent markers. Her hand is poised over the paper as she waits. I glance at her as I wash dishes. The minute I told her my thoughts on telling Kit how I felt, she was on board.

"I sort of thought honesty was the best approach."

Greer writes HONESTY on her notepad, and then looks up at me expectantly.

"I don't have a plan."

She tears out the page and hands it to me. "Don't deviate from the plan," she says, patting me on the head. After that, she retreats to her bedroom. I still haven't seen her damn bedroom. I'm suddenly upset about this. What is she hiding in there anyway? I march over to her door and knock. Probably harder than I should. When she answers, she's wearing a towel like she was just about to get in the shower.

"Sorry," I say, embarrassed. "I … just … I—"

Greer stands aside, and I reluctantly look into her bedroom.

"Whoa," I say.

"Yeah…"

I blink at the nothingness. An empty white room, with scratched wood floors, and a couple of blankets piled in the corner.

"What the hell?" I say. Greer is looking at the floor.

"I just haven't gotten around to doing anything with it yet."

"Okay, no. You don't even have a bed."

I look around, hoping to see something that can explain Greer's lack of … anything.

"The furniture in your room," she says, "belonged to Kit and me. I didn't want to use it. I couldn't. And then I just never got around to replacing it."

"Okay," I say. "But you're sleeping on the floor."

Her face screws up like she doesn't know what to say.

"You want me to fight to be with him, but you aren't over him," I say.

"I am over him," she says quickly. "It was just such a hard time, it all still affects me. It was a really messy break up, Helena."

I nod. I don't remember Kit telling me it was messy. He played it off like it wasn't a big deal. He played off a lot of stuff like it wasn't a big deal.

"Okay. I have to go," I tell her. "But let's order a bed tonight, okay?"

She nods. I can feel her watching me as I walk away. Also, I am sleeping in their former bed. I make a face. I'll be ordering a new bed too.

Della has a wedding date. She knows I'm watching her Instagram. She wants me to see it. June sends me a screenshot after the first wedding countdown post.

J: Are you seeing this?

Yup.

J: She asked me to be a bridesmaid.

I'm not surprised. Della has like three girlfriends, two of them borrowed from me, and my attempt at being social in college. I wonder who Kit's groomsmen will be—if I see them here around town?

J: You should come. Do something about this.

I'm surprised; it doesn't feel like June to say something like that. I think about telling her that I plan on doing just that, but in the end, I put my phone away, try not to think about it. But, I do.

I think about it plenty. I think about the way he looked with the collar of his coat pulled up around his neck, his shoulders dusted with raindrops as he waited for me with a bottle of wine. I think about the way he smiled when he saw me walking toward him, the corners of his lips tugging up into a smirk. I think about the way we lingered for a few minutes longer after saying goodbye to each other, neither of us wanting to leave. I think about the way his lips yielded against mine, the rhythm of our kissing. The way I would have to wrap my hand around the back of his head, and lean against him to keep from toppling over. I'm at work, and I have to go to the bathroom to splash water on my face.

He felt it too. He came back here, to Port Townsend, to feel it. Now it's up to him, because I'm game.

A clock begins to tick, tick, tick. I have a plane ticket. Not a plan. Just words that I need to give him. And that's all I can really do, isn't it? I'll be on my way after that, and the rest is up to Kit Isley. I can't remind him of a dream he never had, but I can remind him of a feeling we shared.

I board the plane with a terrible head cold. I'm shivering and then burning up. I've started thinking about Annie. Wondering if there's a way to see her. I've tried so hard not to think about her these past months, but I have the sound of her breathing memorized. It's just not that simple. And that's what stops me dead in my tracks. Annie. Annie's mom and dad. What the fuck am I doing? I want to get off the plane, but it's too late, and we're taking off. *It's so convenient, Helena, that you just blocked out that part of situation*, I tell myself. I take the pills Greer handed to me when we parted ways at the security line. Then I lower my head to my knees and cover my face. The lady in the seat next to me asks if I'm okay. I mumble something about motion sickness and squeeze my eyes closed. When I wake up, my neck is terribly stiff, and we are landing. NyQuil. Greer drugged me so I couldn't panic. I am the last person off the plane.

June is waiting at baggage claim. She's wearing a dark green cape over a neon pink sundress—sunglasses on even though she's inside. Her strange awkwardness gives me comfort, and I run to embrace her.

"You're so weird," I tell her. "I love you so much."

She pulls away from me and holds me by the shoulders while looking me up and down.

"You still wear beige."

"I fucking like beige," I tell her, smiling. "Long live the beige bitch."

June nods. "You're different," she says. "I like it. Now let's go stop this wedding."

The wedding is in four days. I don't want to stop it. I just want to say my piece and unload this burden from where it presses against my chest. I stay with June in her small cottage. She rents from an elderly couple who rescue parakeets. I'm not entirely sure from what these parakeets need rescuing, but I can hear their chirping coming all the way from the main house. It makes me jittery and anxious. June gives me pink earplugs, but all I do is squeeze them obsessively between my pointer finger and thumb, thinking about Kit and Annie.

"Those aren't stress balls," she tells me. She puts them in my ears, and the parakeets can't reach me anymore.

She feeds me soup, and I take a nap because I'm still sort of sick. Actually, I'm very sick. When I wake up, June has left me a note to say that she's gone to work. I try to take a walk, thinking the fresh air will be good for me, but don't make it half a block before I have to go back. I'm shivering in eighty-degree weather, shamed underneath the palm trees and blue sky. I make it to June's floral print sofa and pull a blanket over myself. Then I have one more fever-induced dream. One more dream to change my life.

47
#DELIRIUM

The house is different. I walk around, looking for the navy Pottery Barn sofa. For the children. But there are no children, and nothing is blue. Everything is black. Black, black, black, black. I try a light switch, and the room I'm in floods with red light. I look at the skin on my arms, glowing soft pink under the raunchy red lights. They are covered in ink—swirls of greenish black. Pictures, and words, and patterns. I laugh out loud. What dream is this that I've tattooed my body?

I walk through the rooms, searching. Kitchens, and bathrooms, and unfurnished bedrooms. I find him outside, French doors swung open—him framed between them.

"Hello," I say.

"Hello."

He doesn't turn around, just continues to look out at … nothing. He's gazing into the darkness. I put my arms around him, because I don't want him to be sucked in.

"Go back in the house," he says.

"No," I tell him. "That's not my house anymore."

"Was it ever?"

"No."

I bury my face in his back, between his shoulder blades, and breathe him in.

"Will you leave me?" he asks.

"No. Never."

"If you do not face the enemy in all his dark power, one day he will come from behind, while you face away, and he will destroy you."

I don't know what to say to this, so I hug him tighter.

He turns to face me, and my breath is caught between his beauty and his words. Muslim.

"Come with me," he says.

"What about Kit?" Kit is leaking into this dream, already the red lights are turning yellow. I can hear a voice calling me from somewhere in the distance.

"You already tried that dream."

I laugh, because I have. In my waking life, I have spent the last year fighting to understand that dream. To obtain parts of it. Maybe I'm tired of trying to fit into that dream. I'm not an artist. I'm not a wife and mother. I'm not anything. Just Helena.

"Then let me wake up," I tell him. "So I can find you instead."

And I wake up.

By the following day, my fever has spiked to 102, and June is threatening me with the emergency room. She looms over me in the most normal clothes I've ever seen her in.

"I'm fine," I tell her from underneath my pile of blankets. "It's just a head cold." But, even as I say it, I know that a head cold has never felt like this. I can't even stand up let alone walk into the ER. I lie curled up in the damp sheets and remember what it was like to be with Muslim. His icy eyes as he led me not to his hotel room, but to a graveyard.

"Why did you bring me here?" I'd asked.

Lips furled into a smile, he'd touched my neck with his cold fingertips and then my hair. I was learning that sometimes he was hot and sometimes he was cold. Both in temperament and body.

"This is where I want you."

"Why?"

"Because you're in love with someone else, and I want those feelings to die."

I'd let him try to kill them. He'd lifted me onto the brick wall of a mausoleum, and I'd wrapped my legs around his waist. Softly, he'd kissed me, and I had been surprised at his gentleness.

Everything about him was lion-like. When you pressed your fingertips to his skin you could feel the power rippling beneath your touch. He was not a normal man.

"Talk to me, Helena," June says. "You're acting weird, and it's freaking me out."

I look at June and nod. Fine. I'll let her take me to the doctor. I just want it to stop. She runs around the cottage, frantically gathering things, then she loads me into the front seat of her car still wrapped in blankets.

I see the worry on her face right before I fall asleep again.

"Helena? Helena, wake up."

I slowly open my eyes. I feel like I am a thousand years old. Everything is heavy and stuck together. We are at the hospital. People are walking toward the car. They help me out and put me in a wheelchair. I fight them, try to push their hands away.

"I'm different," I tell them. But they don't seem to know what I'm talking about. I feel cold air on my skin, and I think of the graveyard. Muslim's mouth sucking, his hands gripping the sides of my panties, and pulling them down. It had been so cold that night.

"Helena, we're moving you to a bed…"

I don't want to be on a bed. I want to be on the wall. There's sharp pain in my arm. Is it the brick? Or a needle? It's a needle. I moan. I don't think I have a cold. Where is June? Where are my parents? If I'm going to die, shouldn't they be here? He's inside of me. He bites my shoulder as I arch in his arms. Need climbs, and then I tumble backwards. An orgasm … sleep … it's all the same right now.

Kit is in the room when I wake up. I lift a hand to my face and groan.

"What the hell?" I say.

"Walking pneumonia," he says. "Extreme dehydration."

"That's ridiculous. It's just a cold."

"Clearly." He leans forward, hands clasped between his knees.

I want to ask him for a mirror, but that's probably not what a hospitalized woman should be thinking about.

"Am I sufficiently hydrated?" I ask. God, I haven't seen him in so long. He's so beautiful.

"You're getting there."

"Why are you being so cold and stiff with me?" I ask. "You're obviously here by choice, so you could at least be pleasant."

He smiles. *Finally.* He gets up and sits on my bed.

"Why are you in Florida?" he asks. "And not in your precious Washington?" He says it in a funny way, and I laugh. *My precious Washington.*

"Two people I love very much are in Florida," I tell him. "I came to…"

"To what?" Kit interrupts. "Stop my wedding?"

"That's very presumptuous of you." And then, "I thought about it."

"Oh yeah?"

"But I'm reconsidering." I don't like the look on his face. Hopeful maybe? If he doesn't want to marry Della, he needs to stop the wedding himself. My God, what's changed in me to make me feel like this?

"Reconsidering me? Or what you feel for me?"

I shake my head. "How do you know I feel anything?"

"I feel it too."

"Fine," I say. "I'm reconsidering you. Because you're a coward. And you're marrying someone you don't even like. And now I don't know if I like you."

He nods slowly, his eyebrows raised. He's not smiling at me now.

"But you love me. You don't have to like someone to love them."

I frown. He's right. But not liking someone is enough fuel to walk away from them. Love can only get you to the first fight.

"Ask me to leave her," he says.

His words scare me. I don't want to have to ask. This is all wrong. Coming here was wrong. I shake my head. "No, Kit. I won't ask you that. If you want to leave, it needs to come from you. It's not fair of you to ask me to drag you out of your relationship."

"Helena, I came to you once; I followed you to Port Townsend. No one dragged me there."

That part is sort of true. I lift my hand to my mouth and lick one of the wires. I want to chew on it, but I'm scared I'll get in trouble. Greer was probably eating dinner right at this moment. Maybe salmon and some risotto…

"Helena! I see what you're doing. Focus."

"Ohmygod, ohmygod, ohmygod!" I rub my temples. "Where are the nurses? Shouldn't they check on me?"

He touches my face. Five fingertips. It pulls me back.

I can't stop the tears when I look at him.

"You're convincing yourself that I haven't done enough, because then you get to walk away from this and be the good guy."

"No," I say. But it's limp.

"Helena, don't lick those—" He pulls my hand away from my mouth and grabs my chin, forcing me to look at him.

"Tell me about your heart right now."

I yank away from him. "No!" And this time it is forceful.

He leans in and rests his forehead against mine, closing his eyes.

"Helena … please."

I'm weak. I am.

"I was supposed to be a coloring book artist," I say softly. "And your wife. And we were supposed to go on that goddamn Blue Train! I never woke up from that goddamn dream, Kit. Do you hear me?" I'm sobbing like a pathetic little shit. He rubs his forehead back and forth on mine.

"So, why are you trying to wake up now?"

What can I say to that?

"I met someone," I say. I feel him stiffen. He doesn't look at me when he pulls away.

"Who?"

"Someone who's not getting married to my ex-best friend tomorrow."

He sits with his hands between his knees and looks at the wall.

"Who?"

"What does it matter, Kit?"

"It matters to me. You know it does."

"He just made me see things more clearly. I don't have to convince him, like I came here to do with you. I don't want to have to convince someone to be with me."

"You never had to convince me of anything. It was a matter of timing. Our timing was off."

He nods slowly. "So, you don't want to be with me? Is that what you're saying?"

"That's what I'm saying. I want him."

I can't even believe I get those words out. I was wrong to come. There's Annie, and Della, and Della's family. I wouldn't just be hurting one person.

"Who's the coward now, Helena?"

He stands up, and I cringe. I want my mom. Is that weird? I don't even like her.

Kit walks out the door, and two seconds later June walks in, wide-eyed, mouth open.

"He—" she says, looking back over her shoulder. "Helena…?"

I shake my head. "It's nothing. It was all nothing. He needs to go live his life. With his family. I told him to go. I was so wrong to do this. I feel like a fool."

June puts her hand on my arm. "You feel like a fool?"

"Yes … June. God. I came all the way here…"

June is shaking her head. "Shit, Helena … shit."

"What?"

She puts her head into her hands and sits on the edge of the bed.

"You slept for so long. The wedding was … should have been yesterday. He called it off. They never got married. He called it off because of you."

I rip the needles from my hand and swing my legs over the side of the bed. This is when the nurse chooses to walk in. I don't even make it a foot before she's *Eh, eh, eh-ing*, and pushing me back onto the bed. What type of from-hell timing is this?

"I needed you ten minutes ago, you know?" I say to her. "Find him, June. Please!"

June looks like a deer caught in the headlights. She is nodding, even as she backs out of the room.

"What do I say?" she asks me.

I flinch as the needle pierces my skin.

"Remind him about the dream. Tell him our daughter's name was Brandy. Tell him I'm so sorry and that I love him."

48
#COKE

This is something I've learned. You can't run away to find yourself. Yourself is there no matter where you go. The difference is, if you're running, you'll be too busy to pick up the sword and face your enemies. Sometimes your enemy will be you; sometimes it will be those with the power to hurt you. Take off your shoes and stop running. Live barefoot and fucking fight. I ran from my feelings—the ones I felt for Kit, the guilt of feeling them. I thought that if I put enough distance between us, my feelings would go away. I should have faced myself back then.

June doesn't find Kit. No one can. He's turned off his phone and vanished. Della calls me in hysterics as I'm leaving the hospital a day later, demanding to know what I did to him. *To him.* Like he couldn't possibly have chosen me of his own accord. I had to use magic or something.

"I didn't do anything, Della. I'm not even as pretty as you." And then I hang up.

"I think it's time to get over that," June tells me. "He obviously made a clear choice between the two of you."

"Shit," I say. "Should I call back and apologize?"

"Absolutely not," she says. "She should suffer a little bit." She looks at me out of the corner of her eye. "She said it again. When he called off the wedding."

"Of course she did."

"You know," June says, "she's so insecure, it almost makes her ugly. Like, she's so unsure of herself, you become unsure of her too."

I make a face. It doesn't matter. All I care about right now is Kit, not Della's perfect cheekbones. I don't know where he is. It's killing me that he doesn't know how sorry I am. He can't hide for long. He won't stay away from Annie.

"He's cooling off," I tell June. "He disappears when he writes, and when he thinks."

"So how are you going to lure him out?"

"I have to go home," I say. "I think he's there."

When I land in Seattle, I rent a car from the first place I see. All they have is a white Ford Focus with Oregon plates and a fist-sized dent in the bumper. No Range Rover this time. I crawl into the driver's seat, exhausted, and take a selfie. I call it, Gut Feeling. I didn't sleep at all on the plane, I read Kit's manuscript. When I was finished I ordered a vodka straight up. He was speaking to me. And I didn't have the guts to read it. When I drive onto the ferry I stay in the car, tapping my finger impatiently on my knee. The ferry has always felt like freedom, but right now I couldn't feel more trapped. I need to find him. That's all I know. There is nothing to even confirm that he's in PT. When I called Greer, she hadn't heard anything. I'm going on a gut feeling. How long has he been in PT ahead of me? Two days? Three?

I have just driven off the ferry into Kingston when my phone rings. It's Greer.

"You have to turn back," she says. She sounds out of breath, like she's been running. "He's getting on the ferry you just got off."

"What?" I slam on my brakes, and someone honks at me. "How do you know?"

"His mom. She just got back from the almost-wedding. He spent two days in his condo, now he's going back to talk to Della and see Annie."

I swing a U-turn, hopping a curb and almost hit a pedestrian.

"I'm going," I say. I hang up the phone and lean forward, almost hugging the wheel. Please, God, please let me make it. I'll never catch him if I miss the ferry.

"You'll have to wait for the next one," the lady in the ticket booth tells me. "This one's full."

"What about if I walk on?" I ask. She nods. I buy my ticket and park. The last of the cars are being loaded, which means that I will have to run to make it up the ramp before they block it off. I leave everything in my car, clutching my purse to my chest, and run.

The porter is closing the gate just as I reach the top. "Wait, wait, wait!" I yell. He holds it open for me as I dash past.

"I love you forever," I say.

I'm on. I'm on. I'm not sure where to go. Would he stay in his car? Wander around the decks? I have twenty minutes to figure this out and I don't work well under pressure.

I quickly walk past the café where most of the passengers are congregated and onto the main deck. There are a few stragglers outside, holding paper cups of coffee as they blink against the chilly wind. I wind around the left side, pulling my thin sweater closer to my body. The loop around the deck takes four minutes, and, by the time I reach my starting point, my nose is running. This isn't going to work; I don't have enough time. He could be anywhere.

I go back inside and take a photo of the Coke machine. I don't know if he's turned on his phone, but I hit *send*, and hope for the best. Kingston is disappearing behind us. I walk out the doors and stand watching the water. I feel defeated, I do. And hopeless. And stupid. And my purse is heavy because I've been carrying Kit's manuscript around for the past few months. I take out the envelope and hold it in my hands for a moment before sliding out the thick stack of papers. I had to let this go, right? Just like the wine cork. If he was on his way back to Florida it was probably to make things right with Della. I hold his book above the water, my knuckles so white they blend with the paper. Then I fling them into the air. For a second it looks as if a cloud of white birds has exploded around the ferry, their thin wings vibrating on the wind. My bottom lip quivers and I grab it between my pointer-finger and thumb holding it still. My body betrays me for Kit Isley, it's not the first time. I walk back inside, my purse lighter, and my heart heavier, and I sit in a chair facing the Coke machine. I cry.

"Have something to drink. You'll feel better." I look up, and an older lady with silver hair is standing over me. Her hair reminds me of Greer. She shushes me and presses six quarters into my palm, then nods toward the vending machine. "The sugar. It will help."

I don't want to offend her, so I scoop up my tears and stand. "Thank you," I say. "That's really nice." She watches until I'm at the machine pretending to consider my options. I smile gaily and wave.

When she's gone I press my forehead against the glass and close my eyes. I'm not even allowed to cry in peace. Blindly, I drop the quarters into the slot, one by one. *Dink, dink, dink.*

And then two hands appear on either side of my head. My eyes shoot open as a body pins me to the glass. I get chills. I know his smell.

Kit runs his nose along the back of my ear as his arm wraps around my waist. My mouth is open, and my eyes are closed as he circles my wrist with his free hand. It's all warmth and the smell of woods and pine. He kisses the back of my neck and I drop the rest of the quarters. I hear them hit the floor before he flips me around to face him.

He's right there. In my face. Forehead to forehead without warning. I'm out of breath as he runs his hands up my arms and cups my face, then pulls me tighter to him. Our lips are touching, but neither of us is moving to a kiss. It feels a little shocking to be pressed right there, against the person you've been wanting for so long.

"Don't ever forget," he says. "That it was my book, and Coke that brought us back together."

"Your book?" I ask. He lifts his hand to reveal one crumpled page of his manuscript. "Page forty-nine." He says. "It floated down from the Heavens and I was lucky enough to catch it before it sank into the Sound."

"Imagine that," I say.

"I thought I was hallucinating until I turned on my phone and saw your text."

"Did you run up here?" I ask.

"Fast as I could."

Our lips are touching a little as we speak.

"Why aren't you out of breath?"

He grins. "It's called working out, Helena."

I touch his scruffy face, and run my hand along the back of his neck. He kisses me with soft lips and hard passion. And it's definitely the best kiss of my life. *Of my life.*

#EPILOGUE

D on't be upset that you can't attain constant happiness. It's the quickest way to feel like a failure in life. If each of our lives represented a page in a book, happiness would be the punctuation. It breaks up the parts that are too long. It closes off some things, divides others. But it's brief—showing up when it's needed and filling tired paragraphs with breaks. Being content is a more attainable constant state. To love your fate without being drunk on euphoria. Brave, determined acceptance removed of bitterness. Be gentle with yourself. Embrace the lows so that you can more effectively enjoy the highs. Love the fight. Love it so much, and let it save you when your emotional muscles have become soft. Kit and I have that. Sometimes, so much joy our hearts ache from it. Sometimes, we have sadness when we're away from Annie or Port Townsend. We feel torn between all the things we love. We fight; we make love. I don't see Muslim again. And after one phone call, I never speak to him again. I hear plenty about him, and I remember our time. And I wonder if you have space in your heart for more than one person. I think you do.

After that day on the ferry, we move back to Florida. We do it so we can be close to Annie until we figure everything out. We keep the condo in Port Townsend and fly back to visit as often as we can. I buy a navy blue Pottery Barn couch for the condo, and hang one of Greer's ripple paintings over it. My heart is there, in Port Townsend. We take Annie back with us sometimes, and walk her around town so everyone can fuss. She's beautiful like her mother, and perceptive like her father. She thinks Greer is a real fairy, and Greer plays the part. Della doesn't ever forgive me, but that was expected. We were for a season. I don't ever become good at art. I dabble here and there. I feel good about that. I'm a dabbler. When Kit's mother becomes ill, I move back to Port Townsend to help her. Kit flies up on weekends, but the time with him never seems like enough. I am stretched, pulled tight. I want to be with Kit and Annie, but I want to be here, too. I am glad for the excuse to be in the place I love.

Eventually, we grow out of the condo and buy a small house in PT. A place where no one can find us. It's a hidden plot. A side street, down a side street, down a side street. It's not that we don't want to be found; we just want to make it difficult.

The house has a wraparound porch. Kit has two chili pepper rocking chairs shipped to us from the goat farm. We set them up on the west side of the house, so we can hear the water from the stream, running over the rocks. Most nights I bring a warm mug of wassail outside, and sip slowly, listening to the creatures of Washington and watching the sun set over the Sound. They are loud, and they make me laugh. It feels like I'm waiting for something, though I'm not sure what. Everything makes me jumpy—noises, shadows, the sound of car tires on gravel.

In early August one year later, my wait comes to an end. Summer licks the sky clean of rain clouds, and the coast blows a hot breath across the Northwest. The weather drives me outside more than usual. I sip wine from an old, chipped mug one afternoon, as a truck bounces down the dirt road at an alarming speed. It hits a ditch, and I think it's going to career into my catalpa, when it suddenly veers right and comes to a halt in front of my house. My forehead dents as I lean forward in my rocker. I am not cool in that moment. Instead, I am like an elderly woman in her rocker, pissed that someone almost hit her favorite tree. The door of the truck swings open and black boots drop into my mud. I stand up, my heart racing, knocking over the mug of wine at my feet. The sun shines in my eyes. Goddamn sun! It doesn't even belong here. I place a hand across my eyes to shield them and step through the wine, leaving footprints of red on the white paint. I see a face, striking blue eyes, and a lion's walk. My whole world rocks. It's been two years, but still, this reaction. I settle back into my chair, lest my knees give. I am too afraid to look, because what the fuck? I can't survive another dream. Palms sweating, heart at a gallop, he lowers himself into the chair next to mine.

He sits. Like he's been sitting there all along.

"Hello, Helena."

"How did you find me?" I ask. He just smiles. "I saw you on the news," I say. "Got yourself into a lot of trouble."

"I blame you for that," he says.

"Oh yeah?"

"You were the one. I could have changed, been better."

"Just like a narcissist," I say, "to blame someone else for their choices."

He laughs.

"You can come with me now…"

I shake my head, though my heart is beating wildly. I almost did last time, didn't I? Abandon everything and go with him.

He stands up to go, our reunion apparently over. The rocker creaks as it releases him and swings back angrily. He stops at the bottom of the steps that lead to the drive and turns around.

"Do you think they'll catch me?" he asks.

I stand up and walk to the edge of the porch, wrapping an arm around one of the beams. I look down at him seriously.

"I think they need to."

"You're the only one who's ever told me the truth," he says, smiling. And then he leaves, the gravel sliding beneath his boots as he climbs back into the truck. "Goodbye, Helena."

"Who was that?" Kit asks, coming to stand beside me. His hair is ruffled from his nap, and I reach up to smooth it. My heart clenches when I touch him. Every time. It was improbable, but he's mine.

"That cult leader from the news I told you about. The one I almost ran away with."

"Shit," he says. "Should I get the gun?"

"Nah. He came to say something he needed to. Now he's gone."

"What did he say?"

"That I was the one."

"I'm getting the gun." Kit turns back to the house, but I grab his arm, laughing.

"I'm *your* one, Kit Isley."

He leans down to kiss me, but his eyes are on the road where Muslim drove away. He's not a jealous man, but he's possessive.

"Do you think they'll catch him?"

I think about Muslim's elusive, flowing personality. The way he can talk his way into or out of anything, and wrap my arms around Kit.

"No. But someone will."

"It's time to get married," Kit says.

I push away from his chest and scrunch up my nose. "What the...?"

"You're not dragging this out another year," he tells me. "Not with *that* guy trying to recruit you. He's like a cult leader pin up model."

I lean back into his chest and close my eyes.

"You're thinking about pulling out your box of socks," he says, kissing the top of my head.

"I am. I believe there's a match for each one and I'm going to find them."

"All right, baby. I'm going to go cook some fish I caught with my own hands while you touch your socks."

He disappears back into the house, but a minute later he sends me a text. It's a picture of our bed. Fuck, Love? It says underneath it. I laugh, and take a selfie because I am happy, and this is a weird night. Before I go inside I glance at the road one last time, wondering where Muslim will go from here. A lion on the prowl. I can hear a noise—something distant—a helicopter, maybe?

Ra

　　ta

　　　　ta…

#ACKNOWLEDGMENTS

I can say fuck love all I want, but over the last few years, people have shown me such extraordinary love. Love enough to restore some of the parts of me I let slip away. 2015 started rough for me, and then continued to be rough. I would like to thank the people who stood with me, refusing to take "no" for an answer, and taking up both sword and shield to fight for me.

Christine Sams is both strange and wonderful and inexplicably kind, despite the bitter little deliveries life has sent you. Thank you for my house. This book is really for you--you who should have said "Fuck love" a long time ago, yet you continue to believe in the goodness of people. Nights drunk on Benadryl are my favorite. One day we will tell everyone your story. Slytherin!

Jenn Sterling, I won't lie to you. Except when I do. I love you. Gryffindor!

Lyndsay Matteo, there's never been a friendship created by a bigger mess. I don't even know what to say. I feel like we can turn any bullshit into something beautiful. Please fight hard for the things you want. I believe in you. Gryffindor!

Ma and Pa Capshaw, for watching my small people so I could write this book. Hufflepuff and Ravenclaw!

Nina Gomez, every time I call you freaking out about something you laugh at me. Like genuine laughter. I have your laugh memorized, because you laugh at me so often. You approach problems like a prophetic ninja. It's half faith, half combat. I've believed in myself more because of your prophetic ninja laughter and the way you always say, "You'll be fine. You're Tarryn Fisher." Seriously, though. Thank you for my house. And for laughing at me. Slytherin!

Thanks to Jennifer Stiltner for answering all of my questions and volunteering part of your story for this book. Slytherin! (Yes, don't argue)

Jaime Eee-what-sue-roo, for that late night text that sent me back to Banks. I needed Banks. I needed you. You are an exceptional human, Jaime. I love you. Gryffindor!

Kavika, my tattoo artist and the most self-evolved human I've ever met. That conversation about contrast, Kavika! I'm still waiting on your blog. Gryffindor!!

Serena Knautz, lover of my soul. We will never have bad blood, though we will drink the blood of our enemies. Too much? Gryffindor!

Claire, the perfect girl for the job. I love your beautiful heart. Gryffindor!

Madison Seidler, for a truly giving and self sacrificial heart. Thank you for always talking things over with me and fixing my serious punctuation issues. You make me laugh, because you make fun of me; also, you're insane. Slytherin!

MariPili Menchaca, thank you for the beautiful cover. You were the right person for the job. I think you deserve the most beautiful love. It will come. Ravenclaw!

Jovana, I really, really appreciate you. You always fit me in. I keep expecting you to tell me to go to hell, and you never do. You are so good to me. Ravenclaw!

My unicorn, Amy Holloway, who brought me to the magical town of Port Townsend. I don't know, if PT is magical because you're there, or if you're magical because you're in PT. But, either way you ain't no Muggle. My soul loves you so hard, Amy. Ravenclaw!!

Lori, you don't speak Parseltongue, that's okay. Tongues! Thank you for warring with me, and dreaming things when I can't see them clearly. All my life I prayed for someone like you. I can't sort you, Lori. I think maybe Gryffindor, but you remind me of myself. We'll leave it to the Sorting Hat.

Do I have to thank Colleen again? God, I'm so sick of thanking Colleen. Shit, she's so great, you know? Thank you, Colleen. You've made a circus out of our friendship. Filthy Muggle.

And finally, Joshua. Who stayed all winter. I love you. Gryffindor!

OTHER BOOKS BY TARRYN

Marrow
Mud Vein

LOVE ME WITH LIES SERIES

The Opportunist
Dirty Red
Thief

NEVER NEVER SERIES

Never Never, Part One
Never Never, Part Two

Tarryn Welcomes Stalking

HTTP://TWITTER.COM/TARRYN__FISHER

WWW.FACEBOOK.COM/AUTHORTARRYNFISHER

HTTP://INSTAGRAM.COM/TARRYNFISHER/

Made in the USA
Columbia, SC
01 June 2022